AURORA SKY
VAMPIRE HUNTER

Hunting Season
Book 4

Nikki Jefford

For The Alaska State Troopers
and Alaska Wildlife Troopers

Thank you for putting your lives on the line every day
and protecting Alaska's natural resources.

"I existed from all eternity and, behold, I am here; and I shall
exist till the end of time, for my being has no end."
−Kahlil Gibran, Lebanese artist, poet, and writer

1

Decoy

A brisk ocean breeze slid up my bare arms, leaving goose bumps in its wake. Fane had an unnerving way of inching up to my side as we closed in on Henry's ornate townhouse in Bootleggers Cove.

He propped a hand against the door, fingers splayed, blocking me at the threshold.

"Ready to do this?" he asked. "It could get rough."

I raised my chin. "Promise?"

Fane shot me one of his half-smirks as his hand balled into a fist. He pounded on the door.

Here's hoping Mason hadn't beat us.

If Noel, Fane, and I were to succeed in capturing Jared, we required bait. Using Jared's wayward daughter Giselle was out of the question, leaving us with Option B: The Setup.

Jared wanted Giselle. Melcher wanted her finished off. All we had to do is start a rumor that Giselle would appear at a certain place at a certain time. And for that, we needed a venue in which to lure Jared—a trap he couldn't resist.

That's where Henry came in.

A few seconds later, the unsuspecting vampire answered the door dressed in slacks and a polo.

Fane pushed him backward before he had time to react to our arrival.

We were quick, Fane and I, busting inside Henry's home and slamming the door behind us with a crack that reverberated across the immaculately clean living room.

Henry barely regained his footing before I took three swift steps across the tiled entry and punched him in the face, relishing the burn across my knuckles on impact.

Henry howled as I shook out my hand.

His face contorted. He started toward me, but Fane stepped in his way.

"Not a good idea, mate."

I looked Henry up and down, lips curling back. We might need him, but that didn't change the fact that he'd drugged me the night before. He'd accused me of being a vampire hunter and Marcus' killer. Okay, yeah, I was in fact a vampire hunter and I did kill Marcus, but that didn't forgive his methods or the fact that in order to throw him off my trail, Fane had bitten me. It had turned into a minor sex show starring Aurora Sky: College girl by day, paranormal porn star by night. Not a chance!

The jackass was lucky we had use of him and had arrived in time to save his uppity ass. Melcher's orders were for Mason to haul Henry back to base. Good thing we got there first.

Fane leaned into Henry's face. "I'd say you had that one coming. What do you think, Aurora?"

I dropped my chin, zeroing in on Henry's groin—another area just begging to receive bodily harm.

"I think we should make him bite himself, but I suppose I'll have to settle for punching him in the face."

Henry's non-swollen eye widened in alarm.

"I told you that was business," he said. "Six months of investigating Marcus' death and I keep hitting dead ends. Richard Stanton is getting impatient. Not to mention all the evidence pointed to you."

"My red scarf?" I asked incredulously. "You're grasping at straws." I glanced at Fane. "We need to go."

He nodded, hand shooting out, grabbing Henry by the arm. Henry tried unsuccessfully to break free from his grasp. It was comical to see his attempt to dip down and pull back. Not much of an effort, as he probably didn't want to wrinkle his fancy shirt.

"Look, I apologized. I won't bother you again."

"Save your apologies," Fane said. "There's a vampire hunter on his way to grab you right now. It's time we split."

Henry stopped struggling. "Marcus' killer?" he asked.

"Your killer if you don't shut up and come with us," I said.

Good thing Mason hadn't shown his face already. He wasn't as fast as his partner, Levi, who had taken Dante's dog Tommy before Fane or Daren could make it in time. The only thing Noel's suck buddy Daren had managed to do is provide me with a quick blood rush, immediately quashed by the reality check that came with it.

Ten months ago, my life had ended. Jared hadn't just run me off the road, he'd removed me from the human race. Time could not touch me, and neither could sickness or starvation. Eating was optional. All my body required was a fresh supply of human blood. As with mortals, blood provided the undead with key nutrients essential to our survival.

Melcher kept his agents' hearts pumping the scientific way—through transfusions. I could understand why vampires preferred the direct approach. Nothing quite beat the high of drinking it from the source, whether it originated from a vein or a blood bag. As it slid its way down my throat, my senses had become supercharged, my state of mind euphoric.

Melcher could try to control his agents all he wanted, but in the end instinct always prevailed. At what point would he admit what he'd done to us?

Fane grasped Henry by the collar, easy enough given Fane's superior height. I led the way out, casting a quick eye down the road for Mason's Hummer. Once I'd verified that the coast was clear, I charged down the walkway to the Pontiac Catalina idling along the curbside. Noel sat at the driver's seat, waiting.

I held open the back door as Fane shoved Henry inside and climbed in behind him. Once I'd given it a firm slam, I sat beside Noel up front.

"Let's blast," I said.

"Where are you taking me?" Henry demanded.

No one answered.

It remained quiet until Henry suddenly asked, "Noel? Is that you?"

Without turning her copper highlighted head, Noel answered, "Yep."

"You're in on this, too," Henry remarked sullenly.

"Afraid so."

"What do you want with me?" Henry asked.

A sick sense of satisfaction filled me from the front seat. I liked being in charge—sure as hell beat following orders. I turned all the way around, resting an arm on the seat back. I didn't have a seat belt on. Why the hell would I? I was undead. Sure, I could get hurt—I could even die—but I had the kind of immune system that rejected sickness and pain. The kind that quickly repaired itself and regenerated with human blood. As Dante once said, we were superhuman.

"It's your lucky day, Henry. We found out who killed Marcus."

Henry sat up, suddenly all business. "Who? How? I want a name."

"Jared," I replied.

Henry's brows knit in confusion. "Jared who?"

"This isn't a knock-knock joke. Just Jared."

Except I knew better. Jared had a last name. He had a different first name, too. Xavier Morrel.

Henry frowned. "How do you know this?"

"It doesn't matter how I know," I snapped. "Do you want Marcus' killer or not?"

"What kind of proof do you have?"

Noel glanced at me briefly. Proof, right, like a cross pendant. Jared was far more clever at deception than I.

"Jared's the kind of guy who covers his trail really well," I said. Truth. "Why do you think you haven't found him yet?"

Henry moistened his lips. "You have my attention."

"Good. Now listen carefully. You're going to speak with your employer and arrange to host a party at the palace next weekend."

Henry's eyes nearly left his head—the one good eye, anyway. The one I'd punched had formed a faint blue circle around the rim, like the rings around Saturn.

"We can't have a party at the palace," Henry said. "Those ended after Marcus died. It would be tasteless. Besides, Mr. Stanton is out of town."

"Hey, Henry," I said, snapping my fingers in front of his face. "Do you want to deliver Marcus' killer to Mr. Stanton or not?"

Henry glared at me so hard I could practically read his thoughts. He wanted to lunge for my neck and rip into me. That would be a very big mistake. He thought I was human. Vampire or not, my blood was poisoned. I'd been juiced up with the agency's post paralytic "antidote" before leaving boot camp two and half weeks earlier.

Normally I wouldn't snap in an angry vampire's face, but I was in a shit-ass mood. My partner and best friend had been kidnapped. His dog Tommy had been taken without a trace. Earlier, Melcher and his minions had pushed me around without a shred of sympathy for Dante or Valerie, to say nothing of myself. All that and the realization that I'd been undead all along after I sucked blood from Daren's open wound.

So yeah, it was one of those bite a boy on the neck, punch a vampire in the face kind of days.

Fane cleared his throat. "All we have to do is get him inside the music room. One hour with me and he'll sing."

I didn't want Jared to sing, talk, or otherwise make a peep. I wanted him bound and gagged, ready to drop off at Giselle's doorstep. But only after she gave me Dante. Until then, Fane said our plan would go a whole lot smoother if Henry trusted us.

I was more in the mood to coerce than sweet talk.

Noel slammed her foot on the brake as the light at the first intersection turned red. I quickly turned and threw my hands forward, catching myself before I hit the dashboard. Henry slammed into the back of our seats. Fane didn't move an inch, like he'd braced himself all along.

I glared at Noel.

"Sorry," she said sheepishly. "The brakes on this thing are really stiff."

"That's nothing. Sometimes they don't work at all," Fane said from the backseat.

"And to think you could be driving a Lamborghini." Noel sighed and shook her head.

Splendid, one of their private jokes. I'd decided to make peace with Fane sucking Noel's blood at the palace. He'd done it to confirm a suspicion that Noel, and everyone else Melcher recruited, had been infected and turned into vampires. I also knew that Fane had helped Noel out of a jam, the details of which I had yet to uncover. But it still ruffled me to listen to their banter.

Rather than laugh at Noel's Lamborghini joke, Fane addressed Henry.

"We have to lure Jared into the open. In order to do that we need him to come to the palace."

"And why would he walk into a trap?" Henry asked.

"He'd come if someone fed him information that a certain vampire he's after was attending."

That's where Noel came in. The three of us—Fane, Noel, and I—had done some fast formulating, which led to a quick grab-and-go at Henry's townhouse. He happened to live only a few blocks away from the palace. What else did Richard Stanton employ him for? The man had reportedly been head over heels for Marcus. But who kept the wealthy gallery owner cold at night with Marcus out of the picture? It wouldn't surprise me if Henry was gay. The only interest I'd ever seen him show in women had to do with the blood pumping through their veins. The first time I met him, I thought he was charming, but appearances could be deceiving.

I'd never forgive the sucker for drugging me at the lodge. If Fane hadn't shown up when he had, it might have been me in the back of Henry's car being transported against my will.

Fortunately, Fane, Noel, and I had joined forces. We now had our in.

Noel's job was to report to Agent Melcher that parties at the palace were starting back up—that and she'd heard a blonde fitting Giselle's description had been seen with Henry. Now we needed to resurrect the parties in truth. Enter Henry.

"You expect me to put a guest's life at risk?" Henry asked.

"She won't actually be there," I said.

The light turned green. Noel floored the gas pedal, causing the tank to squeal in response. She glanced in the review mirror at Fane.

"It might be time for a tune up," he said.

"Time for a new car," Noel muttered under her breath. She had on the same strappy pink and purple checkered dress she'd arrived in earlier after coming home from an all-night party in

Girdwood. I had to give Henry credit for recognizing her from behind. I still hadn't adjusted to Noel's preppy new look.

She cranked the wheel through the intersection.

"Where are we going?" Henry asked again.

"Somewhere safe," Fane said.

"And where's that?"

"You'll see."

"Noel," Henry called out. "Where are you taking me?"

"You'll find out soon enough. Try to relax," Noel answered calmly.

"This is outrageous. Since when do you kidnap vampires, Francesco?"

"This is for your own safety," Fane said, an edge to his voice.

"Even if Richard gives me the okay, how am I supposed to plan a party in one week?" Henry demanded. "It's been over six months. All the regulars have moved on. And what do I tell them? It's beyond tasteless."

The springs on the backseat squeaked when Henry threw his back against them.

"I'll help with the planning," Noel said. "We'll tell everyone that Mr. Stanton believes Marcus would have wanted the party to go on and he'd want his partner to move on as well. Mr. Stanton doesn't have forever. Maybe he's starting these parties back up because he's looking for a new mate."

I found that bit particularly genius. Noel's twisted mind came in handy when least expected.

"How do you know so much?" Henry asked suspiciously.

Noel shrugged. "You're not the only one with a demanding employer."

"Oh yeah, and what does your employer want?"

"Doesn't matter," Noel said with a slight shake of her head. "I'm working independently on this one."

"We all are," I said.

"Why do you care who killed Marcus?" Henry asked in a clipped voice.

I could almost see his eyes narrow on the back of my head.

"Because he tried to kill me, too," I said. "That and we need to deliver him to a vampire named Giselle Morrel. He killed her entire family."

"Is she your employer?" Henry asked.

Employer, commander, puppet master—same thing, right?

"Like Noel said, we're working independently."

"Both Noel and Aurora are vampires," Fane supplied.

"But..."

"You and Gavin did say my blood tasted odd," Noel said. "Remember?"

"I'd heard rumors about AB blood, but nothing definitive," Henry said. "How come you never said anything?"

"Because I didn't know."

Henry's voice softened when he spoke next. "I apologize, ladies. No one knows at first."

Finally, a genuine apology. It made me less likely to punch out Henry's second eye.

Noel pushed through the next intersection, narrowly avoiding a second round of whiplash. Soon we were approaching Westchester Lagoon. Noel took the steep exit ramp, climbing slowly up the hill until we came out at West High School. I'd been a student there for what? A month?

Noel took a right. My grandmother's condo was to the left. I avoided the topic of Dante whenever my mom called to check in. Neither of them could know he'd gone missing. My mom would rush home in half a heartbeat. I needed her in Florida. I needed her safe. That meant lying.

I drummed my nails against the door's armrest.

We snaked our way past posh neighborhoods. Before hitting Northern Lights Boulevard, Noel pulled into a large apartment complex, and slowed inside the parking lot.

"Drive to the far end," Fane instructed her. "You can park behind the maroon station wagon."

As Noel neared the far end of the lot, a beat-up station wagon came into view. From the looks of it, the only thing keeping the back bumper attached to the car was a full roll of duct tape. The right backlight cover was smashed and rear passenger's window outlined in more thick gray tape.

Noel and I sat up in our seats.

"I take it back," Noel said. "Your car is great."

I glimpsed Henry's teeth as his lips curled in the review mirror.

"What are we doing here?" he asked.

I also caught Fane's sly smile as he turned to address Henry.

"Dropping you off. This will be your new home for a while."

"You're putting me under house arrest?"

"Trust me, you're far better off here," I said.

If Mason had gotten to him first, Henry would've been locked in a cell on base never to be seen or heard from again. The complex before us was a deluxe manor in comparison. He'd simply have to vamp up and slum it for a while.

Fane stepped out of the car first and opened my door. What was this? A date?

I swung my legs out, standing carefully so as not to bump into him—he was encroaching on my space again, leaning against the roof of the Pontiac. I had to arch my hips back or else slide against his chest as I rose on my feet.

"Ahem," I said.

Fane shot me a deliberate smile. Those inexplicably sensual, mismatched lips are what had attracted me to him in the first place. Time to put on the horse blinders.

I slid around him, shutting my door before Fane could do it for me.

Meanwhile, Noel stood beside Henry's open door trying to coax him out. "Come on, Henry. This is for your own safety."

Henry didn't budge.

Fane walked around swiftly, a feat he managed gracefully on his sturdy, long legs. Fane didn't ask; he pulled Henry out.

"Let's go."

Noel and I followed Fane and Henry up a flight of outdoor stairs to an open hallway. Our collective footsteps sounded like a stampede over the wood floorboards. We reached a door at the end of the hall. Fane knocked three times, paused, and knocked three times more.

At the end of the last knock there was movement behind the door, followed by the crack of a deadbolt snapping back. The door opened two inches before catching on a chain.

"Who's there?" a voice boomed.

Fane snorted. "Who do you think? I called you thirty minutes ago."

The door slammed shut. Fane released Henry and stretched, causing his subtle six-pack to strain through his black tee. I would have rolled my eyes if I wasn't busy gawking. Noel had her phone out, thumbing over the screen. Boy was I glad washboard abs didn't do it for her. She could keep her bony Goth guys all to herself.

A second later, the door flew back. A lanky dude in baggy jeans, a red hoodie, yellow shoulder length hair and a sideways baseball cap did a series of sideways moves with his arms and hands, as though gaining his footing on top of a balancing board.

"Yo! Fane Donado! My man. What's up?"

Fane lifted his chin. "Yo, Zeke."

"Yo!" Zeke said back louder. "Yo, yo, yo, yo, yo. Come on in, Donado and company."

I glanced at Fane. When he told me he knew someone who could keep an eye on Henry, this wasn't what I'd imagined.

Fane shot me what I assumed was supposed to be a reassuring smile—that or he was trying not to laugh.

Noel slipped her phone inside her purse and walked in first.

"Hey, little lady. You with Fane?" Zeke asked as she brushed past him.

Noel pivoted, eyes narrowed. "I'm a vampire."

Zeke's eyelids stretched back. "Awesome."

I still found it surreal to think of Noel Harper as a vampire—to say nothing of myself—and yet it felt freakishly natural, like finding out I was autistic or gay. Everything I'd struggled with over the past ten months suddenly made sense. My sensitivity to light and garlic. My loss of appetite replaced by an incessant thirst for blood.

I couldn't be the only agent going through this.

I glanced at Noel, whose gaze traveled from Zeke's broad, hopeful eyes to his neck as though considering a treat off the dessert menu. Nope, wasn't just me.

I walked inside the apartment next, Fane hot on my heels, bringing Henry with him.

Zeke shut and re-bolted the door. The entry led directly into a dingy kitchen. Both the oven and stovetop were streaked with grease stains. At one point, a potato must have exploded inside the microwave and never been fully cleaned out—there were bits of it stuck all over the inner window. Dishes had been piled a foot high inside both sinks. It smelled like a full bin on trash day.

Henry's nose wrinkled. I was with him on this one. I was immune to infection, not smell, and this place stank.

Fane didn't venture in much further from the front door.

"Zeke, this is Henry, the vamp we talked about. I need you to keep him safe."

"Not a problem," Zeke said. "This is like witness protection with triple extra pad-locked security. I won't let anything happen to him, man."

Fane reached around to his back pocket and pulled out a wallet. He took out every bill, handing them to Zeke, who stuffed the wad inside his back pocket.

"And make sure he doesn't wander."

"How am I supposed to eat?" Henry asked, eyeing the kitchen disdainfully.

Fane leaned over him. "Noel will bring blood by later. In the meantime, you've got a party to plan."

"Vamp party?" Zeke asked, rubbing his hands together.

"That's right," Fane said. "So don't distract him. If he needs classical music to concentrate, put on Beethoven. And for god's sakes, clean this place up. I don't want to hear about any biting, dealing, rapping, or Walking Dead TV marathons. Noel will check in every day after she finishes school."

"Wicked," Zeke said, eyes alight as he looked at Noel. "I'm human, just so you know. If you ever need a hit, I'm your guy, if you know what I mean."

"Zeke," Fane said in a warning tone. "What did I just tell you?"

Zeke grinned sheepishly.

Noel looked him up and down coolly. "I'll think about it."

"For real? Awesome!"

Keep dreaming hip-hop. I didn't see Noel sucking off a guy not dressed in head to toe black.

"Okay, we're good," Fane said, nodding. "Let's split."

As he, Noel, and I made for the door, Henry called out desperately, "Francesco, don't leave me here!"

"It's for your own good," Fane said. "Don't leave the apartment. That hunter isn't going to stop looking for you."

Henry shrunk back.

Noel gave a quick flick of her wrist. "See you tomorrow, Henry."

I didn't say anything. Pigsty or palace, he ought to be grateful we'd saved his sorry hide. I'd rather have rescued Dante or Tommy, but if Henry did his part, we might have a chance at killing several birds with one stone.

As Zeke closed the door behind us, I heard him ask Henry, "Dude, what happened to your eye?"

2

Scavengers

From the time we grabbed Henry to the time we dropped him off, the sky had morphed from faded pink to a rich red that bled across the pastel horizon. That's how evening worked in the fall. Daylight was fleeting, especially come afternoon when the outside world darkened at a speed similar to time lapse photography. This one changed in real time before the naked eye.

Once Fane, Noel, and I reached the car, I stopped in front of the hood and asked, "Now what?"

Fane lifted his head and looked into the distance. "Now we head to the hillside and find out what Diederick's staff knows about your partner's disappearance."

My chest surged with gratitude. Having help sure beat going about things alone.

"I'll drive," Fane said, holding his open palm in front of Noel.

She rolled her eyes before setting the keys in Fane's hand and climbing into the backseat. I slipped in front beside Fane.

Even on a Saturday, Anchorage's congested traffic made our progress from mid-town to the south side slow going. The Glen Alps rose above the city, their peaks poking the skyline like needles on a compass rose. Termination dust climbed steadily down from the tips of the mountains with each passing week. Winter was coming.

Once we made it out of town and onto O'Malley Road, it was a straight shot along the wooded hillside. Spruce and pine trees rushed by the windows. At the end of O'Malley, the back roads turned to gravel.

The temperature dropped the higher we climbed. I hugged my arms against my torso. Fane glanced over. Without a word, he turned up the heat. For the briefest moment I almost believed I was still a human girl out for a ride with her friends. But we were a car full of corpses—two perfectly poised and one shivering.

Heat blew from the vents. At top speed, it was also top volume. It filled my ears with the force of a gale.

Fane leaned back, one muscular arm manning the steering wheel, the other relaxed on his thigh—perfectly at ease, as always.

He had on a T-shirt, and Noel was wearing a damn sundress. Maybe I really was still human.

"If I'm a vampire, how come I feel cold?" I asked.

"The mind is a powerful force," Fane said. "Your body no longer requires food. You're immune to cold the same way you can't get sick. Hunger, chills—it's all in your head. It takes a few years to adjust."

"And then what?" I asked. "One day I'll wake up as numb and detached as Jared, Giselle, and all the other unfeeling vampires of the world?"

Fane remained silent a moment before answering. "I'm a vampire and I'm not indifferent." He turned his head toward me. "Far from it."

I shivered. "Well, my brain's still telling me I'm cold."

Actually, it was telling me to scoot over to Fane's side and show him I wasn't indifferent, either. Not when it came to him. Not ever. But I played it off as a reaction to the temperature—rubbing my hands together for emphasis even as liquid heat swarmed my insides.

I crossed and uncrossed my legs. The ache of Fane's bite still throbbed on my inner thigh. His teeth marks were still red and raw.

His love bite.

And there went my mind again, whispering nonsense, teasing me relentlessly. I could never turn the damn thing off.

His nearness made me wild with hunger. Fane was both familiar and foreign—like a rock star I'd lusted after from the sidelines, never believing I'd get my hands on him. And yet, he was still out-of-reach, off limits while Dante remained at large.

While I'd been away at boot camp it had been Dante who kept in contact with my family—he even helped my mom move. He'd asked me to give him a chance. He'd never gotten it, and I didn't intend to give him one. I just didn't love him that way, and I never would. But I never got the chance to tell him, and it didn't feel right to make a move on Fane so long as Dante was in captivity.

Noel's phone dinged with an incoming text. My body did a brief jolt, but, once again, it had more to do with my turmoil at Fane's proximity than surprise at the sudden interruption.

A couple seconds later, she said, "It's from Melcher."

I turned down the air vents.

"We need to turn around," she said. "He has an assignment for me tonight."

Fane's posture didn't change, nor did the set speed of the car as it continued up the dirt road. "Not yet. We're almost there," he said.

I glanced from Noel to Fane, once again grateful for his steady presence. When I looked back at Noel, she frowned.

The lodge's valet and butler wouldn't know Dante's whereabouts, but even the tiniest detail regarding his departure was better than nothing. Had Giselle drugged him and dragged him out? I rubbed my lips together. Doubtful. When I left the tasting with Fane, the valet had made sure it was by choice.

At the very least, we could recoup his Jeep. It paled in comparison to Dante's dog, but it was something and it was a start. I wasn't supposed to be up there snooping around, asking questions. Melcher wanted me to return next weekend. He wanted to put a permanent end to the tastings.

"What's your assignment?" I asked Noel, half curious and half hoping to distract her from asking Fane to head back down.

When Noel didn't answer, I turned in my seat to find her reading back over the text. Her eyes lifted briefly and met mine. She turned off her phone.

"What the matter?" Fane asked. "Afraid I'll try and stop you?"

"I'm not in the habit of sharing classified information. It doesn't matter anyway. I'm only gathering intel."

I eyed Noel curiously, wondering how it felt spying on vampires now that she knew she was one of them.

Fane must have been thinking the same thing. "It must be difficult working for these people now that you know the truth."

"The agency isn't all bad," Noel answered. "It's just mismanaged."

I snorted. That was the understatement of the year.

Noel scooted forward on the back bench. "Aside from the underhanded way they've recruited some of their agents, they've also done a lot of good. We've saved lives. The agency has issues, but did you ever stop to consider what would happen if it shut down altogether?"

My jaw tightened.

"No," I said, turning my back to Noel abruptly.

The agency hadn't bothered to consider my future. Why should I give two twigs about its?

The anniversary of my car crash was a little less than two months away. At the end of last year I'd been a straight-A senior in high school. Single. Virgin. College bound.

Earlier, Noel confided that she'd slit her wrists and the agency had saved her. Well, they hadn't saved me. They'd run me off the road and infected me while I was unconscious. There was only one word for that. Evil.

That kind of planning took cold calculation.

"Melcher must have a reason for turning us into vampires and keeping it a secret," Noel said. "Maybe this is a probationary period and he's waiting to tell us once he feels we're ready. Or maybe the antidote didn't work the way it was supposed to—his scientists slipped up. They're still figuring out how our blood reacts with their toxin. Melcher wasn't a hundred percent sure AB positive blood would paralyze a vampire the way type AB negative did... not until my initiation."

Right, because being one of Melcher's guinea pigs made everything all right. The rabies vampire I killed during initiation had nearly killed Noel first. The toxin hadn't protected her from the slobbering fanatic. Being a hunter had its pros.

"Are you sure you want out?" I asked Noel. "Because it sure doesn't sound like you do."

Noel didn't hesitate. "The day I became an informant, I made a commitment to protect people from vampires—even if that means protecting civilians from the agency. No one should be a target based on blood type. We're in this together."

The anger inside me dissipated upon hearing Noel's heartfelt words. I looked over my shoulder. Noel's hands were folded in her lap, head bent.

I'd been so preoccupied with Dante's capture and my new found discovery that I hadn't stopped to consider how Noel was taking everything. When I first returned from boot camp, she appeared all peaches and cream, which was why I hadn't worried about it until now.

The agency might have killed me, but it had saved Noel and given her a sense of purpose. What would she do without the agency?

From the moment I discovered Noel and I were both new recruits, she'd proven herself a sensitive and loyal friend. When

I'd been abducted by Renard and his cohorts, she'd put my safety before the secrecy of the agency by calling in help from a vampire: Fane.

And she'd never succumbed to blind hatred of vampires the way Melcher and Dante had. Noel knew there were shades of grey and that vampires who didn't kill didn't deserve to die at our hands.

"What will you do if we manage to take the agency down?" I asked.

That was a big if... a big as if.

Still, it didn't hurt to talk about the future in case we did manage to somehow outsmart Melcher—even with his unlimited resources, funds, assassins, and government backing.

"I'm not without options," Noel said. "I've made a lot of connections over the past year. Fans of the undead society are much more motivated to help out a lady vamp than a human girl. I'll get by."

She said it like she believed it.

Being a vampire appeared to have put a spell over Noel. She exuded confidence and style. Maybe she had a massive freak out when she first found out. I'd run from her and Fane when Noel's initial realization hit. I'd missed her big moment. I thought I'd walked into something entirely different. Afterwards, I'd disappeared for six whole months. While I was at boot camp, Noel was coming to terms with what she was. I hadn't been there for her, and now I was playing catch up—trying to figure out who this new version of my old friend had become.

"How do you feel about being undead?" I asked. "You seem to have accepted it rather well."

"Because for the first time, I feel alive," Noel said. "I spent almost my entire life acting like a timid little mouse, hood over my head, hiding in the corner. There are two types of people in this world: criminals and quarry. That's what I used to believe until I became an informant and a vampire. Once that happened, I realized there was a third category of being: champions." Noel lifted her chin. "I don't owe my family or the agency anything. I have no fear. My purpose is clear and that is to do what's right at all costs."

Fane turned my way. When I looked over his eyebrows jumped. "Is this when we applaud?" he asked.

"Shut up," Noel said with a laugh. "And hurry, will you, so I can get home and change."

"Into your warrior princess costume?" Fane asked.

Noel snickered. Even I cracked a smile. It was becoming easier to relax around Noel and Fane now that our secrets were out in the open. Well, maybe not Fane, but that's because my heart did funny things in his presence.

"By the way, you forgot a fourth category of people," Fane said. "Loyal subjects. You stole a couple of mine. Daren. Reece. How are my old groupies?"

"More like quarry," I said.

Noel shrugged. "Even a champion's gotta feed."

As the stone pillars marking the mansion's driveway appeared in the headlights, Fane slowed the car. The road smoothed out as we rolled onto the paved driveway leading up to the three story stone mansion.

"Just don't get carried away like these fools," Fane said, nodding at Tasting Headquarters.

Three gray stone chimneys rose from the towering rooftop. One was near the entrance of the mansion, another on the west wing and a third on a separate possible guest home, which the driveway skirted and disappeared around what I gathered was a hidden parking lot or industry-sized garage.

"Holy smokestacks, look at this place," Noel said, leaning against the back window. "It has to be five times the size of the tasting Dante and I crashed in Fairbanks. It's as big as a castle."

"I call it the lodge," I said.

"Cozy," Fane said. "We'll take three mugs of warm blood in front of the fire."

"Can I have marshmallows in mine?" Noel asked.

The Pontiac squealed to a stop in front of the stone stairway. We stared in the direction of the big bay windows flanking the entrance.

"Where's the valet?" I asked.

"Obviously not expecting company," Fane remarked.

He exited the car and slammed the door shut. Noel and I were right behind him. We followed Fane up to the front door, where he pounded against the wood.

The butler answered. If he was surprised to see us, he didn't show it. He held the same aloof posture and spoke in an even voice. I wondered briefly if there was such a thing as boot camp for butlers.

"Mr. Donado, may I help you?"

He even remembered Fane's name.

For the price vamps paid to partake in the tasting, I imagined the staff was as knowledgeable about their esteemed guests' names as the wine selection.

Fane smiled. "Our friend went home with a woman last night and asked us to pick up his car."

"Ah, yes," the butler said.

I leaned on the tips of my toes listening closely for the butler to say something about Giselle. Instead, he retrieved one of the wicker baskets from the wall and pulled out a cell phone and keys.

"Mr. Dante's Jeep is parked in back." He handed the phone to Fane. "Wilkins is off tonight, but if you wait out front I will bring the car around."

The butler held the door open for us. Fane swept a muscular arm out for Noel and I to go first. As he followed, he paused in the doorframe and looked back at the butler.

"Say, Smithers, I hope my friend wasn't too far in his cups. He's a bit... new. I trust he behaved himself upstairs? Didn't get kicked out for misbehavior? Or dragged out for drunkenness? " Fane lifted one eyebrow.

The butler stiffened.

"I assure you, your friend behaved himself perfectly. He was in a bit of a hurry to leave with the blonde, but in no way disorderly."

"And did you see what kind of vehicle they left in?" Fane asked.

I held my breath waiting for the answer. How long would it take to search every driveway in Anchorage if we knew the make, model, and color of Giselle's car? Too long, especially if she stowed it inside a garage. But we didn't have a whole heck of a lot else to go on.

"I'm afraid I didn't see. Wilkins would know." The butler frowned. "Sir, is something the matter?"

"Not at all," Fane said.

"Very good. I will bring the car around."

"Smithers?" I asked Fane once the three of us were alone, waiting in the drive. I could have sworn the guy's name was Foster or Forester.

"Veronica's butler in the Archie comic books," Fane said.

I rolled my eyes. "Your knowledge of pop culture astounds me."

"I've been in America longer than any living American."

"Now you're just bragging."

Fane smirked.

Noel cleared her throat. "He wasn't dragged out against his will. She must have tricked him or threatened him in some way."

"Or invited him home," Fane said under his breath.

A bolt of outrage jolted me. My insides boiled at Fane's suggestion. "Dante would never leave me behind in the middle of a mission."

Fairbanks didn't count. His departure had been part of the plan, which he was up front about from the very beginning.

Noel nodded her agreement. While I glared at Fane, she looked him over with a disapproving frown. "Aurora's right. Dante wouldn't do that."

Fane made no answer, no apology. He gave a slight shrug that suggested his disinterest in Dante's motives or true character.

Headlights cut across us like laser beams when the butler drove the Jeep into the front drive.

Noel stuck her hand out in front of Fane. "Keys." When Fane made no move for his keys, Noel said, "I don't know how to drive stick so I'm stuck with the tank."

Fane handed over his keys.

The butler stepped out of the Jeep, keeping it running.

"We hope to see you and Mr. Dante again soon," he said to Fane before heading back to the lodge.

"Aurora?" Fane asked softly. "Will you ride with me?"

I twisted my lips to the side, considering. Part of me really wanted to. Another part was totally annoyed by his implication that Dante tried to leave the party to hook up with another woman.

As flirtatious as Dante could be, he'd waited six months for my return from boot camp on the off chance there might be something more than friendship between us. If he thought I was in trouble, he'd drop everything in an instant to come help.

My eyes met Fane's. "I'll ride back with Noel."

He stared at me a long moment before answering. "Okay," he said before turning toward the Jeep.

I watched his long, lean, muscular form as it moved away. My heart dropped as he receded into the fading light. Why did it feel like I was the one who had insulted him?

The Pontiac started up with a squeal that jolted me out of my reverie. I hurried in beside Noel who threw the car into drive—jerking us forward.

"So you and Dante," she started in immediately, as though the words were a breath she'd been holding in. "That's real?"

I shook my head before realizing her eyes were on the approaching stone pillars.

"No. I love him as a friend, but that's all."

"Good," Noel said without pause. "You should give Fane another chance. You obviously still care for each other. Plus now you know you're both vampires. I realize I wasn't supportive of the relationship in the beginning, but that was before I knew we were all undead. Personally, I've decided only to date other vampires. Daren and Reece are casual, you know? Suck buddies."

Daren and Reece weren't my idea of a hot threesome, but now I understood what Noel really wanted them for. I'd gotten a taste, too. We were blood-sucking vampires and it was Melcher's damn fault.

"Only vampires, huh? Any vamp in particular? Say, Gavin?"

"I'll help with his rescue, but he had his chance with me, and he blew it."

From the sudden flush in her cheeks, I didn't buy it. I'd told myself something similar about Fane. Now I wasn't so sure.

I pressed my back into the seat. "Before I do anything I need to talk to Dante, which is impossible at the moment since he's been captured." I said it as much for my own benefit as Noel's.

Noel glanced over quickly. "I want to get him and Gavin back as much as you."

She pointed the Pontiac down the gravel road outside the stone pillars. Anchorage lit up below. The city lights extended to Cook Inlet, where the mountains across the ocean dimmed against the impending twilight.

A second pair of headlights reflected off the Pontiac's review mirror as Fane followed us in the Jeep from a distance.

"This not being able to drive thing is really starting to blow," I said.

Noel made a puff sound when she exhaled. "No kidding. Why don't you do something about it?"

I grinned. "Driving the convertible might help motivate me."

"No, way," Noel said. "My baby isn't a practice car."

I glanced at the Jeep in mirror. "Maybe I'll start with the Jeep." Dante wasn't around to object. Besides, he'd once told me to get back in the saddle.

"It's stick," Noel said.

"Yeah, well, why do things the easy way when you can do them the hard way? Speaking of which, want to tell me about this secret mission tonight?"

Better Noel than me. I'd had enough excitement for one day.

When I looked over, Noel made a face.

"Nothing exciting. Just some vampires dealing drugs at a party on the eastside. I've been keeping an eye on them ever since the doors of the palace closed. Not my favorite assignment."

"I thought you said Melcher didn't have much work for you these past six months."

Noel shrugged. "Just the usual informant, spy stuff. I'm playing it cool. What about you? You have to go back up to that place next weekend?"

"One last time," I said, barely audible.

I stiffened as Melcher's voice echoed through my brain.

"We're going to shut down Diederick's tastings permanently."

35

I wanted no part of it. I especially did not want to partner with smug-mouth Levi and the lackluster Mason. No, I wanted to team up with Noel and Fane to rescue Dante and take down Jared and Melcher.

Hopefully I made it through the next mission in one piece to carry out my own.

3
Defensive Measures

Once we reached home, Noel yanked the keys out of the ignition and thrust them at me.

"Give these to Fane, will you? I've got to dash."

The moment the keys slipped from her fingers into mine, Noel rushed off to the house. I waited in the driveway, expecting Fane to pull up in the Jeep at any moment.

He didn't.

I planted my feet firmly over the concrete and swung my hips in figure eights to keep busy and stay warm. When a car drove by, I stopped until it passed and started again as though slow dancing with myself.

What was taking Fane so long? Did he decide to upgrade to the Jeep? Sure, insult a man's integrity then keep his ride. Real sportsmanly... and so not Fane.

The door to our house slammed shut as Noel raced toward her convertible. I blinked when I saw her dressed in black fishnets covered in a knee-length, high collared purple Gothic jacket.

"Halloween isn't for another month," I said.

Noel grimaced before answering, "I'm blending in." She opened her car door and squinted into the dark street. "Fane's not back yet?"

"No."

"Why don't you wait for him inside?"

"Because then I'll have to invite him in," I said. That wasn't why I waited outside in the cold. The real reason I stood fidgeting in the shadows had more to do with guilt over not riding home with him after he asked so nicely.

"Yeah? And?" Noel said and chuckled. "Invite the man in. I won't be home for hours."

She winked and dove inside her car before I could respond. As the convertible zoomed down the road, I groaned inwardly.

Sure, invite Fane inside. Why not invite him to spend the night again while I was at it? Meanwhile, who knew where Dante was? I was still waiting for a phone call. I'd told Giselle I wanted to talk to him and make sure he was all right. She said that could be arranged. When? My phone had yet to ring with Dante's voice on the other end. Where was Giselle keeping him? And where was Fane?

It wasn't as though he'd get hungry along the way and stop for pie. That was Dante's M.O.

I checked my phone for any missed calls or texts, but nothing new had come in.

Impatience finally got the better of me. I called Fane.

It was a relief when he answered, even when he skipped the pleasantries to say, "Be there shortly." With that he ended the call.

Fine. No sense standing around in the dark.

Once inside, I paced around the kitchen and listened for the Jeep. Fane obviously knew how to handle a stick shift. Big surprise. If I asked him to teach me, I knew he'd agree. He was the one who'd started my car rehabilitation. He might as well finish it.

The Jeep didn't announce itself the way the tank did, with a start-up or stopping squeal, which was how I missed its arrival. Plus Fane parked it on the street rather than in the driveway.

The sound of his pounding fist kick-started my heart rate. He had been doing that all day. No doorbells for Fane Donado, no, he liked things more hands-on.

The porch light lit up one side of his face and cast a shadow over the other side, making it appear as though he were wearing half a mask like the Phantom of the Opera. Goosebumps rose to the surface of my skin.

"Did you run out of gas or something?" I asked.

"No, I stopped by Frigid North Company to pick up a security system for you."

Fane turned his head. That's when I noticed the big box on the porch. In bold lettering it said: EXTREME SERIES. Complete 2 Camera Pro Security Camera System.

For me? I thought, my eyes lifting quickly up to Fane's. My brain fuzzed over briefly and my heart flipped. Nothing said "I care about you" like an extreme series security system.

"Do you have a ladder?" Fane asked. He pulled out a pocket knife, crouched beside the box, and slid the blade through the wide tape.

I stared at him, unable to answer as my throat constricted.

"Or a stool?" he asked.

"I'll check the garage," I said, quickly turning before he could see my face. My eyes had an annoying tendency to tear up when my emotions flared. Kindness was hard to come by and his filled me with affection. Car rehabilitation could wait.

Searching the garage gave me time to collect myself. When I failed to locate a chair or stool in the garage, I returned with a dining table chair. In the meantime, Fane had unpacked the box and laid out the cameras along with the extra pieces and parts on the porch.

"I couldn't find a ladder," I said. "Hope the chair works."

Fane grinned. "Good thing I'm tall."

Tall, dark, and so damn hot. I'd had a thing for Fane ever since I first saw him stroll by at Denali High School in his black garb and blond mop of hair on top of his head. He was the only Goth boy I'd ever seen who didn't dye it all black. No, not Fane. He went for Barbie blond. And like a little girl, I had a sudden urge to play with it—more specifically, run my hands through the thick patch up top.

At times, I felt like our time together had only been a dream. A fantasy. A figment of my imagination. Two weeks together. Not nearly enough time.

Fane moved the chair by the far corner of the door and stepped on it—effectively transporting his hair out of reach from my twitching fingers.

"Will you hand me one of those cameras?" he asked.

I crouched down, grabbed a camera, and handed it to Fane. I stood below watching his every move as he hooked up the security cam. Once finished, he inspected his work, flashed me a pleased grin, and jumped off the chair landing in front of me with a thump.

"Smile, you're on camera."

I stuck my tongue out at the camera, instead.

Fane chuckled. "Grab the chair. I've got one more to install by the sliding glass door in back."

❋ ❋ ❋

After Fane finished installing the second camera, he lingered inside the living room. He didn't sit, nor did he show signs of leaving.

"So Noel's out on mission?" Fane asked.

"Yeah."

He took a step closer, both eyebrows raised in question. "Want me to stay over?"

Did I want Fane to stay over? Did bears shit in the woods?

If I wasn't so worried about Dante, I'd say we most definitely deserved a do-over. But the timing was never right. I'd once spent the night at Fane's. He'd taken the couch and given me his room. His bed. The week before, he'd slept on my couch, not that I'd known he spent the night until the next morning. One of these days we needed a sleepover that involved actually sleeping together—same room, same bed.

I cleared my throat. "That's nice of you to offer, but I have a lot of sleep and homework to catch up on."

Fane smiled slightly as though seeing right through my excuse.

"I won't bite this time."

My cheeks burned. I screwed up my face and scowled. Smug bastard.

"How's your thigh?" he asked, eyes dropping to the tender spot near my groin.

"How's your tongue?" I shot back. He'd bit it hard enough to draw blood.

"As good as new. See?" The fiend ran the tip over his upper lip.

Rather than recoil with indignity, my body quivered in hunger. Blood cravings were one thing. Fane cravings were a hundred times more demanding. He had a knack for getting under my skin anytime he desired.

Before I could respond, my phone rang.

Relieved by interruption, I moved away from the heat surrounding Fane to fish my phone out of my pocket.

"Hello?"

There was a moment's pause. Fane raised one eyebrow.

"You wanted to speak with Dante," Giselle said through the speaker.

"Yes," I replied, my heart rate speeding in a new direction.

"You have one minute."

I held my breath. Was Giselle really going to let me talk to Dante?

A door groaned open, followed by a low thump. The sound of creaky footsteps increased in volume until they stopped.

"Aurora?"

Dante's voice flooded me with relief.

"Dante! Are you okay? Has Giselle harmed you in any way?"

Fane folded his arms and leaned back, watching me. I turned my back to him.

"I'm okay," Dante said solemnly.

He didn't sound okay. His voice was withdrawn and moody. Well, what did I expect? I'd feel the same way if I'd been imprisoned against my will. I thought he'd perk up a little if he heard my voice.

"We're going to get you out of there. We'll have Jared this Friday. Once we capture him I'll demand an exchange."

"Tommy," Dante said as though he hadn't listened to a word I'd just said.

My chest tightened.

"Tell me you didn't forget him."

Far from it. The golden retriever had been running around in my mind from the moment Melcher told Levi to scoop him up.

"Of course not."

Dante breathed a sigh of relief. "I suppose I can hang tight a little longer, though the accommodations leave something to be desired."

"Where is she keeping you?" I asked, eager to move away from the subject of Dante's dog.

"In a basement with a vampire."

Oh god, if Gavin was locked up with someone he thought to be human...

"He hasn't tried to..."

"She gives him plenty of blood," Dante said. "The vamp's not interested in me, anyway, says this is what he gets for going out with Valerie. Is he a target?"

"No, but he and Valerie are going out."

"The girl said she stabbed Valerie, and she'd do the same to anyone who didn't do what she wants."

"Melcher said Valerie's going to be fine," I said.

"And you? Are you all right?"

I balled up my toes inside my sneakers.

"I just want to get this over with and get you back," I said, regretting my word choice as soon as I finished speaking.

I wanted to get Dante back safe and sound, not back, back— as in back together. Not that we'd been together, though Dante had tried and I'd never gotten a chance to set him straight.

My shoulders hunched into my neck. Hopefully Fane knew what I meant. I turned and found him staring at me steadily, expression unreadable. I cleared my throat.

"I want to help you," Dante said, "But the she-vamp won't let me out."

"I'll get Jared."

"You need me," Dante said.

"I've got help."

The sound of a door creaked open on Dante's end. He sighed.

"Vampire Hitler wants the phone back."

"Just hang tight, Dante," I said quickly. "We'll have you out of there in no time."

God, I sounded cheesy. That's what bad circumstances did to speech—reduced words to lace covered bull crap full of holes.

Dante didn't say "bye." The next words I heard were Giselle's from afar.

"Set the phone on the middle stair and back away."

The speaker picked up light movement before Giselle spoke into my ear.

"Are you close to securing Jared?"

"This weekend," I answered.

44

"Good."

"I want you to release Dante once we get him."

"That wasn't the deal," Giselle said.

"I need Dante's help to trap Melcher." Heck, I'd probably need a whole army of hunters to get Melcher.

I didn't like the way Giselle played the game, but at least we had a shared interest in the end results.

The line went quiet a moment.

Finally Giselle said, "I'll think about it."

That answer gave me about as much hope as a "maybe." I'd take it.

"And can you please give Dante some real food?"

"Unnecessary," Giselle said. "He's a vampire."

This was true, but Dante didn't know it.

"He likes to eat," I said.

"I'll think about it," Giselle repeated. "This will be the only time I contact you," she said next. "Call me at this number when you have Xavier."

Giselle ended the call, apparently not requiring an answer. I set my phone on the kitchen table, frowning down at it.

"That was Giselle, she..."

"I think I got the gist of it," Fane said.

I lifted my eyes. Fane frowned. Okay, Mr. Moody, sorry to interrupt our earlier conversation-slash-flirtation with this hostage situation.

"In that case, I guess there's nothing more for me to say," I said peevishly.

Fane's shoulders dropped. "That's not what I meant. I'm not happy because I'm not in control of the situation. I don't like Giselle calling the shots."

"You and me both," I muttered.

"But I do like the plan of capturing Jared."

I nodded.

Fane stepped up to me and touched the side of my face gently.

"I don't want you anywhere near this freak on Friday."

I inhaled, holding my breath for several beats. "I can't go to the palace, anyway. I have to be at the lodge."

Fane nodded grimly. "I don't want you there, either, but at least you'll be far away from Stanton's place."

It sounded weird hearing Marcus' home now referred to as Richard Stanton's. It had always been Stanton's, but it never seemed that way. It was the palace, Marcus's domain. Bet he never expected this raven-haired teenager would take him down. I hadn't seen it coming, either.

"At least I'll have an alibi when Jared's abducted," I said. Had to stay on the positive side.

"I'll let you rest up," Fane said. "Call if you need me."

Oh, I needed him, all right, but I didn't call. I didn't catch up on homework, either. Instead, I slept through all of Sunday.

Apparently even vampires weren't immune to sleep.

❅ ❅ ❅

Monday morning, I brushed the tangles out of my long black hair, dressed and headed out the door to walk to campus. I wasn't in a learning mood, but it beat putzing around home waiting for the weekend.

When I stepped outside in my skinny pleather jacket and saw Dante's Jeep across the yard, I half expected him to climb out of the car and come ambling up to greet me with a cheerful, "Looking good, Sky. Real good." Wink, wink.

If only I'd just imagined the last forty-six hours.

I took a steady breath and walked up to the Jeep.

"I'll get him back," I said to it. "I promise."

What then?

Everything had changed. How would Dante deal? His feelings for me were no longer the big issue. He had forever to work them out of his system. He didn't strike me as a dweller. He'd move on—once we freed him. At least I hoped he would.

I knew now what I'd struggled to realize before. Dante was my best friend. I loved him to the moon and back, just not romantically. There was more than one way to love a person. I hoped he'd understand that.

That left me with the riddle over what to do about Fane. Confusing as usual. Didn't matter. I had plenty of time to deal with the Dark Prince. I had all the time in the world.

There. Now I could make jokes about time, too.

The sky was solid white. Not quite dreary, but not especially cheerful, either. I walked past the homes of my neighbors, none of whom I'd met. If the apocalypse ever hit Anchorage, I wouldn't have anyone within an eight mile radius to count on for help or so much as a cup of sugar. Not that I needed their sugar. One juicy vein would do just fine.

Fane said blood was enough to get by on, but that morning I'd stuck to my usual breakfast routine—toast with tea.

I needed normal. I clung to it like a straightjacket in a sea of crazies.

The sound of traffic increased as I approached Lake Otis Parkway. I made my way up the stairs to the pedestrian bridge, morning commuters whizzing by beneath my feet. A horn honked. It didn't startle me the way it once would have. In fact, my fingers were itching to get back behind the wheel.

I had no desire to spend the remainder of my undead life squirreled away like Fane's roommate, Joss. He wasn't cold like Giselle, but he acted just as detached.

I needed to be able to take care of myself. I wasn't about to call up Fane every time I had to go someplace. And I could pass on the public bus. All I required was a vehicle, and I had one temporarily. At least I hoped it was temporary—so long as this weekend went according to plan. But it was a start. Too bad the Jeep had a manual transmission.

Once on the opposite side of Lake Otis, I made my way to Campus Drive and the stadium-sized parking lot in front of the University of Alaska Anchorage's first set of buildings. Clearing the lot was a hike in itself. Even if I took up driving again, it would still make more sense to walk to campus. By the time I warmed up the car, waited at the intersection, and circled the lot looking for an empty spot, I would have made it by foot to the Professional Studies Building.

I entered now, taking the stairs to the second floor, passing the journalism department until I reached my Written Communications class.

Class started in five minutes. The room was already more than half-full of students making chit-chat.

"Who's the easiest math teacher on campus?" a woman asked a guy in plaid as I passed between them.

Good question. Numbers had never been my friend. I tried to listen in, but his answer got obliterated under the smack of the next student's textbook dropping on his desk.

I took a seat and arranged what I needed on the tiny desk. The din continued around me. Funny how weird it seemed not knowing anyone. It wasn't as though I'd always had a friend in every class at Denali High, but I recognized their faces.

The college students surrounding me were complete strangers. It struck me how few people I really knew.

I'd lived in Anchorage all my life, yet a rush of loneliness came over me with such magnitude it threatened to suck the breath from my lungs.

I rubbed the desk surface with my middle finger for no other reason than to look busy.

Striking up conversations with strangers had never come easy to me. Not to mention it was pretty much pointless. Why would I want to make friends with someone who would up and die one day?

The only friendships worth investing time and emotion in were with other vampires.

Fane had no trouble befriending humans. He was a social king among society's rejects.

I still remembered the group of misfits that flocked to him at Denali High—Goth kids who all looked the same. At some point Fane added grunge to his repertoire of followers, as Zeke colorfully demonstrated.

The point was, he didn't let everlasting life bum him out. He had fun and thrived. It made me flush to think that out of his hordes of adoring groupies, he'd chosen to fixate on me. It didn't matter that he couldn't suck my blood. He didn't care whether I was human or vampire. I suspected it made him happy I'd live forever... in theory.

Even when I pushed Fane away, he loomed at the edges of my life like a shadow—backing me up one minute, gone the next.

I frowned. The gone part was the current problem.

Suddenly we weren't vampire and hunter. Suddenly I knew why he'd bitten Noel at the palace. The playing field had evened out. The game changed. But where did that leave us? As teammates? A high-five, good job, see you at the next meet?

You're just lonely, I tried telling myself.

Loneliness was worse than being drunk.

I glanced sideways at my nearest neighbor, a young woman with blue streaks in her auburn hair. Her stockings were ripped—on purpose I was pretty sure—beneath a tweed skirt and tank top. A snakelike Chinese dragon was tattooed over her arm.

Nobody talked to her. I should have made an effort to strike up a conversation. Instead, I stared at her tattoo and wondered how much it had bled.

I opened my textbook over the desk to prevent a finger burn if I continued to rub away at the surface.

A guy wearing a UAA Seawolves baseball cap sat down in front of me. He leaned back. Sure, why didn't he shove his neck in my face?

My eyes darted back and forth between my textbook and the few inches of skin between his shirt collar and cropped hair.

I rubbed the bridge of my nose.

Why did I have to walk over so early? This was turning into the longest five minutes of my life. What was I even doing at university? I didn't belong here. I wasn't on campus to make friends or date or pursue a career. I was only fooling myself.

I got up. I had to get out of there.

Inside, my heart raged, but nobody noticed the vampire in torment. After stuffing my textbook, notepaper and pen inside, I grabbed my backpack by the top loop. The moment I walked out of the classroom, I felt instantly better. Free.

My feet carried me quickly down the hall, past corkboards papered in fliers, students walking in pairs, and professors headed to teach class.

I practically ran down the stairs until I pushed through the double doors leading into an open courtyard. Students sat at picnic tables and sprawled out across the lawn while the weather still permitted. Everyone around me looked like they belonged there.

Meanwhile, I felt like a dowager at a rock concert.

I was an old soul. That was the problem. Even though I was from this century, I had trouble relating to my generation.

I took my phone out and dialed Fane. Instantly, I felt less alone with the promise of someone to talk to. Better yet, he answered after the first ring.

"Is this a mission related question or do you just miss me?" Fane asked in a devious voice.

"I'm having a problem," I said.

"What is it? What's going on?" Fane asked, instantly switching his tone. "Where are you?"

"I'm on campus. I was in class, but I walked out. I couldn't sit there anymore. My classmates were starting to look like walking, talking blood sacks."

The line went quiet. Suddenly Fane laughed.

Once he'd regained his breath, he said, "Welcome to my world."

"The underworld," I said sarcastically. "What about you? How do you fill the void now that you're no longer Denali High's number one delinquent?"

Fane had told me he was taking a break from the whole high school charade this year. Since Joss was the one who supported them with his online rare books business, I wasn't sure how Fane passed his time without any kind of daily routine.

"The real question is how does Principal Romero pass the time now that I'm gone?"

"I'm sure he has one less grey hair on his head this semester," I said, watching that I didn't run into anybody as I circled the courtyard.

"Two less," Fane said. "As I recall, you paid a visit to his office at the beginning of the year—three days suspension for fighting." Fane clicked his tongue. "Bad girl."

Sizzles ran up and down my spine, humming like a power line along a mountain pass.

I remembered that day clearly. Fane had followed me onto the public bus after Principal Romero finished suspending me. But I was the one who'd jumped into Fane's lap and stuck my tongue down his throat.

"And now you're cutting class," Fane observed.

I circled around a building, leaving the courtyard behind. It wasn't exactly a telephone booth, but I had the shaded corner to myself. Was this what my life had come down to? A vampire watching humanity from the shadows?

My eyes watered. I'd been holding it in since I first walked onto campus.

Betraying nothing with my voice I said, "I don't know what I'm supposed to do with myself. I don't know how to spend forever. I don't even know what to do today or right now, this second."

Fane was silent a moment before answering. "All you have to do is take it one day at a time."

My face dropped. "I expected something better than a bull-shit answer from you, Fane Donado." The next pause was longer than the last. I couldn't hear so much as a crackle or breath on the other line. Finally I asked, "Did I lose you?"

"Not a chance," Fane answered right back. "You want to know what to do with yourself?"

"Yes."

"Live each day in the present. To regret what might have been is to live in the past. To worry about what's to come is to live in the future. The question is, what does Aurora Sky want to do right now?"

You, I thought. I want to do you. I want you to taste me the way no man or vampire has tasted me before. I want you to make love to me for so long I can't think of a damn thing besides how good you feel inside me... finally. I want to forget everything—yesterday, today, tomorrow, the present, the past, the future. I don't care what moment I'm living in. I want you.

Naturally, I said none of the above. I said something almost worse.

"Can you come over?"

The silence that followed was different. If a smile had a sound, this was it—the soft exhalation, the half-chuckle that came before Fane answered.

"I take it you're skipping the rest of the day?"

I shrugged beneath the building's shadow. "Old habits die hard."

"I'll be right over."

"Good. I'll see you soon," I said, ending the call before he could answer.

Aw, hell, what had I just done?

4

Co-Pilot

jammed my phone into my coat pocket and booked it off campus, retracing my steps home. Even on foot, I figured I had a ten minute lead on Fane. I raced up the stairs to the overhead crosswalk and back down to the other side of the street.

So much for making the Dean's List. I'd missed my high school graduation. What were the odds I'd make it through college?

I smiled at the security cam Fane installed above the front door.

"Back so soon?" I asked it. "Why yes, I am."

I ran upstairs and gave my hair another quick brush through. The walk back and forth to campus had introduced a couple of minor tangles back into my dark hair. I shook my head in the mirror.

"What are you doing, Aurora?" I asked my reflection.

Nothing. This wasn't a booty call. I simply wanted to finish car rehabilitation. The more I could rely on myself, the less I had to count on anyone else, including Fane.

I waited on the front stoop, not wanting Fane to get any ideas by letting him in.

He pulled in soon enough, the bottom of his car scraping the driveway as he came up. I winced. From behind the windshield, Fane grinned. At least the little things still amused him.

As Fane stepped out, I moved toward him. He pushed his car door shut with his shoulder and straightened. My eyes traveled up and down his body before I could stop myself.

He wore combat boots, black jeans, a black belt, and a black V-neck taut across his chest. No man dead or alive had ever made a T-shirt look so sexy.

There was a wide black leather bracelet wrapped around his right wrist. It looked like the kind used to shackle a person's wrist to a bedpost.

My feet stopped working. Fane had no trouble closing the distance. He stopped in front of me, shoving a hand into his front pocket, thumb resting over his belt, which caused me to look down, directly into the danger zone. My eyes shot back up. Fane smirked, missing nothing.

"Aren't you going to invite me in?"

I nodded in the direction of the Jeep. "Can you teach me to drive a stick?"

Fane studied me a moment. "This is a car we're talking about, right?" The bastard stroked his belt with his thumb, drawing my attention back down.

"Of course I mean the car," I said. "Can you teach me?" I made a point of leaving the stick part out the second time.

"Whatever you want," Fane said.

I pulled the key from my pocket and dangled it by Dante's Alaskan Brewing Company keychain.

"Great, know a good parking lot?"

Fane grinned mischievously. "I know a great parking lot."

I knew Fane wouldn't take me back to Denali High's parking lot, not with school in session, but the last place I expected him to drive up to was a big-ass compound with an even bigger cross raised on top of the roof.

"Really?" I asked. "A church parking lot?"

"It's spacious and it's empty."

"You really are the Dark Prince," I muttered.

This made Fane's smile widen.

"Fine, let's get on with it before lightning strikes us down."

Fane had already gone over the gears on the way over, narrating his actions: first gear to second, second to third, third back down to second in a curve, and so on. I'd only half-listened as I watched his fist over the shifter and the black leather around his wrist moving with each thrust of the hand-lever.

Fane pulled into a parking spot in front of the church. He turned the car off.

"Ready to trade places?" he asked.

I pulled off my jacket, tossed it in back, and jumped down from the Jeep. We crossed paths in front of the hood, Fane grinned in passing.

Back inside the vehicle he said, "You can start by backing up."

I reached for the key to turn on the ignition. Fane put his hand on my arm.

"Wait a second. The vehicle's in gear."

"Right," I said, exhaling. "I need to put it in neutral before I start it up."

I put my hand on the gear shift and jiggled it until it loosened up and settled into the middle position. I glanced at Fane. He shot me a relaxed smile. I loved the way he didn't make me feel rushed, like I could spend the entire morning just backing up and he wouldn't utter a word of complaint.

I turned on the ignition, right foot on the brake. I pressed the clutch down with my left foot.

"Good job," Fane said. "Now put the car into reverse."

I pulled the gear shift down carefully and let up on the clutch and brake. The Jeep grumbled and quaked in response. I quickly put it into neutral and hit the brake.

From the corner of my eye I saw Fane's lips pucker, holding in a laugh.

"What?" I demanded.

"You put it into second."

I shoved the clutch back down, keeping my foot on the brake and yanked the gear stick back roughly.

"You're still in second," Fane said, voice turning serious. "You don't need to manhandle the gears that way."

He put his hand over mine. I nearly let my foot off the brake.

Fane guided my fist around the gear shift sideways until it would no longer move.

"Now bring it down gently," he said.

My skin tingled from his touch, even the parts of me not connected to his hand.

Fane took his hand off mine. I pulled back.

"That's it," he said. "Now take your foot off the brake and give it a little gas while releasing your foot gently off the clutch."

This was the tricky part; the balancing act—one foot up and one foot down. I hadn't paid much attention to Fane's combat boots on the drive over. I'd been far more focused on his arm, wrist, and hand.

I imagined my left and right foot on opposite ends of a teeter-totter and alternated pressure. The Jeep rolled back gently. I let up on the clutch some more, backing up several feet before stopping.

"Excellent," Fane said.

Yeah, it was just driving, but I was beaming inside.

"Now put it back into neutral and try going from first to second."

Getting into first proved easy with one gentle push up. As long as I was mindful, managing the pedals wasn't so bad, either. I drove across the parking lot in first, no problem, a little jerky, but nothing I couldn't manage. As the Jeep rolled over the pavement it struck me that I was more than ready to drive again. I felt my independence returning—my sense of freedom. Driving a manual really wasn't so bad.

Everything was going great until the car choked, sputtered and died. It gave a dramatic lurch before the engine cut off.

"What the hell?" I said. I looked from the windshield to Fane. "What did I do?"

He grinned. "You tried to change gears without using the clutch."

"Stupid stick shift," I said. "Pain in the ass. Why would anyone want to drive one of these things, anyway?"

"You're doing great," Fane said.

"Don't patronize me," I grumbled.

"We've been here less than five minutes and you've already gotten the car into reverse, backed up, put it in first and driven across the parking lot. Imagine how well you'll be doing in another hour."

My shoulders relaxed. I no longer felt like beating the steering wheel. We really had just begun the lesson.

"You're right," I said. "All I need is a little patience."

"You've got this."

Fane's words engulfed me in a warm jet stream of confidence. This went beyond flirting. He believed in me. At the moment, I needed it far more than honeyed words or terms of endearment.

Fane was right. An hour later I could get all the way up to third gear—the fastest I dared inside the parking lot—without killing the engine. I spent less time thinking about what I was doing, and more time doing it.

"You're doing great," Fane said. "Now why don't you drive us home?"

"On the road?" I grinned. "Okay."

After rounding the far corner of the parking lot, I put the Jeep into second gear and headed for the exit. There, I shifted down to first and eased onto the road when the coast was clear. From first, I shifted to second. From second, to third.

I was feeling pretty awesome until I killed the engine trying to get going at the first intersection.

"Oh shit!" I cried, trying unsuccessfully to start the car back up. It made no noise when I turned the ignition. "Shit! It's not starting!"

"Just relax," Fane said, like we were still inside the deserted parking lot, not blocking traffic on the Old Seward Highway.

I put my foot on the brake and tried the ignition again, and again nothing happened.

"Pretty soon people are going to be pissed," I said.

"They can wait."

"This is taking too long. We should trade places."

"Aurora..." Fane said.

When I looked over his lips puckered as though, once more, attempting to hold in a laugh.

"You're still in gear."

I looked at the gear shift.

"Oh, right," I said. "Clutch."

I pressed the clutch down and tried again. This time, the Jeep started.

"Ha, ha!" I cried out, inching forward in first gear.

"Look at you," Fane said. "When we first met you wouldn't even get inside a car. Now you're driving manual. What's next? The Dakar?"

"The what?" I asked after shifting into second gear.

I could keep up with traffic in second, maybe I could stay in this gear the remainder of the way home—so long as no lights turned red. Dang nuisance, traffic lights.

"The Dakar Rally," Fane said. "It's an off-road race that used to run from Paris through Spain and Northern Africa, ending in Dakar, Senegal. It takes place in South America now. It's one of the most dangerous sporting events in the world."

"In that case, sign me up," I said sarcastically. "Driving around Anchorage is dangerous enough already, thank you very much."

Fane shrugged. "No ice in the desert."

"Right, just sandstorms, wild animals, and who knows what else."

"You're right about the sandstorms—they're blinding. But the animals are absolutely incredible."

"Wait a minute." I peeled my eyes off the road for a split-second. "You didn't participate in this race, did you?"

Although I had my eyes back on the road, I caught Fane sit up an inch taller.

"I did," he said proudly. "I was one of the original participants in the late seventies. Did my first race in a Renault 20 and came back the next year and did it on a Yamaha. I'll try anything once."

"Or twice?"

Fane stretched in his seat. "Once by car, once by motorcycle."

"Daredevil."

I took a quick glance at Fane. He raised his eyebrows.

"It's the Mt. Everest of motor racing. Life changing." Fane leaned into me. "You told me you were worried about becoming cold and unfeeling. The best way to feel alive is to experience life. That sense of discovery never has to end. Life continually evolves. Just imagine the things you have yet to see."

Fane had it down, all right. A never-ending bucket list that included travel and adventure. The truth was, he lit a fire inside of me. I not only craved that kind of freedom, but for the first time I felt like it could truly be mine.

Where would I go first once I got off Melcher's leash? What new experiences would I have? Suddenly I didn't care about a degree. College was for career-minded people entering the rat race. I was more of an adventure-minded woman who wanted to see the world and everything it had to offer.

When I first met Fane, I felt like he'd woken me out of a coma. Now it was as though he'd pulled me from the fog.

I didn't have to stop at the next two intersections. I wasn't so lucky at the third.

"Oh, crap," I muttered.

This intersection rested on a slight incline.

"You can do it," Fane said.

I shifted down to first and stopped. That done, I was able to look over at Fane and roll my eyes.

"Were you ever a motivational speaker in one of these former lives?" I asked.

Fane's lips twisted in thought. "No, I just happen to view life as a gift."

Said the man dressed in black.

"So, you and Joss? Is that some kind of cosmic joke?"

Talk about yin and yang. Joss was about the gloomiest vampire I'd ever met. He looked like a sad and depressed Adrien Brody.

Fane was quiet a moment before answering, "Joss is my responsibility."

I wanted to respond to that, but the light turned green and the moment I lifted my foot off the brake, the Jeep would roll backwards. The current balancing act was a bit more delicate. I gave the car gas while still on the brake. The engine revved. Better to jump the gun than roll into the car behind me. We lurched forward, but I didn't kill the engine, which brought a huge smile of triumph over my lips.

I waited until I'd made it home and parked before turning to ask Fane the question that had niggled at my brain the remainder of the drive.

"What about me? Do you feel like I'm you're responsibility?"

Fane tilted his head when he looked at me, his expression unreadable.

"That's not how I see you."

I waited for more. How did he see me? But that's all he said. Sometimes it was the things left unsaid that drove me the craziest.

Fane jumped out of the Jeep. While he walked around the hood, I reached behind the seat for my jacket. I opened my door as Fane reached for the handle. He readjusted by resting his arm over the top of the door and leaned in.

"I'd say your car rehabilitation is complete."

"Wonderful. Can I get out now?"

He had an unsettling way of invading my personal space. Maybe it was the European in him or maybe, like me, he felt the inexplicable cosmic pull between us.

Fane stepped aside and grinned as I slid out.

"Are you going to invite me in this time?" he asked, slipping his hand inside his front pocket.

I wished he wouldn't do that. From the corner of my eye, it looked like he was stuffing it down his pants.

It seemed rude to send him away when he'd spent the morning teaching me to drive the Jeep.

"Would you like to come in for a drink?"

Fane smiled slowly. "I thought you'd never ask."

✻ ✻ ✻

Now that the vamp was out of the bag, Noel had stocked our fridge with blood. She'd stuck one inside a small cooler that morning to deliver to Henry after school. I had yet to rip into one of the bags, but offering Fane a mug seemed like the hospitable thing to do.

He followed me to the kitchen dining area. I draped my coat over the back of a chair before setting a mug on the kitchen counter. Fane raised one eyebrow.

"You're not drinking?"

I shook my head. Sipping on blood still struck me as unnatural. What would happen if I started? I might go crazy and rip into all the bags. What next? Ripping off all of Fane's clothes? Blood increased my adrenaline. It was an aphrodisiac—one of the ways vampires got off during sex and foreplay. I did not need to be drinking blood around Fane.

At least he'd been around long enough to know how to control himself.

I filled the mug halfway, resealed the bag, and set it on the bottom shelf of the fridge.

"How long do I heat this up?"

Fane leaned over me to look inside the mug.

"Thirty seconds is good."

I popped it into the microwave. The time on the digital clock showed five minutes to noon.

"Aren't you hungry?" Fane asked beside my ear.

Actually, I was. Now that the stress of driving was behind me, I felt more famished than usual.

"I'll make myself a sandwich," I said.

I returned to the fridge and pulled out a jar of peanut butter and jelly, followed by two slices of bread, a plate, and a knife.

Fane tsked and shook his head slowly from side to side. "Jelly is a sad substitute for blood."

The microwave beeped. I pulled out the mug and thrust it into Fane's hands.

"I'm not trying to substitute blood," I said, returning to my sandwich assembly.

Fane slurped.

I turned and glared at him as he lowered the mug, revealing a wicked grin.

"Enjoying the blood?" I asked.

Rather than answer, Fane tipped the mug back and drank down the rest. Once finished, he set it on the counter and licked his lips.

"May I have seconds?"

I'd only managed to get peanut butter on one slice of bread.

"Since you asked so nicely," I said, returning to the blood bag in the fridge.

I filled the mug a little more than halfway and heated it, but when I tried to hand it to Fane he shook his head and said, "That one's for you."

Our eyes locked.

Fine, if Fane wouldn't take it, I'd set it on the countertop beside him. His eyes followed my movements.

"Why deny yourself the things you want most?" he asked.

I swallowed, which drew Fane's eyes to my throat.

Why did he have to torment me this way? Anger swelled inside me. Life was an ocean breeze for Fane Donado. I'd never met a person more comfortable inside his own skin. He drifted through life all Joe Cool, doing whatever he wanted. He was a globetrotter, a daredevil, a high school delinquent—whatever struck his fancy at the moment, the way I did now.

How long would that last before the next new experience beckoned him?

I shoved my plate aside, not bothering with the clumpy jelly, which reminded me too much of blood clots.

"I don't want the blood."

Fane's eyes widened at my gruff tone.

I want you to want me forever, I thought. Oh, what a sucker I was. If I let Fane have me, he'd ride me just like a motorbike over the rough and tumble desert then move on at the finish line. He'd said it himself; he'd try anything once.

Fane's eyebrows furrowed. "What's wrong?"

I took a step toward him.

"Do you believe in soul mates?" I asked.

Fane leaned forward. Without a moment's hesitation he answered, "I do now."

I searched his face for signs of mockery. Fane gazed back. He didn't so much as blink as he stared into my eyes.

Screw, "You had me at hello." Fane had me at, "I do."

I lost it.

I went straight for his provoking lips. He stood steady even as I launched myself against his chest and wrapped my arms around his neck and pulled his head toward mine.

Once more, I was the girl on the public bus—the one wild with desire—unable to resist the pull of Fane's magnetism. I longed to lose myself in the moment. I expected his lips to split apart into a wide Cheshire grin, but his eyes widened in surprise.

Dread stabbed at my insides. Had I misread the signals? His earlier response?

For one tortuous second, humiliation appeared imminent until Fane seized me in his arms—embracing me as though answering a long-awaited question. Our lips met with a crushing force that spread warmth through my entire body. Kissing him was like coming home to my most happy memories.

Fane scooped me up into his arms. I wrapped my legs around him as he lifted me, my arms grasping his neck firmly. One glance at his fingers gripping my thigh and his leather bracelet was enough to make me squeeze him tighter.

Where Fane was concerned, I didn't need blood to go into an all-out lust frenzy.

I sucked greedily on his tongue, coaxing it inside my mouth. When Fane let out a deep, shuddering breath, I smiled without breaking contact.

He carried me out of the kitchen and backed me against the wall. His pelvis rocked against mine—push, push, push—as he kissed me roughly.

The relentless rubbing made me want to lose the clothes already and take it all the way.

I grabbed Fane by the shirt collar—breaking away only to gasp for breath between kisses.

"I've missed you," Fane rasped, following his words with a blaze of kisses all up and down my neck.

I shuddered and squirmed between his abs and the rough wall. My body throbbed—begging for immediate gratification. I grabbed Fane by the butt cheeks and shoved his pelvis into mine. Fane inhaled sharply.

A deafening crash shattered the space around us. At first I thought we'd knocked over a vase, but there wasn't anything against the wall to break.

Fane's head snapped back—eyes wide and alert. I lowered my legs to the floor. They were still shaky. Fane, meanwhile, sprang to action. The muscles in his arms tightened, his nose lifted as though catching a scent right before he stormed down the hallway toward the front door.

5

Red October

Once my legs were stable, I hurried after Fane. He stopped in the entryway and stared down. There was a baseball-sized rock on the linoleum floor surrounded by shards of glass. Cold air streamed in through the splintered gash in the front windowpane.

Fane ripped the front door open by the handle. I had to peer around him to see into the street. All appeared quiet in the front yard.

Fane stepped outside and tramped across the lawn to his car. He stopped in front of the hood and just stared. With my heart lodged inside my throat, I made my way to the Pontiac. It took me a second before I noticed the front windshield had been cracked all across the front.

Web-like fractures splintered the entire window. The worst damage appeared over the driver's side with hairline cracks so dense they'd turned the glass white and all but obscured the steering wheel from sight.

It would have taken a solid object to cause that kind of damage. I looked on the ground, but didn't see anything.

Maybe it had been a baseball bat or the same rock pitched through my windowpane.

My stomach dropped. A tingly sensation came over me like a sixth sense.

Valerie. It had to be her.

She'd threatened Fane Saturday morning. How would she feel if she saw him parked outside my house two days later?

Two days later.

I shook my head. She'd been stabbed. Surely she wasn't already out roaming the streets of Anchorage. Giselle had left her in critical condition Saturday morning. Then again, she'd been rushed to base, where Melcher's white coats had a lightning-speed knack for bringing agents back from the almost-dead.

Fane's jaw clenched as he appraised the damage.

My stomach double-knotted.

Valerie—if it was her—couldn't have known we were kissing. But she would know Fane was inside.

As Fane moved away from the car, so did I.

Once we reached the porch, he waited for me to go inside first then looked up at the security cam as he followed me inside. "I need to borrow your laptop," he said.

I nodded. "It's upstairs."

As I skirted the broken glass, Fane said, "Be careful."

Good thing neither of us had removed our shoes. I hopscotched my way over and around the jagged shards then hurried up the stairs to my room. My laptop was on top of my desk in sleep mode. I unplugged the power cord, closed the lid and clutched the machine against my side.

When I came back down the stairs, Fane had already begun picking up fragments of glass, which he tossed inside the trash bin we kept beneath our kitchen sink.

Cold air prickled my skin. Shutting the front door did little good blocking the chilly stream flowing through the gaping hole in the window. A shiver ran down my spine.

It's all in your head, I chanted. The cold is all in your head.

"Watch your step," Fane said. "There's still glass everywhere." He straightened up as I moved carefully around the glass to the other side of the hall. "I was just about to phone the window repairman."

"I'll call the agency," I said. "They'll cover the cost."

Fane shook his head. "The less they're involved, the better."

"What about your window?"

"I'll take it in for a replacement."

I made my way through the land mine of shattered glass a second time to retrieve a hoodie from upstairs. When I returned, Fane made swift work of cleaning up the last of the glass with a broom and dustpan. He'd duct taped a black trash bag over the opening in the window.

I knew he was eager to look at the footage and appreciated the time he'd taken to patch up the entryway. I wanted to see it, too, though I wasn't in any rush. At the moment, a nameless hooligan had thrown a rock through my window. Once we watched the video feed, we'd have a face and, likely, a name.

There wasn't anything left with which to distract ourselves.

Fane had cleaned up and called the repairman. I'd turned down the thermostat and set up my laptop at the dining room table—pushing a second chair in front of the screen.

Fane and I took a seat side by side. His fingers reached forward and zipped over the keyboard. A security website appeared on the screen asking for a password, which Fane typed in rapidly. I liked watching his hands in motion. They looked very skilled. I suspected they'd be gentle but firm in taking off my clothes.

My face flushed. Fane leaned closer to the laptop and didn't seem to notice.

His fingers hovered over the keyboard. "What time would that have been?" he asked himself. "Ten, twelve minutes ago?" He peered at the time on the lower right corner of the screen, leaned back and entered a number on the screen.

"Here goes," he said.

We both leaned forward.

The video feed showed the porch in front of the door vacant. It didn't capture the window. I held my breath waiting for someone to walk up and chuck a rock toward the house. A timer with seconds raced by beneath the video display. No one was there. Suddenly there was.

Valerie, dressed in skinny jeans and a beige sweater, walked up to the camera. She looked directly into the camera, at us, and flipped it off. Just as quickly, she pivoted and stormed away, disappearing from the screen.

I gripped my arm while waiting for the inevitable. It wasn't instantaneous like I'd expected. Maybe she'd gone off to smash up Fane's windshield first. Over a minute went by before the camera picked up the rock sailing past. If I hadn't seen the rock in the entryway, I might have mistaken it for a bullet, despite its size, as it blurred past in a flash of silver-gray.

Caught, red handed, or in this case, red haired.

"That stab wound certainly didn't slow her down," I said.

Fane's fingers tightened into a fist.

He soon appeared on the footage bursting through the front door with a fierce scowl that matched the one on his face now.

Fane stopped the video feed and closed the screen of the security site.

"Do you think it's out of her system now?" I asked.

"Doubtful," Fane replied.

Fane's hip suddenly rang. He stood up, pulled the phone out of his pocket, glanced at the screen and answered.

"What's going on?" He sounded serious. It wasn't a breezy, "Hey, what's happening" kind of what's going on.

I watched Fane curiously, but his gaze looked a million miles away.

"I'll be right there," he said abruptly.

He jerked the phone from his ear and squeezed it so hard it looked like it would crack inside his fist.

"I have to go," he said.

"What's going on?" I asked.

Fane shook his head, lips pushed out.

"Who was that?" I asked.

"Joss."

"Is he okay?"

Joss was gloomy, but he was the closest thing Fane had to family.

"He's fine."

Okay. I waited for Fane to elaborate.

"The window repairman will be here in an hour or two. He has my credit card information. We'll talk later," he said, heading toward the door. He stopped, spun around, and hurried back to me. Fane put his hands on my cheeks and kissed me hard. My heart fluttered. A second later, it was over. Fane turned his back and practically sprinted out the door.

I stared down the hallway after he'd gone, wondering what the heck had just happened—not just with the vandalism and phone call, but with us.

I suddenly felt weak and shaky in the hungry sense. I remembered the blood on the kitchen counter. Getting it back into the bag without staining the counter would be nearly impossible. I could stick the mug in the fridge. Or I could stop kidding myself and drink the damn thing.

Why fight nature?

❉ ❉ ❉

Once the front window had been replaced, I retreated to my bedroom and sat at my desk, the start of an English paper open on my laptop and my hoodie zipped to my chin. Try as I might, it was a little hard to concentrate on homework after Valerie's surprise attack.

Who was I kidding?

My concentration had blown out the window long before she threw the rock. It had shattered the moment my lips touched Fane's.

Then there was the other issue. I had trouble seeing myself sticking around long enough to complete a college degree.

There was still the question of what I would do once free of Melcher. How would I support myself? I had no skills, no experience that mattered in the real world. How many companies were looking to hire ex-vampire hunters? None that I'd be interested in.

Maybe I could get a fresh start in another country or state—another do-over to add to my list.

I wasn't really in the mood to be alone. I tried streaming music online, but it only made the house seem emptier.

Shortly after eight o'clock, I heard the front door open and close, which gave me a brief start. I'd been so caught up in my own thoughts, combined with online radio, I hadn't heard anyone pull up.

"Noel?" I yelled from the stairs. I was pretty sure it was her, but these days I could never be sure.

"Yeah," she called back. "I picked up a pizza if you're interested."

"I'll be right down."

I paused the music and headed downstairs.

Noel had plates and napkins set out on the kitchen beside a pizza box. Her back was to me as she rummaged through the fridge.

"Wine cooler?" she asked.

"No, thanks."

The blood had satiated me quite nicely. I wasn't even hungry, but the pizza smelled good, and I could use some normalcy to end the day. Noel had missed all the action.

I grabbed a plate and slice of pie. "How'd it go with Henry and Zeke?"

Noel put two pieces of pizza on her plate. She took it to the table and rested her elbows on the surface.

"I'm exhausted," she said.

"That bad?" I bit off a piece.

Noel lifted one of her slices, took a bite, chewed and swallowed. "It was like trying to convince a three-year-old to bathe."

I wrinkled my nose. Henry bathing was not the visual I wanted to have while eating.

"But he ran it by Richard and got the green light. Henry refused to invite anyone until we came up with an appropriate theme. Friday night is going to be a tribute to Marcus. Everyone is to dress in black."

I snorted. "Won't be a problem for Fane."

Noel put her pizza down and frowned. "Unfortunately I won't be able to attend."

Not that I'd been thrilled about Noel and Fane teaming up together at the palace, but what the hell? Noel had as much motivation as me to get Dante and Gavin back. She knew what Jared looked like. This was our mess, and I didn't like leaving it all on Fane, especially with Valerie on the loose.

"Why not?"

"I phoned Melcher after school to tell him about the party at the palace and let him know I heard Giselle had been invited."

I sat up straighter. "Did he buy it?"

Noel shrugged. "It's a tribute party. The palace was the last fête Marcus and Andre ever attended. It's possible Giselle might want to speak with some of the last vampires to spend time with her father." Noel shrugged again.

"Okay," I said. "That's great, but why can't you go?"

"Melcher said he wants me back on the eastside Friday night."

I groaned. "Melcher and his missions. Well, I guess you'll have an alibi, too. I just don't like this. Does Fane know?"

"I tried to call him, but he didn't pick up."

My fingers curled into my palms. "He was here earlier. He taught me to drive the Jeep, then came in to talk. Shortly after, Valerie came by, smashed Fane's windshield, and threw a rock through our front window."

"Holy shit," Noel said, craning her neck around to the hall as though she'd missed the broken window.

"It was replaced a couple hours ago," I said.

Noel's head snapped back around. "I thought she was still in the hospital."

"Apparently not."

"You actually saw her?"

"On the security cam." I tapped my fingers against the table. "Fane got a call from Joss after that and left."

"Shit," Noel said. "What's the deal? She's with Gavin now."

"Before Giselle stabbed her Saturday morning, she came by and found me here with Fane. She made threats."

Noel's eyes expanded. "Oh, crap. Are you going to report her to Melcher?"

"And tell him what exactly? That I was entertaining a vampire at the time?" I shook my head. "That would put me in even deeper shit."

Noel sighed. "I suppose you're right." She lifted the wine cooler to her lips and drank down a third in one go before returning to her pizza. Between chews she said, "I take it you won't be inviting her over for any more sleepovers?"

I screwed up my face. "Never again."

"Good." Noel reached under the table, leaning to one side as she dug into her pocket. She set a small baggie filled with white powder on the table. "Or you could invite her over for happy hour and slip this into her drink." Noel's teeth flashed white when she grinned.

I leaned forward. "What is that?"

"Ground up sleeping pills," Noel said.

"Where did you get that?"

"From Henry. I figured it wouldn't hurt to have some on hand with all the unwanted company we've had coming through."

Noel stood and snatched the bag from the table, retreating into the kitchen. I turned and watched her open the cupboard by the sink. She pulled out a tea tin and popped open the lid.

"I'll stash it in here," Noel said. "In front of the bottle of chloroform Daren and Reece scrounged up for us."

Noel closed the cupboard and helped herself to a third slice of pizza. She rejoined me at the table. "Now that we've established that the no vampires allowed rule doesn't apply in our house, I think we should instate a no psychotic vampires allowed rule."

I snorted. "Deal."

"I can't believe she actually threw a rock through our window. Who does that? Oh, right, Valerie." Noel pulled her hair over one shoulder and pushed it back a second later. "Fane and Joss might want to find some place to hole up until this blows over."

I snorted. "Maybe Zeke has an extra room."

Noel didn't break into even a small smile at my joke. She held one slim hand over her neck. "They should check into a motel or something, at least for a while—until Valerie has a chance to cool off."

"I don't think Valerie is the kind of person who ever cools off," I said.

And Fane wasn't the type to be intimidated. Somehow, that worried me more.

* * *

Once Noel cleared out of the dining room to start on homework upstairs, I tried calling Fane, expecting to hear my name on his lips at any second. But he didn't answer.

This was the first time I'd heard his voice message—he'd always picked up before.

"Hello, this is Death," Fane said in greeting. "I'm not in right now, but if you leave your name and number, I'll get right with you."

Beep!

If I weren't so anxious, I would have laughed.

I hesitated before saying, "Hi, it's me. Is everything okay?"

I hung up and stared at my phone for two minutes, sure it would ring. But it didn't.

Now what the hell had happened? Could we not get through one damn day without a new catastrophe knocking us over?

I walked upstairs. Noel sat with her back to me at the desk inside the office. Even after clearing the air, I wasn't sure I wanted to move my desk back in. I liked having my own private domain to study and sleep.

I knocked on the open door.

Noel's head remained bent over the desk. I picked up the faint sound of music playing from her ear buds.

I knocked louder. Nothing.

"Noel!" I shouted.

She gave a start and whipped around. Only when she saw it was me did her shoulders relax. She took out the ear buds.

"Fane's not answering my call, either," I said.

Noel frowned. "Want me to drive you to his place? Make sure everything's all right?"

I considered it a moment. "If he wanted me to know what was going on, he would have called."

"Are you sure?" Noel asked.

"Yeah, thanks. I'll try him again in the morning."

I kinda did want to go check on him, but he didn't seem like he wanted me around when he left. I was touched that Noel had offered to drive me without a moment's hesitation. Technically I should be able to drive myself, but I wasn't keen to do my first solo drive in the dark.

He was fine. This was Fane Donado we were talking about. Joss was probably having an existential crisis or something that required Fane talking him off the ledge. That was all. Nothing to worry about. Maybe it was something as silly as Joss spilling tea on a book that would have paid a month's rent. Who knew? I didn't. If it had been something I needed to worry about, Fane would have said something.

I needed to stop stressing over it and try to finish at least one assignment.

I took a detour to the bathroom to brush my teeth first. I put toothpaste onto my brush, but didn't stick it inside my mouth. Instead, I stared at my pearly whites in the mirror. Vampire teeth, no fangs. Nevertheless, they were teeth that had bitten a boy and drank blood.

I paused only a second longer before brushing them so hard my gums bled—making me brush them more rigorously still.

Pajamas on, I set my phone on my nightstand and crawled under the covers. I turned off the bedside lamp. My phone lit up a moment later, ringing. Fane's name displayed over the screen.

Thank goodness!

"I was worried," I cried into the phone.

"I'm sorry I didn't call sooner," Fane said.

I sat up straight.

"Fane, what happened?"

He took a deep breath. "Valerie came by my place and broke out every window with Joss inside."

My gut twisted.

"Oh my god. Is he okay?"

"Shaken up, but fine otherwise."

"Did she throw rocks?"

"Yes."

The line went silent. Fane sounded more angry than sad.

"Fane, I'm sorry. If I hadn't asked you over..."

"I'm the one who dated her," Fane said, voice hardening. "This is entirely on me."

My back straightened. "This isn't on you or me. It's the agency's fault. The agency did this to us."

Fane sighed. "And this is only the beginning."

"No." I shook my head. "Like you said, we can stop them. Starting with Jared. He's Melcher's right hand."

"We'll be ready for him," Fane said. "I only hope Noel made a convincing case to your boss and that Valerie stays out of it."

My heart sunk down to the covers.

With Valerie once more operational, Melcher might assign her back to the lodge, or worse, the palace. She could throw a great big wrench into our plans.

"Maybe I could talk to her," I said. "She has as much motivation to take down Jared as I. and as for the trade, Giselle still has her boyfriend."

"Do not get her involved," Fane said.

I bristled at his command.

"But if I sent her a text..."

"Aurora, you need to stay as far away from her as possible."

Even though I knew he was right—Valerie was beyond reasoning with—I didn't appreciate his tone. Fane wasn't Melcher. He couldn't order me around. I didn't have a choice in the matter if she and I were put on assignment together. Wouldn't it be better if we were on the same page?

"She could screw everything up," I cried into the phone.

"And you can bet that if she knew what we were up to, she'd screw it up worse," Fane said.

I inhaled and held it to the count of five before releasing slowly. I knew he was right; I just found the whole thing frustrating. Why did Valerie have to be such a psychotic bitch? We could have teamed up. If only she'd listened to reason when I tried to explain what happened with Fane at the tasting. It was as though she expected any guy who ever dated her never to care about another woman again. What a prima donna.

"Okay," I said. "The less people who know about our plan, the better. We need to be on our toes—you especially."

"So long as she stays away from Stanton's Friday, I can handle her and any stones she throws my way."

"Fine," I said. "Just promise you'll be careful."

"Only if you promise first."

"I promise," I said.

The trap had been set. All that was left was for Jared to take the bait and for Valerie to keep the hell away. I hated having to worry about her.

Just what we needed this week—Evil Red resurrected, released, and raising hell while we were in the midst of a rescue mission.

6

Hit Squad

A single snowflake flew at the windshield and melted as soon as it touched the glass. Another wet flake quickly followed, then another, until a whole flurry flew at my face like spittle. I blinked despite the protection of the windshield. I fumbled for the lever to activate the windshield wipers, but they didn't budge. I tried to slow the vehicle down, but my foot hit empty air where the gas pedal and brake should have been.

Then, through the blizzard, a dark SUV appeared, barreling straight toward me. My hands dropped to the steering wheel, which had been driving itself a moment before. I cranked the wheel to the right then noticed it hadn't moved at all, only my hands—sliding along the surface.

Frantically, I attempted to open the door only to find it lacking a handle.

Fear seized me by the throat.

I looked up even though the oncoming vehicle was the last thing I wanted to face.

The SUV had closed in enough to see inside—to notice that no one manned the vehicle. Headlights glared into my eyes.

No, not again. Not when I'd faced my fears and taken the wheel.

A movement to my right caught my eye. I saw the blue bandana tied around his forehead first.

Jared sat in the passenger's seat, a bag of theater popcorn in his lap. He pulled a puffy kernel out and plopped it inside his mouth, followed by a crunch.

Jared didn't look at me. He stared ahead.

"This is going to hurt," he said in a matter-of-fact voice.

I turned my head just as the SUV came at us full speed.

My body jerked, reaching out on both sides for anything to grab hold of. This time, my fingers slid over cool, smooth bed sheets.

Slowly, my ragged breaths abated. I opened my eyes to find no blinding headlines aimed at my pupils, only darkness inside my bedroom.

It was only a dream.

Real or not, it didn't bode well. Call it a premonition, an omen, instinct... It could mean only one thing. Jared was back in town.

❋ ❋ ❋

I half expected to find a dusting of snow on the ground when I looked out the window later that morning, but the sidewalks were clear.

As I organized my backpack, my phone rang, displaying a blocked number.

"Hello?"

"Hello, Agent Sky," Melcher said.

My breath caught inside my throat. A queasy sensation, similar to the one I'd experienced in the dream, roiled around my stomach.

I wanted to scream, to shout—to tell Melcher I knew what he'd done to me. Instead, I swallowed my anger down like a lump of coal and replied, "Good morning, Agent Melcher."

"I need you on base in an hour."

"But I have class in twenty minutes." I'd blown it off the day before, but I wanted to give college a fair shot. Fane was right. I should live in the moment, experience life. The agency had no right to take away my college experience.

"School can wait," Melcher said. "This can't. Do you need me to send someone to pick you up?"

My jaw tightened. "I can get there myself," I informed him.

"Good."

"By the way, how's Valerie doing?" I asked.

"Miss Ward lost a lot of blood, but no vital organs were damaged. Once her transfusion was complete, she was cleared to go home."

Uh-huh. Home. Hers. Not mine. Not Fane's.

"See you soon, Agent Sky," Melcher said.

"Yeah."

I hung up the phone and immediately dialed Fane.

"I've been called on base for a meeting."

"Did they say why?" Fane asked.

"No, but that's normal." I sucked in a breath. "What if he called in Valerie, too? What if Jared shows up?" Rage sparked across my body. "This is my chance. I should do something with it. If Valerie was called in, she could take Jared and I could take Melcher."

"Aurora, stop and think a moment. Even if everyone was there and even if you could convince Valerie to cooperate in a split second, how would you clear the building, let alone the base, with hostages?"

My shoulders sagged. Man, reality checks sucked. "I don't know. I guess it was more wishful thinking than anything else."

"Go in and stay calm. Find out what they're planning. Remember, we have the upper hand."

I liked the sound of that even though it wasn't true. Melcher had an army of hunters at his beck and call, including a particularly nasty vampire. He had backing from the government and his own team of scientists. How were we supposed to go up against that?

"We'll get Jared," Fane assured me. "But we have to be smart about it. Get him where we want him. So play along today and find out what you can."

I should have been grateful for Fane's level head. But he sounded like someone else. Someone who hadn't kissed me yesterday. His actions indicated that he cared for me, maybe even loved me. But until he said the words, I wouldn't know for sure.

Fine, Fane wanted to be all business, I would, too.

"You're right," I said. "This is my chance to find out what Melcher's up to."

"Just remember to keep cool while you're on his turf," Fane said. "Once we lure them into the open, they're fair game."

Fair game? More like bargaining chips.

Jared ought to be thrown into oncoming traffic for what he'd done to me.

Patience, Aurora. Let Giselle rip his heart out. I didn't care who did the honors so long as it was done and Jared—The Recruiter, The Killer—was no more, followed by Melcher. With those two out of the picture, maybe I could finally begin living a normal undead life with a decent undead guy.

❋ ❋ ❋

Fane's voice provided only temporary relief. Finding out as much as I could from Melcher made perfect sense, but it didn't mean I was happy to meet with the man. Then there was the immediate dilemma of driving the Jeep.

My hands shook as I opened the driver's door. The keys weighed down my hand.

If only Dante were there to drive me... or Noel.

Scratch that!

What kind of assassin feared cars? Self-reliance meant getting from point A to point B without a chauffeur.

Unless—the dream had been a warning not to get behind the wheel.

The jagged edges of the keys bit into my palm as I squeezed them. I didn't have much choice. I'd rather take my chances behind the wheel than call Melcher back and say I required a ride after all. No way.

I started the Jeep and put it into neutral, the way Fane had taught me. I got it into first gear and eased onto the road.

No problem, I told myself.

On the way through town, I watched the cars in front of me carefully. I down shifted and stopped at red lights, which, luckily, weren't on any hills. When the light turned, I eased up on the clutch and tapped the gas, paying attention to every foot maneuver and shift. Somewhere along the way, I began humming Christmas tunes, stopping briefly to have a one on one conversation with myself about how it was way too early for caroling.

By the time I reached base, my temples were sweaty.

Two cars waited in front of me. At my turn, the guard checked my ID then handed it right back, his face expressionless. The gate lifted, and I drove onto Elmendorf Air Force Base toward the top secret compound on the outskirts.

Melcher certainly knew how to protect himself. If Giselle was correct, and he was a vampire, how had he ever rallied government aid?

If only I could get some information out of Jared before Giselle offed him.

Triumph flashed through me as I parked the Jeep. I'd made it on my own—conquered the mountain—all thanks to Fane and his car rehabilitation tactics.

Suddenly, I wanted to call him and thank him for believing in me all along. For having patience. For giving me my independence back.

But it would have to wait until after the meeting.

I walked toward the compound, chin up. As I tromped through the dank halls, the Christmas carols humming inside my head were replaced with positive affirmations.

I am strong. Superhuman. Vampire. An asset to the agency. They'll never see me coming.

Once I turned the final corner, two sets of eyes looked at me. Levi and Mason sat in plastic chairs in the hallway. Levi slouched back, one leg propped over his knee. Mason sat ramrod stiff, at attention like a good solider boy. My nose wrinkled.

I kept my head up and walked straight over to Levi.

"Where's Tommy?"

Levi sat up straighter. "Well, hello to you, too," he said, grinning from ear to ear.

I couldn't believe I ever compared him to Kurt Cobain. He smiled way too often and with too much teeth.

"You can go in now."

I barely noticed the secretary, and it wasn't because of her camouflaged uniform.

I continued glaring down at Levi. "We're teammates, remember? So, why don't you play ball and tell me where you took the dog?"

Levi stood. Our noses were practically level. His smile dropped briefly from his face.

"If your partner hadn't gotten himself kidnapped, I wouldn't have to take care of his mutt."

Anger flared through me at the same time hope blossomed. If Levi was taking care of Tommy that meant he was safe, for now.

Melcher should have let me take care of Tommy from the start. This was probably some sort of punishment for questioning orders. He acted like we were a team, like I mattered, but I knew the truth. Melcher didn't give a damn about any of his recruits. He didn't want us to have pets or any kind of relationship that interfered with our commitment to the agency. All that mattered was the mission. Follow orders. Period.

"Agent Melcher is ready for you," the secretary said louder.

Levi brushed past me, Mason right behind him, toward Melcher's office. They let themselves in first. I walked in last and shut the door behind me. While my back was turned, a voice sneered.

"Is this all you've got for me?"

My body went rigid at the sound of Jared's voice.

I turned. His eyes drilled directly into mine from the far corner of the room. There stood the vampire responsible for all my woes. He wore a dark blazer over blue jeans—casual cool. There was a five o'clock shadow over his chin and cheekbones covering his face in a sinister looking mask.

Melcher stood between his desk and chair.

"Jared, meet agents Levi Parker and Mason Hicks. You and Agent Sky have already met."

Oh, we'd met all right—on a cold wintery road ten months ago. Jared had robbed me of my humanity. If that wasn't bad enough, Melcher later forced me to work alongside my killer.

Why did he want us all to meet now?

I glanced at Melcher who had taken a seat at his desk.

"Do you two know how to follow orders?" Jared demanded, looking from Mason to Levi.

"Yes, sir," Mason said.

Jared's eyes narrowed on Levi. "What about you, Jeans?"

I expected Levi to glower back, but he grinned instead. "You can count on my full cooperation."

Something in the way Levi said it made Jared grin back. "Good."

Jared sat behind Agent Crist's old desk. The vamp had a lot of nerve taking her seat after killing her.

Mason and Levi lowered themselves into the two chairs in front of Christ's desk. I crossed over to a chair in front of Melcher.

"Now here's how Friday night is going down. You three have the upstairs," Jared said, aiming his finger at us in one arc. "I'll handle everything below."

My body jolted as though shocked inside the chair.

Handle everything below? What? No! We needed Jared to go to the palace, not the lodge. But I couldn't protest without raising suspicion.

"Everyone dies, except Diederick," Melcher said.

"What about the wine girls?" Levi asked, raising an eyebrow.

Melcher rested his arms on his desktop. "I've got an informant on the inside. He'll slip something in their wine before your arrival. They'll be asleep during your operation. He'll also take care of disabling security cameras at the front door and entryway. Diederick doesn't have cameras upstairs. He keeps the tasting rooms private."

"What about the valet and butler?" I asked.

Melcher pursed his lips. "They'll have seen your faces. Allowing them to live would put my agents in danger."

Mason nodded. "Collateral damage."

"They aligned themselves with the enemy," Melcher confirmed. "That's the risk they took."

"What about Diederick?" I demanded. "He'll have seen our faces." Well, mine, anyway. I'd attended the tasting twice and made a scene at the bar with Henry. I hadn't exactly flown beneath the radar.

Melcher had warned Dante, Valerie, and me off killing Diederick the first time we scoped out the hillside tasting, claiming the vamp was more valuable to him undead than forever dead.

"We've already lost track of dozens of vampires since Marcus' departure," Melcher had said.

"Diederick has vast connections to the underworld. For now, we need him to coax his underlings out of the shadows."

"Diederick won't see what any of you are doing upstairs, and there won't be any survivors to describe you later," Melcher said now. "Jared and his team will go in below with ski masks."

Just what we all needed after Sitka had gone sooooo smoothly. If anyone could massacre a house full of vampires, it was Jared.

I sat up in my chair. "But if we kill all his clients and staff, what good is he to you? It's not like he'd be dumb enough to set up new tastings. His reputation will be ruined if it gets out that his patrons all died at the hands of hunters."

Melcher nodded. "He'll leave the state, or Anchorage at the very least. My informant will stay with him and keep an eye on future endeavors."

"So we're just going to let Diederick walk out the front door?" I pressed.

"My man will help him escape," Melcher said.

"Now listen up," Jared's voice boomed. "I want you three to go in first. Take out the valet and butler. From there, go directly upstairs. You will find one of Diederick's associates overseeing the tasting rooms above. Kill him. Jeans will take his place," Jared said, nodding at Levi. "Don't let anyone leave until they've visited the room at the end of the hall. That's where Raven and Mason will be."

Melcher cleared his throat. "My informant says there are eight rooms above. You will need to move the woman in the eighth room to another location and close the doors on any unoccupied rooms. That indicates that they are occupied. Aurora will pose as a wine girl. Once a vampire has fed on her, Mason will come out of hiding and finish the infected off. Quietly." Melcher leaned forward. "We don't want to scare off the vampires still feeding in the other rooms."

My nose wrinkled. So he still had me going in as bait? Snaptastic.

"Any questions?" Jared asked.

Levi and Mason exchanged a look. "Sounds pretty straightforward," Levi said.

"Good. Then keep to the upstairs, get the job done and stay out of my way."

I winced. Although Jared addressed Levi and Mason, I couldn't help thinking his words were meant for me.

Levi and Mason stood up. I remained seated. I leaned forward, addressing Melcher. "Can I speak to you in private?"

Melcher nodded. "Parker, Hicks, you two are dismissed. Shut the door on your way out."

We sat in silence until they're footsteps had receded and the door clicked shut.

Melcher straightened his back. "We actually want to speak to you, Agent Sky."

Jared got up and moved in front of the door, arms crossed, blocking me inside.

My mouth went dry.

"But first, what is it you wished to speak to me about?" Melcher sat as still as a statue, only his eyes moving to focus on me.

I didn't want to go first. I wanted to know what exactly he and Jared planned on talking to me about. Did they suspect I knew I was a vampire? Had Valerie said something about Fane staying the night with me? Did they know what Fane, Noel, and I were up to? Is that why Jared wasn't taking the bait?

Melcher hadn't moved a muscle, but his eyes zeroed in on me.

I cleared my throat. "What about Giselle? Noel said there's a good chance she'll be at Stanton's party this weekend. Shouldn't we be going after her?"

Melcher's eyes narrowed. "Agent Harper should not have shared that information with you. Allowing the two of you to live together might have been a mistake."

I glared at Melcher. As if he'd put us together out of the goodness of his heart. Noel had confided that he did it so she could keep an eye on me. To make sure I wasn't succumbing to blood cravings. Nice try, Melcher.

Jared snorted behind me. "Giselle would never show up at a party. She's got the social skills of a wolverine."

My heart dropped. Jared wasn't buying it. We'd set up the party for nothing. I turned slightly, catching Jared's eye. He grinned.

"Though I did hear Henry Fisher will be there. The big guy let him get away." Jared looked over at Melcher. "I hope he's not that clumsy at the tasting this Friday."

Melcher frowned. "There's been no sign of Henry at his townhouse. He dropped off the radar until now."

Jared moved to the front of Crist's desk and sat on the edge.

"Send Ginger after Henry. If he gives her any trouble, she can always shoot him." Jared's eyes slid to mine.

Our eyes locked. Mine began to sting, my whole body prickled with frustration and anger. We needed Jared at the palace, not Valerie.

I sat up and looked at Melcher. "If there's even a chance Giselle might be there we should check it out. You told me we'd get her once Jared got to town."

Melcher's chest puffed. His nostrils flared. "I said you could help with the retrieval mission after we put an end to the tastings. Our work doesn't stop because one agent was kidnapped."

My lips pressed into a tight frown.

Nice to know Melcher would throw us to the wolves—or in this case, wolverine—without a second thought.

The show must go on. But how were we going to capture Jared if he didn't go where we wanted him? At least I had the advantage of knowing where he'd be Friday night. On the other hand, I couldn't bring Fane or even Henry into it without putting their lives at stake.

Melcher must have taken my silence for cooperation.

"Now that that's settled, let's move onto the next order of business." Melcher pressed his hands together, as though in prayer, then folded his fingers into one tight ball. "Jared's not only here to apprehend Giselle. He's here to recruit."

My stomach filled with acid.

If Fane were there, he'd tell me to keep a cool head, but I couldn't. He'd remind me to keep Melcher in the dark as much as possible. He'd point out my precarious position on base, seated between Jared and Melcher. He'd tell me to keep my mouth shut.

But I couldn't.

I rose from my chair.

Screw this.

"Recruit? Don't you mean kill?" I pointed at Jared. "I saw you behind the wheel of that SUV that rammed into me."

Jared didn't even flinch. He looked me up and down before saying, "As I said before, I was at the right place at the right time."

I swung toward Melcher. "Is this how you recruit agents? By forcing them into accidents?"

Melcher's lips twisted. He stared at me a long time, not speaking.

Say something! I wanted to scream, but I didn't. I closed my mouth, heart hammering up my throat and pounding in my ears.

"Hunters are a rare breed," Melcher said slowly. "As you know, AB negative blood is one of the rarest in the world. It's the only type that can poison a vampire. You are nature's most powerful weapon against man's biggest threat. You were created to protect mankind. Nature decided."

My fingers balled into fists.

"I don't care about my blood type. You decided. Not nature. You stole my life from me."

"Not I," Melcher answered calmly. "We are but humble servants serving the greater good."

"By ruining peoples' lives?" I demanded. "And now you plan on going after more innocent victims? Is everyone with AB negative blood on your hit list?"

Melcher stared at me, unblinking. "I admire your compassion. It's one of the many qualities that make you a good hunter. We can teach recruits to kill, but we can't teach them to care." Melcher glanced briefly at Jared then back to me. "Jared, as you know, is infected. Centuries ago, he murdered innocents, no better than the creatures we hunt today. But he is atoning for his sins."

I glanced at Jared, dubiously. He studied the cuff of his sleeve without comment.

"It occurred to me that if a killer such as Jared could reform his ways, why not others like him?" Melcher asked, voice rising in excitement.

My jaw dropped. "Wait a minute. You're not suggesting what I think you are... are you?" I took a step toward Melcher's desk. "Are you saying you're going to start recruiting vampires?"

Already-turned vampires, that was. At least I'd kept my mouth shut on that little tidbit. Despite my outburst, they probably figured I still thought I was human, albeit one who suffered a near-death experience at the hands of a madman.

Melcher lifted his chin. "It is the perfect solution. No more accidents. No more initiation. No more mandatory infection. We have only to poison their blood and send them into the field."

"And why would a vampire willingly kill another vampire?" I asked.

Melcher straightened his back. "They would if they want to be on the winning team. Being an informant or a hunter offers certain protection. We look after our own."

Yeah? Tell that to Dante.

"Some agents recognize their duty to serve from the start. Others require incentives."

Jared smirked.

I looked from him to Melcher.

"Why are you telling me this?" I asked.

Melcher leaned back. "Miss Ward tells me you got close to Selene Ericson on your first tasting assignment."

Selene? Melcher had wanted me to kill her... now he wanted to recruit her?

"We played pool together, that's all," I said. "I thought you wanted her dead."

"Yes, she's been something of a troublemaker, but we're already spread too thin in this state. If Ericson attends the tasting Friday, she's dead. If we recruit her now, she can make her life count for something. We are fighting a war, and we need all the soldiers we can get. Once Diederick flees, we'll need an insider to keep an eye on the vampires who run in other circles—the ones attending Stanton's party, for instance."

"What does that have to do with me?" I asked.

"I want you to come with us when we recruit Selene," Melcher said. "She'll likely be more receptive around an agent she's familiar with."

Selene had been all friendliness and charm. It had been a huge relief not to run into her when Melcher instructed me to end her life the weekend before. Now here was a way to save her, grab Jared, possibly Melcher, and get Dante back.

I folded my arms. "And if she refuses?"

"She won't refuse," Jared said. "I guarantee it."

Right, because Jared did whatever necessary to get what he wanted. I only wished he'd start putting that kind of tenacity into locating Giselle.

"What about her partner?" I asked.

"Randal Hammond," Melcher said with a nod. "We need you to go into their home first and put him to rest."

Kill him. Why couldn't Melcher come out and say it like it was?

"When?" I asked.

Melcher reached under his desk, pulled out a smart phone and set it on his desk. "I want this done while Miss Ericson is out of the house." Melcher looked at Jared. "That will give her further incentive to join our ranks if she comes home to find her benefactor is dead." Melcher turned his attention back to me. "I have an informant on her around the clock. I need you to be ready at a moment's notice to go in when we receive word of an opening."

I tilted my head. "We're all going together?"

Melcher had said "come with us" to recruit her.

"That's correct. Once you have put Randal down and Jared has convinced Miss Ericson to join the agency, I will bring her back to base for debriefing."

Just like that. Snap, snap.

I couldn't do anything about Jared and Melcher while they were on base, but if they were to leave base...

I had to fake cough to cover my smile.

This was better than the setup at the palace. Thanks, boys, for making things easier all of the sudden.

I still had to play along. I straightened my spine. "If I do this, I want you to turn Dante's dog over to my care."

Melcher didn't make an immediate answer. I could practically hear him gathering his thoughts, like papers shuffling through his brain.

"You've been under a lot of stress," Melcher said slowly. "One of your partners was abducted, another stabbed." A long pause followed before he continued, "I will have Agent Parker bring you the dog."

I breathed out, overcome by gratitude even though Melcher had been the cause of my turmoil from the beginning.

"However," Melcher said, voice deepening. "If the animal interferes with your missions in any way, I'll take him away for good."

"Understood," I said between clenched teeth. "When can I expect him?"

"By the end of the day."

Guess I wouldn't be going to school that afternoon, either. I wasn't in the mood anyway, but I certainly wouldn't go now, not at the risk of missing the drop off.

I stood up. "Can I go now?"

Melcher nodded. "Be ready for my call."

I nodded and turned quickly, afraid my face would betray my thoughts. I'd be ready, all right. Once Jared and Melcher stepped off base, I'd go Armageddon on their asses. Now I just needed Fane and Noel to help me plan exactly how to pull that off.

7

Dirty Work

The Jeep sputtered and died when I first started it up. I wasn't paying attention to what I was doing. I was too excited.

We needed chloroform and rags. Better yet, sleeping gas. Throw a couple of those smoking canisters inside Selene's house with Melcher and Jared inside and go in after them with gas masks on. Or shoot them with tranquilizing darts.

If we didn't have access to that sort of weaponry, we could always go old school and taser the suckers.

The Jeep started and kept running on the second try. I drove through the parking lot in first gear then went up to second and third on road to the gate.

I was dying to get home and call Fane. We wouldn't have to wait for Friday. One of the biggest challenges was not knowing when this operation would go down. As Melcher had said, we needed to be ready at a moment's notice.

The sight of the gate always filled me with relief, especially once it appeared in my review mirror. I slowed the Jeep as I approached the manned booth and waited for the gate to lift. I waited and waited, anxiety beginning to creep into my fingers. I tapped at the steering wheel.

A young man in camouflage stepped out of the booth, gun holstered at his hip, and approached my window. I rolled it down.

"Agent Sky, Agent Melcher would like you to wait for him here."

My heart plummeted.

I had an insane urge to press down on the gas pedal and keep going—smash through the gate. I wondered how far I'd get before Jared caught up and headed me off or—more likely—ran me off the road again.

"You can park in one of the spots to the right."

The guard looked me over with mild curiosity. Why wouldn't he? I was a teenage agent. Did he realize what kind of agent?

I looked at his expression to see if I could detect anything, but he'd already taken a step back to return to his post.

With one last longing look at the gate, I pulled over into a single row of parking spots. A larger lot across the way flanked a visitor's center. Getting on base was usually the challenge, not getting off.

Once parked, I snatched my phone and dialed Fane. A black SUV approached the exit then veered over into the lot where I'd parked and pulled in beside me.

I quickly turned off my phone and shoved it inside my pocket.

Jared stepped out of the SUV's backseat. He slammed the door shut behind him, walked around the front of the Jeep, and sat in the passenger's seat.

"Selene's on the move, let's go," he said.

"Now?" My heart couldn't drop any lower than it already had.

First the palace, now this. Why couldn't I catch a break?

"Yes, now," Jared said. "Follow the SUV."

The SUV had already backed up and re-entered the exit lane. I shifted into reverse and eased back.

"Hurry it up," Jared said. "The point is to get in before she returns."

I glared daggers at him, biting my tongue to keep from informing him that I'd only just begun driving again after the accident he'd caused.

We'd barely made it through the gate when Jared asked, "Who were you calling?"

"What?"

"When we pulled in you had your phone out. Who were you calling?"

"I was checking messages."

"Sure you were," Jared said.

I shoved the Jeep into third gear a little too roughly and the vehicle lurched forward.

"You're not half as sneaky as you think you are, Raven. Don't think I doubt for a moment that you'd hand me over to Giselle without a second thought if you had the chance."

Well, if it was honesty Jared wanted...

"You're right," I said. "I would. It's your fault we're in this mess. If you hadn't dragged me into your revenge mission, she wouldn't have gone after Dante."

"This one's on you," Jared said. "You just had to let Giselle go, didn't you? That's what I get for taking women into the field."

Venom rushed through my blood. "Excuse me?"

"I know," Jared said, waving a dismissive hand in the air. "This is the twenty-first century. If you ask me, the good old days are behind us, but I adapt to the times."

My eyes narrowed to slits.

"It was a straightforward mission," Jared continued. "Leave no vampire alive."

"You're a vampire," I said, through clenched teeth.

"Reformed," Jared said, puffing up his chest. "Once my benefactor showed me the blasphemy that is my kind, I vowed to help him put an end to this evil plague." Jared leaned into me, cupping a hand over his mouth as though sharing a secret. "And can't beat the benefits."

"How can you joke?" I demanded. "You killed Agent Crist then pinned it on Andre Morrel so you could murder him and his family for revenge."

Jared's smile dropped. "I didn't kill 'ol sourpuss."

"Andre didn't," I countered. How else would Jared have gotten her cross pendant unless he removed it from her cold body? Who else would have a motive? But Jared looked genuinely affronted by my accusation.

Jared swiped a hand down his blazer as though killing Crist was beneath him and just the thought needed brushing off.

"That part is true," Jared said. "Andre never had the backbone to do what it takes to survive in this world."

107

I lifted my chin. "It looked to me like he was doing quite well for himself. The whole family looked better off without you."

Jared's eyes narrowed. Of course, I had to go and pick a fight with him in a moving vehicle—one that required both hands and both feet to operate. I wasn't just playing with fire, I'd stepped directly into the inferno.

"Pull over," he said.

My heart rate picked up. "Why?" I demanded.

"You're taking too long. Now pull over and let me drive."

"Like I'd ever trust you behind the wheel of a car," I said.

"This isn't about trust," Jared said. "It's about following orders."

"I need to drive home first and get my dagger." I thought of the sleeping powder Noel had hidden in the tea tin. I couldn't imagine Jared pausing for a drink. It's not likely he'd allow me to take any type of detour, but it was worth a shot.

"I told you, we don't have time. You can borrow my knife. Now pull off onto the shoulder."

I flicked the blinker on and pulled onto the side of the road. Cars zipped past. I imagined running into the road shouting that a killer had kidnapped me. But working for the agency was worse than being held hostage. There was no getting away. Beating them at their own game was the only way out and so far they kept blocking my moves.

With the car in neutral and hand brake lifted, I jumped down from the Jeep and cast one last wistful glance at traffic.

I gave Jared a wide birth as we crossed paths in front of the Jeep. He glowered at me as we passed, eyes dropping to my arm. If we weren't on route to Selene's, I had no doubt he'd grab me as he'd done at the totem park in Sitka.

As soon as we were both seated, Jared pulled onto the road in front of another vehicle, speeding up before the driver had a chance to rear end us.

I forced a neutral look onto my face.

"They're dead," Jared said smugly.

His eyes were on the road as he sped through traffic until he'd caught up with the SUV. Once he had, he glanced over at me and smirked. "My family. The traitors are dead, and I'm not. Who's better off now?"

This didn't seem like the right time to mention Giselle wasn't technically dead. I ought to consider myself lucky Jared hadn't snapped my arm in half. Not yet.

I'd never forget the way he snapped Henriette's neck or crushed my arm in his grip when he showed up at the palace and said, "Don't ever disobey me again."

"And no one knows Giselle better than I," Jared said.

So he hadn't forgotten her.

"If you ever hope to see your partner again, you're going to need my help."

I needed Jared's help the way a tire needed a nail. What I really wanted was to have him bound and gagged, ready for delivery.

"You think I'm bad," Jared said, "but you never witnessed my precious daughter slicing open a victim with her sword. 'Fastest way to the vein,' she used to say."

And Dante was currently stuck with the psycho vamp. "You said you can help get Dante back. How?"

"Simple," Jared said. "We go hunting."

My frown deepened. This wasn't what I had in mind, but if the end result was the same, I guess I could alter my plans. They weren't exactly going smoothly thus far.

"Okay, so how do we hunt down a vampire whose whereabouts are completely unknown?"

"We go to her." Jared lifted his chin. "You have her phone number. Call her. Tell my precious little pumpkin that you've captured me and want to make the swap."

"Just like that?"

Jared grinned. "Just like that."

I sat up. Real hope filled my belly. Maybe I would actually manage to rescue Dante before the week was out.

I moistened my lips. "When?"

"After you complete your assignment Friday."

I sank back into my chair. I wanted to make the call right then and there. Not kill Randal. Not help Melcher corner and coerce Selene. Not kill a house full of vampires. But what choice did I have? Jared wasn't going to the palace, and he hadn't given me time to set a trap at Selene's. Things would go a lot smoother if he arrived at the swap willingly.

"What happens at the swap?" I asked.

"I kill her, and we get an agent back."

I chewed on my lip. "She's not just going to let you walk in and kill her."

"Never mind that. She'll come up with a plan, and we'll let her think she's the one calling the shots... at first."

Everyone seemed to be trying to call the shots on this one. It made me worry about how it would all play out.

Jared sat back, expressionless.

I took note of the intersections we passed. As we neared mid-town, the SUV entered a turn-only lane and slowed at the light. Once the light turned green, it passed an industrial area that turned into a neighborhood.

Most of the homes in the neighborhood we entered were one-story, ranch style, older structures. They were modest and slightly run down with paint peeling from the sidings, but they looked cozy.

The SUV passed more houses before entering a large parking lot in front of a community center. It stalled in a deserted row in back. Jared pulled the Jeep alongside it and parked.

"Get out," he said.

I glared at him then stepped out of the vehicle. Jared headed me off, opening the backdoor to the SUV.

"In you go."

His tone really annoyed me. I clenched my teeth together. Damn if the mother sucker wasn't right. I needed him if I wanted to get Dante back.

I hoisted myself into the SUV, noticing Melcher had a driver beside him in the front.

Jared quickly got into the back through the opposite door. As soon as the doors were shut, Melcher's chauffeur drove out of the lot and back through the neighborhood. He slowed when he reached a detached one car garage beside a narrow gray house that reminded me of a trailer.

Is this where Selene lived? I'd pictured her in something nicer—something more like the palace or lodge, not this modest house. This was worth putting up with her keeper, Randal?

Perhaps a home was better than nothing, but I thought Selene would have been able to do a lot better.

The SUV stopped in the road.

"Take care of Randal and call me as soon as it's finished," Melcher said. He lifted his wrist to look at his watch. "It shouldn't take long."

I turned to Jared. "You said you had a knife?"

"Did I?" he asked, tapping a finger to his corner lip.

I narrowed my eyes. "Yeah, you did."

"Well, I don't. Guess you'll just have to find something in the kitchen. Any pointy object will do."

"Thanks for nothing," I grumbled as I exited the vehicle.

"We'll be waiting," Melcher called after me.

Sure, send the teenager in to do the dirty work.

When I stepped outside, I caught the scent of wood smoke. It drifted from the chimneys, the only motion on the street in the middle of the day. I noted the house numbers nailed to the side of the house.

If only I could have one private minute to call Fane and update him on my status. I glanced over my shoulder. The SUV remained idling in the road, probably waiting to make sure I entered the house.

The front door was in a narrow outer entry between the garage and house.

I pounded on the wood then wrapped my arms around myself. There were no windows by the door and no way of knowing if anyone was home.

I didn't hear footsteps until they were almost at the door. Then they stopped.

"Who's there?" a male voice asked sharply.

"I'm a friend of Selene's."

The sound of a deadbolt clicked. As the door swung back, I saw Randal peering through the frame. He pushed his glasses up the bridge of his nose and looked me over as though regarding a specimen beneath a microscope.

"What are you doing here?"

He was about as friendly as the first time I'd met him at the tasting, which was to say—not friendly at all.

"I'm here to see Selene."

"Well, she's not in at the moment." Randal began shutting the door.

"Can I wait for her?" I asked.

The door froze. Randal eyed my neck.

"She called you over to feed, didn't she?"

"Look, I'm already here," I said. "Can I just come in and wait until she gets back?" Rather than wait for an answer, I pushed my way into a small mud room. A wood bench and shoe rack lined the wall beside the door.

Randal wore a dress shirt untucked, probably to try and help hide his protruding gut. As far as I knew, blood wasn't fattening. He must have retained a hearty appetite even in the afterlife.

"I don't have time to entertain Selene's friends. I work from home, you know. You're interrupting my work day."

I narrowed my eyes. "What do you do?"

"Tech support," Randal answered, puffing up his chest.

Tech support, not grave robbing. All in all, it didn't sound like a bad job for a vampire, especially working from home where clients wouldn't notice he didn't age.

All right, Aurora. Time to go for the Achilles heel.

"Then perhaps you could use a pick me up," I said, raising an eyebrow.

Randal's gaze flitted to my neck then back to my face. "I am not in the habit of drinking from strangers."

Yeah? And what did he call the wine girls at the lodge? Maybe he was more comfortable paying to suck.

"Suit yourself," I said, heading into the house.

"Hey," Randal called. "We have a shoes off policy."

I rolled my eyes and turned slowly. "Fine."

I plopped down onto the bench and yanked off my slip-on shoes. From there I stepped into a connecting kitchen barefoot. This half of the house was all open. The blinds were shut on the windows of the dining room facing the street. To the right, there was a living room furnished with a cream-colored couch, wood coffee table, and medium-sized TV propped on a simple wood stand.

No, not the posh digs I would have pictured worthy of Selene.

I returned my attention to the kitchen, into which Randal had followed me. After a quick scan of the countertops, I found what I'd been looking for—a wood knife block filled with black handles jabbing out. I walked up to it and removed one of the blades.

"What are you doing?" Randal demanded.

"Opening a vein," I said, calmly.

If Randal was the stuffy shoes off kind of guy, he probably preferred a clean cut over biting through.

Randal stared at me bug-eyed. "We use that for cooking."

Yeah, he was anal all right.

"Relax, I'll clean it in a moment," I said.

"What blood type are you?"

"Type I don't know."

Randal frowned. "You don't know your own blood type?"

"You got a type-O fetish or something?" I asked back.

Randal scowled. As far as enticing a vampire to bite me went, I wasn't doing a very smooth job. If I didn't convince him to bite the bullet soon, Selene would return, and we'd have a real problem on our hands.

I turned my arm over, wrist facing the ceiling, and traced a blue vein with the tip of the blade.

Randal leaned forward, suddenly quiet.

At this point, I hadn't put any pressure into the stroke. Cutting into myself gave me the willies, but it had to be done. I pressed harder. It stung. Using care, I sliced open the skin above the vein. Blood followed the edges of the knife like ink trailing a pen.

I set the knife down and balled my hand into a fist, squeezing more blood out. I lifted my wrist.

"Go ahead. I'll let you have a taste if you leave Selene and me alone when she returns."

Randal's eyes narrowed behind his glasses. "I told Selene not to do this kind of thing at my house. She and I are going to have a little chat when she returns."

"Well, I'm already here, and I'm bleeding," I answered sweetly.

Randal's eyes narrowed further. "I want you to leave."

"Fine," I said, matching his irritated tone with my own. "Do you have a Band-Aid or something?"

Randal huffed. "Wait here."

He walked through the kitchen and disappeared around a hallway to the right.

Damn it.

Did I really have to shove my wrist into his face? Or maybe I should pick the knife back up and go directly for the kill. If Randal fought back, that wouldn't be fun. He might not have an athletic build, but there was a lot of him than me, and that could present a real problem.

Picky vampires were the worst.

Before I could make a decision, Randal returned. He stopped two feet away from me and held out a single Band-Aid.

I stared at it between his fingers. "How about something to clean up the blood?"

"Oh, for Pete's sake," Randal said, sounding more annoyed than ever.

He moved toward me with sudden speed and grabbed my arm with surprising strength, lifting my wrist to his face. His head bent forward. A warm, wet trail followed his tongue along my cut. Now I really wanted to clean it. I tried to pull my arm away to go for the knife and prepare for the kill, but Randal's grip tightened.

He licked again.

And again.

But he wasn't swallowing.

My nose wrinkled in disgust as his saliva mixed with my blood.

I yanked my arm back. Randal smacked his lips, a hazy look in his eyes. He swallowed. A moment later, down he went—hitting the kitchen floor with a resounding boom.

I hadn't made a vampire convulse in ages. The sight, which had horrified me in the past, gave me sick satisfaction when Randal began to twitch. A second later, the sensation passed. I'd killed way worse vampires than Randal.

I grabbed the knife, avoiding eye contact as I crouched beside his shaking body. Hand on his chest, I pressed down and felt for his heartbeat. Once located, I let my fingers linger over his racing heart. Time to do the deed. I positioned the tip of the blade over the area of his heart as I'd done above my vein.

My hand shook.

I didn't like Randal, but I didn't hate him, either. As far as I knew he'd never killed before.

The knife shivered between my fingers. Randal and I were both shaking.

A car horn shrieked from outside.

Really? That was just like Melcher and Jared to signal me to hurry up and kill all ready.

I grabbed my quivering wrist with my free hand to steady myself. In this manner, I plunged the knife in.

Randal gasped. When he did, the shaking abruptly stopped. He rose several inches off the floor as though curling into his abdomen. The small checkered boxes on Randal's shirt filled with blood.

I got to my feet and backed away, leaving the knife in his heart. Randal clutched the area below the knife, his breaths turning to rasps.

Instant death was a luxury. Most people fought it—like chickens with their heads cut off, trying to run away from the inevitable.

I gripped the counter in front of the kitchen sink and leaned forward, sure I was going to hurl into the steel basin. Instead, I dry heaved a couple times. Once finished, I squirted liquid dish soap into my hands—way too much—and spent the next couple minutes drowning out Randal's gasps, trying to rinse and rub off the thick, slimy goo.

By the time I shut off the water, Randal was silent.

I dried my hands on my pants.

Call Fane, I thought. And tell him what? To bust in on Melcher and Jared single-handed? I might as well tell him to jump off a building. Either one of those actions would result in a broken neck. No, I couldn't lose Fane, and I needed Jared to get Dante back. Because Jared was right. He was my best bet if I ever wanted to see Dante alive again.

8

Recruitment

Once I gave Melcher and Jared the signal, they entered the house without removing their shoes. I went ahead and slipped mine on. Randal wouldn't mind.

Jared walked straight up to Randal and glanced down. "You want me to call in the cleaners now or after we talk to the beauty queen?"

Melcher looked around the dining area, slight frown on his face before taking note of Randal's body on the kitchen floor. "Call it in," he said. "I'd prefer they get him out of here before Miss Ericson returns."

"Could help motivate her," Jared said. He pulled his cell phone out, typed quickly and returned it to his blazer pocket.

"We have all the motivation she needs right here," Melcher said, removing a large manila envelope from inside his coat. His footsteps creaked over the wood floor as he walked over to Jared and handed him the envelope. "You'll go over this with Miss Ericson."

"What's inside the envelope?" I asked. "A contract?"

Sign your life away right here next to the X. Yeah, sure. I hadn't been offered that opportunity. My mom's hands had been tied. I would have died without her signature.

What did Melcher have to hold over Selene's head?

I didn't have to wait long to find out. The cleaners arrived within ten minutes of Jared's call, entering the house in their biohazard gear.

"Do you keep them on standby or something?" I asked.

Neither Melcher nor Jared answered. While the cleaners removed the body, they performed a quick search of the house, including the kitchen.

"Blood bags," Jared announced, opening and closing the fridge.

"That's better than a dead body, right?" I asked.

Again, no answer.

I sucked in an exasperated breath and released it slowly. Calming breaths, sure. The company and environment didn't exactly lend themselves to a Zen moment.

Randal's blood had stained the front of his clothes and not the linoleum floor, which made the cleaners' job extra quick. As far as kills went, it was clean.

A cell phone rang. Melcher reached inside his suit pocket and answered it. "Very good," he said before ending the call. He looked at Jared. "She's on her way."

My heart picked up speed. Why did recruitment feel so similar to a kill?

Melcher went over the plan briefly. He and Jared would stand out of sight. Seeing me inside her house would be enough to startle Selene, but Melcher didn't want to put her into an all-out panic. At least not at first.

"What if I wait for her outside?" I asked. "That would be even less startling."

"And give you an opportunity to run or warn her off," Jared said. "Keep dreaming."

I rolled my eyes. "You have trust issues."

Jared's forehead wrinkled as he zeroed in on me. "Need I remind you of Giselle?"

I pressed my lips together.

"Didn't think so."

As unpleasant as it was biding time with Jared and Melcher, all too soon "she's on her way" turned into "she's here."

A car rumbled into the driveway, followed by silence. Twenty long seconds passed before the jingle of keys could be heard at the front door. The dead bolt snapped free, and the door swung open. A light flicked on.

Light spilled out from the mud room. With baited breath, I waited for Selene to enter the kitchen and see me to the left in the dining room. The sound of wood creaking was quickly followed by the plop of one shoe, then another.

The biggest one was yet to drop.

Selene entered the kitchen, turning her back to me as she set her purse on the counter.

Panic rushed through me. Home invasion. Murder. Jared was right. I did want to warn Selene. But I wouldn't. At least she got a chance to live.

My fingers balled into fists. "Hi, Selene," I said, relaxing them.

Selene whipped around, a hand over her heart. "Aurora! You startled me. What are you doing here?"

Selene's brown hair hung loose around her shoulders. She had on a red sweater with a silk scarf fluffed around her neck.

"Did Randal let you in?" she asked when I didn't answer her immediate question.

"He did," I said.

Selene lifted her chin. "Where is he now? His office?" She started walking through the kitchen. Jared appeared from around the corner, blocking her way. Selene screamed.

I moved to block the way back to the mud room.

"Randal is dead," Jared said, taking a step toward Selene.

Her eye's widened. She scrambled back into the kitchen, eyes darting side to side. Selene turned toward the stovetop and snatched a frying pan resting on top of a burner.

"Stay back!" she cried when Jared advanced on her. He stopped and lifted his brows almost in challenge. "Who are you, and what are you doing here?" she demanded.

Melcher stood up from where he'd been sitting in the living room. He circled around the room divider, going through the dining room to take his position near me.

"Aurora," he said, keeping his eyes on Selene. "Why don't you tell Miss Ericson why we're here?"

I swallowed and stepped forward. "This is Agent Melcher and Jared. They belong to a special division of the government, and they want to recruit you."

Selene lowered the pan a fraction. She looked directly at me. "What do you mean, recruit me?"

"They want you to become an informant for their agency."

"What kind of informant?" Selene asked sounding scared and confused.

Melcher cleared his throat. "Our agency is tasked with protecting mankind against the demonic beings who feed on the innocent. We are committed to an ongoing battle with terror, Miss Ericson. It will be your duty to keep your eyes and ears open and report back to me."

"Aurora? What is he talking about?"

"The agency hunts down killer vampires," I said. My lips pursed. The irony wasn't lost on me that I was playing Crist's role of clarifying Melcher's ramblings.

Selene's eyes expanded. "You're vampire hunters."

"Melcher runs the agency, and Jared is a recruiter," I said. "They want to bring you in as an undercover informant to keep an eye on Alaska's undead."

"You mean spy on my friends?" Selene asked.

Melcher took a step toward her and stopped. "I'm sure you've seen and heard enough in your lifetime to know the undead can be dangerous when they go unchecked. It is our duty to maintain peace and order for humanity. You can help us."

Selene lowered the pan, holding it limply at her side. "But I've never hurt anyone in my life," she said.

Melcher straightened his back. "We are aware of that, which is why we are making you this offer rather than locking you up."

"But you want me to give you information that could get my kind killed?"

"Only the ones who deserve it," Melcher said. "Ruthless killers. What about their victims? Should vampires be allowed to end lives without consequences for all eternity?" Melcher's forehead wrinkled.

Selene looked at me. "How long have you been part of this?"

"I was recruited ten months ago," I said.

Both Selene's eyebrows shot up. "You're a vampire, too?"

My heart summersaulted. Melcher and Jared stared at me. The air stilled.

"No," I said. With that one word, Melcher and Jared visibly relaxed. Their shoulders, which had lifted, sunk back down below their ears. "I'm a vampire hunter."

Selene's eyes widened. She leaned back. "So your blood is... poisoned?"

"You know about that?" Melcher asked, his head lifting in interest. "I see we already have a lot to discuss."

"What happens if I refuse?" Selene demanded.

"You've been damned," Melcher said, lowering his head. "And there is only one way to atone for what you are. You must stop others like yourself. Lives are at stake, Miss Ericson, including your family's."

The pan slipped from Selene's fingers and clattered to the floor. My heart gave a startled leap into my throat.

"What have you done to my family?" Selene demanded.

"Your family is safe, and they will stay safe so long as you obey me." Melcher turned. His voice rose. "Jared."

Jared entered the kitchen with heavy footsteps. Selene took a step back as he walked up to her. Once at her side, Jared pulled a stack of photos from the manila envelope. He set the first one on top of the kitchen counter. Selene leaned forward, the color draining from her face.

"Here's your father playing dominos with his friend, Ralph, the retired optometrist, in Valley Home's courtyard," Jared announced.

He slapped the next photo down.

"Here's your sister coming out of church with your mother." Jared began dropping photos faster. "Your sister walking a rat or maybe a dog, I can't quite tell." He leaned forward. "And here's your brother eating his morning sausage and eggs at the Country Skillet, though judging from his waistline he might want to rethink his diet."

Selene turned away from the counter abruptly. Tears gathered in her eyes when she looked at me. "Did you know about this?"

I couldn't speak. All I could do is shake my head.

Jared gathered the photos, hitting the edges on the counter as he lined them up before stuffing the stack inside the envelope. He set it on the counter and leaned back, eyes on Selene.

"Don't cry, Geisha. This is your lucky day. Agent Melcher over there is offering you an opportunity to make a living, a chance to be independent."

Independent. Ha. Was that what they called a life of servitude?

"No more hiding. No more holing up." Jared's eyes flicked around the kitchen. "You could do a lot better than this."

Selene must have made a decent impression on Jared. He could call her a lot worse things than a geisha.

Selene folded her arms beneath her breasts. "Where am I supposed to live? You killed my partner."

"Your housing will be provided for you," Melcher said.

Selene's lips puckered. She lifted one hand to her face and twirled thick strands of hair around her finger rapidly as though winding up a toy. "What kind of allowance can I expect to receive?"

Jared smirked.

"More than enough to keep you comfortable," Melcher answered.

Selene pulled her finger away. The strand she'd twisted unraveled into a loose wavy curl. "And all I have to do is spy? Nothing messy?"

"You will need to know how to kill if necessary," Melcher said. "You will either be trained on base or sent to boot camp."

Selene's lower lip folded over. "I'm afraid that's out of the question. I simply cannot suffer through something so physically grueling."

Poor Selene. I wouldn't wish my life on anyone. She was a socialite, not a serial killer.

Melcher's eyes narrowed slightly. "That is for me to decide."

Jared pushed himself away from the counter. "I'm sure onsite training will be more than enough for our lovely geisha. No sense sticking her in with the new recruits. I'm sure she can hold her own out in the field."

Melcher looked at Selene with both eyebrows raised. "Then we can count on your full cooperation, Miss Ericson?"

Selene frowned. "You leave me no other choice, and you know it."

"Then it's settled," Melcher said. He clapped his hands together then dropped his arms and headed to the mud room. "You will accompany us on base where we will go over the terms of your contract."

I looked at Jared, who inclined his head in Melcher's direction. My eyes slid over to Selene, who fiddled with the scarf around her neck. I wanted to explain things to her. I wanted to express my deepest regret for getting her involved in all of this, no matter how little control I had over the situation.

"Selene," I said in a whisper. "I swear to you, I had no idea about any of this until today."

Selene made no eye contact. She stared at the manila envelope on the counter.

"We're done here," Jared said. He tapped his foot on the floor.

"I'm sorry," I said one last time before pivoting on the ball of my foot.

Melcher left the front door open. I walked out, followed closely by Selene and Jared. Melcher had already seated himself in the passenger's seat of the car.

Jared opened the door for Selene and shut it after she got inside. As we walked around the SUV to the other side I said, "You were awfully nice to Selene."

Jared ran his fingers over the stubble on his chin. "I recognize talent when I see it. Besides, I know her type—responds better to flattery than threats."

Lucky Selene, I thought sarcastically. I didn't want Jared's flattery, but I didn't care for his threats, either.

The ride to the Jeep was short, but not short enough to avoid one last question from Selene. She stared at me pointedly.

"Did you kill Randal?"

"I'm sorry," I said.

For several seconds she looked at me, not blinking. Her eyes were on mine, but she looked miles away, as though she didn't see me at all. Finally, she nodded once and turned to face forward. Silent.

Melcher's driver pulled up alongside the Jeep. I'd done what they asked. I could go home.

Meanwhile, Melcher and Jared still walked free, stronger than ever.

"I want Tommy," I reminded Melcher.

"Like I said, you'll have him by the end of the day," Melcher said.

Jared jumped down from the SUV to let me out. He lifted his chin as I stepped out. "Run along, Raven."

When he turned his back to me, I flipped him the bird.

❄ ❄ ❄

Noel wasn't home when I walked in. She wouldn't be home for another few hours. Nope, she was just wasting her time planning a party Jared had no intention of attending.

I tossed my purse onto the dining table and slumped into a chair.

Damage control. Where to begin?

Jared had offered his assistance with Giselle. Fane wouldn't like it, but what other choice did we have?

Fane, Noel, and I needed to meet, but I couldn't leave until Levi came by with Tommy, and I wasn't about to put Fane at risk by asking him over before then. If I called him, it would be too hard not to mention my latest killing assignment and everything else that had gone wrong that day.

I brought Fane's number up on my phone. I'd never texted him until now.

Me: Dog safe
Fane: Good

I chewed on my lower lip and stared at my phone, grateful Fane had replied instantly.

Me: Windows fixed?
Fane: Yes. What happened at the meeting?
Me: Can we talk later?
Fane: You in the middle of something?
Me: Got something I have to do
Fane: OK

The phone felt heavy in my hand. I stared at it, not sure what to type next.

Me: Do you think V would try to hurt you?
Fane: Don't worry about me

Of course I'm worried about you! I thought. Valerie had threatened Fane, smashed up his windshield, and broken every window in his house. I'd seen her cut down vampires before. She was merciless.

Before I could type anything else, there was a knock on the door.

I set my phone on the table and went to answer it.

Levi stood outside, leash in hand, Tommy attached to it, sitting on the concrete. The moment Tommy saw me he stood up, his golden tail wagging like crazy.

That seemed quick. How close did Levi live? Maybe the agency owned every house on the block. I shuttered to think it. Now wasn't the time, not with my heart bursting with relief.

"Tommy!" I cried, falling to my knees. I wrapped my arms around the big fur ball, tears of happiness gathering in the corners of my eyes.

"Score one for Aurora Sky," Levi said.

His blond hair was lighter at the roots rather than the ends, curling slightly an inch below his ears. He had the whole grunge look down from his frayed jeans to his flannel shirt.

I gave Tommy several pats on the head before standing. Levi had a big smile on his face as if nothing gave him more pleasure than delivering Tommy to me. I knew better.

Still holding onto the leash, Levi asked, "What did you have to do to get Melcher to change his mind?"

"I negotiated with him," I said.

Levi raised both eyebrows. "I'm impressed. But don't let it go to your head. Melcher will make you pay for it later down the road. He's not the kind of man you bargain with."

I grabbed the leash from Levi and gave it a gentle tug. Tommy stepped into the foyer.

Good boy, you're safe now.

Levi glanced down briefly. "All I'm saying is be prepared for this to come around and bite you in the ass when you least expect it."

Not if I got to Melcher first.

Levi craned his head around me.

"Nice ass, by the way," he said, grinning from ear to ear. "I wouldn't mind being the one to bite it," he added.

I folded my arms over my chest. "We aren't the ones who do the biting."

Levi smirked. "Says who?"

I narrowed my eyes, watching him suspiciously. Did Levi know we were undead? If I asked, he'd know I knew, and I didn't want to show him any of my cards. He was probably just making a sexual innuendo. Funny how it came across cute and annoying when Dante did it, as opposed to sick and sleazy coming from Levi.

Melcher sure knew how to round up the cream of the crop.

I reached for the door handle. Before I could grab it, Levi pulled it open wider and stepped into the open space. Because he was down one step, his eyes were about level with my breasts.

"What about some kind of reward for bringing you the dog?"

"Not a chance," I said. "Now get off my property."

I stepped down to reach the door handle, pushing Levi aside so I could close it. He gripped the edge, engaging in a tug-of-war with the door. My heart sped up. I was strong, but Levi was stronger.

"Let go!"

Tommy growled.

I loosened my grip on the door, suddenly calm.

"You know who else likes to bite?" I asked, looking down at Tommy.

Levi's smile faltered. He didn't look so sure of himself anymore. He also glanced at the security camera aimed directly at him. He smiled again. "Never was fond of dogs, except for bitches. Pick you up Friday. Wear something sexy."

"Screw you," I said, lips curling back.

Levi lifted his hands in the air. "Melcher's orders."

We'd see about that.

Now that Levi was no longer blocking the door, I yanked it toward me, slamming it on him. Once shut, I dead bolted the lock and turned to Tommy.

"Oh, Tommy. Tommy, Tommy. I am so happy to see you!"

Tommy's ears perked up. He resumed wagging his tail as I crouched beside him and ran my hands through his golden fur.

I was so happy to see him. Besides, it wouldn't hurt to have a dog in the house. I'd sleep a heck of a lot better.

I unclasped the leash from Tommy's collar and straightened out. "Are you thirsty, boy?"

Tommy turned his head sideways when I asked.

"Come on."

I led him into the kitchen, filled a bowl with water, and set it on the floor. Tommy began drinking immediately. Damn, Levi! Had he given Tommy anything to eat or drink?

Once the bowl was emptied, Tommy set about exploring the downstairs. His nails clicked against the kitchen's linoleum floor, the noise stopping when he reached the carpet inside the living room.

I followed Tommy, watching him sniff around.

I needed dog food.

"Hey, Tommy," I said.

He stopped, looked at me, and wagged his tail.

"Want to go for a ride?"

He wagged his tail harder.

I put Tommy back on the leash before unbolting the door and locking it behind us. As we approached the Jeep, Tommy pulled at the leash, tail going crazy.

"That's right, boy," I said. "Got two back, one left to go."

When I saw how happy Tommy was inside the Jeep, it boosted my courage about driving on my own. I started the vehicle up, put it into first gear and headed to the pet supply store where I purchased dog food and treats.

After I paid for the food, I called Fane, followed by Noel, telling them we needed to talk right away.

9

Reinforcements

Noel arrived home first.

As soon as she entered the kitchen, Tommy hurried toward her, tail wagging.

"Dante's dog!" Noel exclaimed.

"I convinced Melcher to turn him over."

"Thank goodness." Noel gave Tommy a pat on the head. "This is great news."

My shoulders slumped forward. "If only I had more of it."

Noel's eyebrows furrowed. "What is it? You sounded pretty serious over the phone."

I sighed. "Melcher's gone and messed up all our plans. Jared's going to the tasting instead of the palace. I'd rather talk about it when Fane arrives."

"Is having Fane over such a good idea?" Noel asked.

Fane and I had already thought about that.

"He's going to park around the block."

Noel nodded. "Good, because if Valerie smashes my windshield, she's dead." She opened the fridge. "Sounds like we're going to need some drinks." She pulled out a wine cooler. "Want one?" she asked, holding the bottle toward me.

Blood sounded better, but if Noel wasn't having any, I didn't want to be the one giving into cravings.

"No thanks."

Noel twisted the cap off and tossed it on the countertop. The bottle lifted into the air as she tilted it back and took a big swig. Once she'd swallowed, Noel smacked her lips. "These don't do much in the way of a buzz, but damn, they taste good."

I lifted an eyebrow. "Better than blood?"

"Depends on the source. Blood from a bag..." Noel shuddered. "Gross. Blood from a boy..." She grinned big, eyes lighting up like twin monitors. "Delicious."

I snorted.

Noel lifted her head. "I like to bite, and I like to be bitten, and I'm not ashamed to admit it." She took another swig of her drink.

"Which do you like better? You know, now that you know you're a vamp?"

Noel pursed her lips. "Hmm. Good question. I really liked being bitten, but once I learned I was a vampire it made me really want to bite people." She took another sip from her wine cooler.

I leaned forward. "You know, I think I will try one of those. I could use a drink."

"Sounds like you could use more than one," Noel said, setting her bottle down to grab me one from the fridge.

As she handed it to me, I said, "Thanks."

Cap off, I took my first drink. I'd tried champagne, wine, vodka and beer, but this was my first wine cooler. It tasted cool and fruity. I remembered Noel telling me one of her favorite perks of working for the agency was a fake ID. It was weird to think we'd never reach the official legal drinking age no matter how long we lived. The agency could have at least had the decency to let us reach twenty-one.

I lowered the bottle and nodded. "This isn't bad."

"What did I tell you?" Noel asked. "Tasty." She pointed her bottle at me. "While we're waiting, why don't you spill? How did it feel sinking your teeth into Daren?"

The sound of Daren's moan when I bit into him filled my head. It had both encouraged and repelled me. Hunger had fueled that bite. Exhaustion. Desperation. Followed by disgust in myself. But it beat thinking about how I'd killed Randal earlier and stood by while Melcher and Jared threatened Selene.

I grimaced. "I wasn't thinking straight when I bit him."

"No kidding," Noel said. "You were acting on instinct."

Tommy's wet nose nudged my free hand. I glanced down as I ran my fingers over his silky head.

What would Dante have thought if he'd seen me acting on instinct? Out of everyone in the agency, I pictured him taking the undead thing hardest.

He saw himself as a superhero— a Van Helsing, not Dracula.

When we got him back, what would I tell Dante first? That he was undead or that I had feelings for another vampire? Talk about cold.

"What's the matter?" Noel asked.

"What do you mean?"

"You have a funny look on your face."

I met Noel's eyes. "I'm just thinking about Dante. How's he going to handle all this?"

"Dante's a big boy," Noel said. "He can deal." She sucked down the remainder of her wine cooler and set the bottle with a hollow clink on top of the counter.

I'd always wondered how Noel ended up at the agency—what tragic event had claimed her life, but her sensitivity on the subject had always deterred me from prying. That was until she admitted the reason herself.

Noel had attempted to commit suicide.

In the craze of Dante's abduction and my undead discovery, I'd had no time to ask her about it further.

Now here we were, standing face to face, a rare private moment without hostile vampires bursting in or rocks shattering windows... at least not yet.

I hesitated to ask, but in the end, curiosity won. "Why did you try to kill yourself?"

Noel frowned. "It doesn't matter anymore."

"Then why not tell me?"

Noel's voice turned to ash. "I was abused by my father, okay? I let him smack me around for years until one day I couldn't take it anymore, so I climbed into the bathtub and slit my wrists. When I regained consciousness, I was on base. Melcher took me in, trained me, and gave me a second chance to make something of my life. He helped emancipate me from my parents. He found me a place to live."

"And you haven't seen your family since?" I asked.

Noel slumped against the counter, reminding me of the vulnerable side I noticed when we first met, even when she talked tough.

"My father found me last February."

"While I was still in town?" I asked.

Noel nodded solemnly. "He showed up at my apartment. At first he stayed in his car, watching from outside."

I shivered. "That's creepy."

"Then he got one of my roommates to let him inside."

"What the hell?"

Noel shook her head slightly. "He didn't hurt me, but he wasn't going to leave me alone, either, so I left, only I didn't know where to go. Whitney was grounded and Hope had just been kicked out."

I had a sense of where this was headed. "Why didn't you stay with Daren or Reece?"

"That was before I bonded with those guys."

"Before you knew you were undead?" I asked.

Noel nodded. "I didn't know who to call, so I called Fane."

"I wish you would have told me what was going on," I said. To think of all the turmoil we could have all been spared if only Noel had opened up to me in the first place.

I stared at Noel, waiting for an explanation.

Tears suddenly swarmed her eyes. She blinked rapidly and looked down at the floor.

"I don't like telling people," she said. "It's humiliating."

"But—"

"I don't want to be a victim." Noel squeezed her fingers into fists.

"You're not," I said. "You're an undercover vampire agent."

"What about if we succeed in taking out Melcher?" she asked. "Then I'm just another predator feeding on innocent victims."

I snorted. "I wouldn't call Daren and Reece innocent victims. They want to be bitten. You make them feel special, as messed up as that is. We can't help what we are."

Noel cocked her head to the side when she looked at me. "You feeling all right? You don't sound like yourself."

I shrugged. "A lot's changed in the last week. We're assassins and informants, and we're vampires. Melcher's stuck us smack dab in the middle of no man's land. I don't know whose side I'm supposed to be on any longer."

"I don't think we have to choose a side. We just have to do the right thing."

I gripped the wine cooler by the bottle's neck.

"We need to stop Melcher and Jared from endangering peoples' lives. That's the right thing to do. That's our mission."

Noel sighed. "We need reinforcements."

"We need Dante."

Noel lifted her chin. "And Gavin."

When it came to taking down bad guys, Dante didn't hesitate for a second. The more inner agency help we could get, the better. I couldn't see Gavin offering much in the way of assistance. He'd be a liability more than anything else. We had enough trouble brewing between Valerie, Fane, and me without adding Noel and Gavin into the mix.

Why did Valerie have to go manic? We needed her on our side.

Too bad that ship had sailed—right on into the Dead Sea.

❊ ❊ ❊

A knock at the door sent Tommy barreling down the hall barking.

Security cams and a guard dog—I felt better already.

"Good, boy," I said to Tommy, placing a hand on his fury head as I peered through the door's peephole.

My heart gave a lurch that was quickly followed by flutters when I saw Fane on the porch, one hand in his pocket, jaw tight, arm flexed.

Joss stood beside him, eyes darting around the porch.

I turned to Tommy. "Okay, boy. These are my friends. Can you sit?"

Tommy's ears perked up. His tail swished from side to side.

"Sit," I commanded.

Tommy's tail stopped wagging. He sat and looked up at me.

"That a boy," I said, ruffling the fur on his head quickly before turning to open the door.

My cheeks heated even as the outside air met my face.

"Hey," I said, my eyes meeting Fane's.

Until then, I never realized one word could come out so breathless and soft, like an invitation to my soul.

Fane's head perked up, as though startled by my tone. His shoulders relaxed. "Hey," he said back.

His smile made me smile, or maybe I'd been grinning from the moment I looked outside and saw him.

Joss stomped one foot against the ground. "Well? Are we going in?" he asked.

I opened the door wider.

Fane broke eye contact to turn his head to Joss. "After you."

Joss made no move forward. His lips pursed when he looked at me. I hadn't seen the vamp in eight months—not since I spent the night at their house, in Fane's bed, minus Fane. Joss hadn't liked me back then and from the scowl on his face now, I'd say he hadn't missed me much.

"Come in, Joss," I said.

He had the same ghastly pale skin and narrowed eyes underlined by dark circles. "It's Josslyn."

Oh, right. Only dude in the whole wide world who would grumble at someone for failing to call him by his girly name.

"Joss," Fane said in a warning tone.

Joss stuck his nose in the air. He stepped forward into the house. Fane followed right behind him, slowing as he passed the place where I stood pressed against the door. While Joss' back was turned to us, Fane paused inches from my face and looked down at my lips.

The hooded look of his eyes made me lightheaded. Fane leaned toward me, as close as he could without actually touching.

"Hello, Josslyn. Hi, Fane," Noel called from down the hall.

Fane lifted his head toward her voice, and the moment was broken. I hurried to shut the door behind us.

"Can I make you tea?" Noel asked.

"That would be most kind of you," Joss said.

I did a double-take. How come Mr. Moody was all charm and manners to Noel but not me? Maybe because she said his full name.

"Come on in and make yourselves comfortable," Noel said.

Joss followed after her. Fane lingered in the hallway.

Fane leaned into me. "You and I have unfinished business."

I glanced involuntarily up the stairs.

Fane broke out into a Cheshire grin. "That's not what I meant, but I like the way you think."

I folded my arms across my chest. It didn't hide my blush, but it helped mask the awkwardness encroaching all around us.

Fane dropped the smile. "I'm tired of being split apart every time an obstacle comes between us."

Obstacle? Try juggernaut.

As long as Melcher had me on his radar, I wasn't free to love anyone—let alone another vampire.

"Hopefully we don't have to wait much longer," I said.

"What happens once we free your partner?"

I met Fane's eye. "Once Dante's free, he's on his own."

"You and I can start fresh?" Fane asked. "No more romantic feelings for your partner?"

"I told you. Dante's my friend. That's all."

Fane's eyebrows rose. "You never slept together?"

My nose wrinkled. "No."

Fane smiled when he saw my expression. "Don't forget, I know all about you and your stash of Trojans."

I'd nearly forgotten about my pit stop at the Jewel Lake Quickie Mart on my way to Scott Steven's house. Fane had the unfortunate timing of buying smokes at the same time I was buying protection.

"Your face turned so red when you saw me in line behind you," Fane said. "Sorta like it's doing right now."

He reached his hand forward to touch my cheek. I uncrossed my arms and batted it away.

"That's because I'd just come in from the cold," I said.

Fane shook his head. "You were embarrassed."

"You were an ass."

"Don't forget, I offered to drive you home. Should have taken me up on it."

I sucked in a breath.

Fane moved his chin back and forth lightly as though saying, you know I'm right.

In the end, it would have been better to return home. I could have avoided the worst sex ever. I didn't have anything to compare it to, but I was convinced it couldn't get worse than Scott Stevens. Doing him ranked somewhere up there with stabbing a vampire to death.

Schools ought to hire me to preach abstinence.

"Hey guys, don't do it. It sucks—unless you meet a nice vampire because he probably knows what he's doing and I bet he does it really well. Plus you won't get pregnant or any STD's. Remember, don't take him to bed, unless he's undead."

Not only should I have accepted the ride home, I should have made Fane my first.

He searched my eyes. His lower lip puffed out. In his eyes, I saw concern. What happened that afternoon wasn't something I wanted to dwell on, and I didn't want Fane to worry about it, either.

"It's all in the past." I waved a limp hand in the air.

"Not us," Fane said.

My mouth opened slightly. Our eyes locked. He cupped my chin gently in his hand. His fingers were surprisingly warm.

"Not us" echoed through my head over and over like a wild drumbeat. If Noel and Joss weren't waiting in the kitchen, I would have grabbed Fane's hand and dragged him upstairs to my bedroom.

My inexperience couldn't hold a candle to my desire to take Fane inside of me. I craved that kind of closeness. I wanted more between us than rubbing and kissing. I wanted to connect body and soul.

I also really wanted to please Fane. Not that I imaged that was too difficult to do. It wasn't as though sex required instructions.

Insert man part here. Rock hips and ride partner until you are both moaning and screaming your heads off. Do not stop until you reach climax and release. Take as much time as you need to do it right.

Yeah, I think I had it pretty well figured out. I just needed practice.

"What are you thinking about?" Fane asked.

He spoke gently, as though he knew his words had touched me on a purely romantic level. If only he knew the true direction of my thoughts. I had to bite down on my lower lip to keep from laughing.

Fane straightened. "What's that look? Now I'm curious."

Fane was a hard person to take off guard. I went for it.

"I was thinking about you naked."

His jaw dropped. Good, he hadn't been expecting that. I shot him a cheeky smile and headed past him into the kitchen with Tommy at my heels—Fane a close second, hurrying to catch up.

10

Hunting Party

"Damn it!" Noel said after I shared what I'd learned from Melcher at our morning meeting on base. "Now what?"

She sat at the dining table beside Joss with another wine cooler. Joss sipped his tea and set it down. Tommy's head lifted briefly off the floor after Noel cussed before lowering it once more and closing his eyes. The retriever had followed me to the end of the table and laid on the floor beside my chair once I sat down.

Fane stood, gripping the back of a chair. "We can't allow Henry to go to the palace Friday," he said. "If Valerie takes him in, the gig is up. He'll tell your boss the names of everyone involved in setting up the party."

Fane was right. Henry knew too much.

"We can't cancel the party, either," Noel said. "How's that going to look to Melcher that I reported it taking place then all of a sudden, nope, cancelled?"

Fane's frown deepened. "You're right. One way or another, there has to be a party."

I looked at Fane. "You can't go, either. Not when they're sending in Valerie."

Noel released an exasperated breath. "Then who the hell is going? This party isn't going to throw itself."

"I'm going." Fane let the chair go and straightened up. "When Valerie shows up, I'll deal with her."

"No way," I said. "It's not worth the risk."

Fane folded his arms. "I wasn't asking."

A flash of hurt, followed by anger shot through my body. It festered inside me like an open wound. Friday night filled me with enough dread already. The body count at the lodge would be substantial with Levi, Mason, and I upstairs, and Mr. McCreepy and his team down below.

I had enough to stress about without having to worry about Valerie and Fane going head to head at the palace.

Noel looked from me to Fane and cleared her throat. "It does seem really risky."

Fane gave Noel the same hard stare. "Not half as risky as going into Diederick's tasting to kill every vampire inside."

A hush fell over the room. What could I say to Fane? He was right. My neck was on the line in more ways than one. There's no way he'd be content to sit back doing nothing while I entered the lion's den. The one thing that had pacified him was coordinating the trap for Jared at the palace. Fane was like a missile that had been fired, and there was no calling him off.

Joss set his mug on the table roughly. "We need to leave the state."

"Here we go again," Fane said.

"Better yet, the country."

"Leave?" My heart fell. I turned my head toward Fane. "You can't leave."

"Don't worry, I'm not going anywhere until this matter is settled."

I hadn't realized until that moment that it was possible for my heart to sink any lower.

Until. He's said until. What then? Once the matter of Jared, Giselle, and Melcher was resolved would Fane leave Alaska? Leave me?

Leaving me implied that we were together, which we weren't. We'd flirted; we'd kissed, but we hadn't discussed much beyond the present crisis.

"In the meantime, that madwoman might burn our house down in our sleep," Joss said.

Fane's shoulders relaxed. "Which is exactly why I need to be at the palace to ensure Valerie doesn't leave."

Noel tapped her fingers lightly on the table. "What do you mean?"

Fane walked over. "I'll trap her inside the music room. That way, she won't be able to cause any more problems. Once we've dealt with Jared, Giselle, and this agency business, I'll send her packing."

"It would be nice if she were out of the picture," Noel said.

It was hard to miss the smile on her lips, no matter how faint.

I leaned into the table. "What happens after she goes on mission and disappears? You think Melcher's going to sit around scratching his head in confusion? No. He'll send someone to check it out."

"She took off after Sitka. She could take off again." Noel shrugged.

"Exactly," I said. "If Valerie disappears a second time, Melcher will be on her like a blood hound. He'll tear the town upside down to get to the truth."

"So I'll move her someplace else," Fane said.

"Where?" I asked.

"I don't know. The bottom of the ocean."

"Not a bad idea," Noel said under her breath.

I knew Fane had a personal vendetta against Valerie, but I wished he'd take her connection with the agency more seriously. True, she was a ticking time bomb, but if Valerie went missing, we could end up with a more explosive problem when the agency went to investigate her whereabouts.

Joss looked around the table. "What if it appeared that she had died?" he asked.

Fane looked down at him. "What do you mean?"

"Secure her, as you said, but send the agents on a false trail."

Fane smiled suddenly. "Joss, you're a genius. I'll drive her car down some backwoods road out of town. Let your agency chase their tails on that one." His head lifted triumphantly.

Noel nodded. "It would buy us more time without arousing too much suspicion."

I chewed on my lower lip. "Wouldn't that make you a suspect?" I asked Fane. "I'm pretty sure a vampire ex-boyfriend would make the list no matter how well you've behaved in the past."

"You said they already have their eyes on me," Fane said. "Might as well give them a reason to look."

My nails dug into the table. Fane had once accused me of having a death wish. What about him?

"The fact that they have a file on you should be reason enough to lay low."

Fane's eyes flashed. His chest rose. "I'm not the sort to lay low." He backed away from the table abruptly. "I need a cigarette." Without another word, he walked out of the kitchen toward the connecting living room.

I pushed away from the table and planted myself in front of the kitchen sink where I began scrubbing at dishes. There wasn't much to keep me occupied, only my plate and cup from breakfast. Noel was an exceptionally tidy roommate. I wouldn't have expected her to be Miss Clean, not after I first met her and saw the disarray of her room in her first place, but she'd cleaned up her act quickly.

"Can I get you another cup of tea?" I heard Noel say behind me.

I didn't hear Joss' answer over the rushing water in the sink.

Noel sidled up to me and whispered, "Go to him."

"Clearly he wants to be alone," I said.

Noel clicked her tongue. "He wants to protect you, but he knows he can't stop you from going on this mission."

"I want to protect him, too," I said.

"I know you do," Noel said. "It's frustrating, isn't it?" She raised her eyebrows. "I'll entertain Josslyn. Now stop pouting and go talk to Fane."

I shut off the water.

"Fine. I'll talk to him."

How had I gone from thinking about him naked to thinking about what a stubborn ass he could be within the space of half an hour?

❄ ❄ ❄

There was a rectangular slab of concrete just outside the sliding glass door in back. The outside light illuminated Fane's back, spotlighting him against the dark. As I pulled the sliding door open, Fane turned to watch me. He took a drag from his cigarette, lifted his head skyward, and blew out a smoke cloud.

As soon as I shut the door, Tommy appeared behind the glass and stared out. I re-opened the door several feet to let him join us. He immediately stepped into the grassy part of the yard and began exploring.

Fane took another puff off his cigarette.

Noel had told me to go after him, but now that I was here, I didn't know what to say.

I had to go to the lodge. I didn't have a choice. Fane didn't have to go to the palace. This wasn't some kind of competition to see who could bag the biggest prize at the end of the night.

Fane pulled his cigarette out of his mouth and pointed it at the security camera. "The cameras aren't enough. They can't keep you safe. Joss is right. If we don't succeed in crippling the agency. We all need to leave the country. I can arrange that."

I let out a humorless laugh. "So that's Plan B? Flee the country?"

"Better a globe trotter than ash." Fane lifted his cigarette and flicked the top for emphasis. The tip sparked and gray ash drifted to the ground.

"What if Dante wants to leave? Would you help him, too?"

Fane studied me a moment. "You said he's like family?"

I nodded.

"I understand what that's like. Yes, I'd assist him, too. If he wanted my help."

"I'm worried about my mom and grandma." I thought back to the surveillance photos of Selene's family. I didn't want Melcher to ever use them as leverage against me.

"I'll take care of it."

I shook my head. "It's too much to ask. Besides, how would we get by?"

"I can show you how," Fane said. "I'm not without experience or resources."

I gave my head a bitter shake. "We aren't the ones who should be running."

Fane's cheeks compressed as he sucked in another lungful of smoke. After blowing it into the air, he crouched down and rubbed the cigarette out over the concrete.

"We'll try things your way first," Fane said as he straightened. "But if it doesn't work out, we do them my way. Agreed?"

I started opening my mouth, but before I could respond, he continued. "And if I take my clothes off for you, you better be prepared to do the same. And I do mean everything." Fane let his eyes drift down my body slowly.

Every inch of me tingled and shivered. I didn't know whether I was hot or cold.

I folded my arms across my chest and met his stare when it returned to my eyes.

"Just don't go getting yourself killed before you get a chance," I said.

Fane chuckled. "Very well, you've convinced me. I'll be careful, but you have to promise to do the same."

"No one's killed me yet."

Fane sobered. "Aurora..."

"I'll be careful. I'm not about to let my friends and family down." I stepped to the edge of the concrete and patted my thighs. "Come on, Tommy. Back inside."

The golden retriever lifted his head and looked my way. A second later he lowered his nose to the ground.

"Tommy, come," I said louder.

This time, he trotted over. I let Tommy into the living room and stepped in next, Fane right behind me.

We rejoined Noel and Joss in the dining room. They both sat with a mug of tea at the table.

"Lenard Oneal," Noel announced when we walked in.

I shook my head. "Is that name supposed to mean something to me?"

"He's a vampire with a thing for redheads. Everyone knows it. Best of all, he's already on Melcher's radar. I'll have Henry invite him to the party."

It couldn't hurt. Who else could Henry invite? Maybe if we were lucky, Valerie would get abducted for real. Right, because everything had been falling into place so beautifully already. Lenard was in more danger than Valerie, but at least he would give Melcher a potential target other than Fane.

Fane nodded. "Now let's settle the matter of Jared."

"If he wants to walk into a trap, I say we let him," Noel said.

"We should surround him on all sides," Fane said. "Leave nothing to chance."

Nothing to chance. Famous last words. We were playing a game of Russian roulette, and I just hoped that when our turn came, the chamber would turn out empty.

❅ ❅ ❅

Friday afternoon, Levi texted me to say he and Mason would pick me up at ten. I dressed early. I wanted to be ready to go as soon as they arrived. I'd already worn two long dresses to the tastings, so I selected a short black dress with a halter top that crisscrossed over my breasts. My arms and shoulders were bare. If I had to be tonight's bait, I might as well give the vamps easy access. The quicker we got this over with, the better.

I parted my hair on the left in front of the bathroom mirror, gathered it all into one hand and twisted it into a bun, which I secured at the nape of my neck with a metal clip.

As I put on a pair of chandelier earrings, Noel walked in wearing a midnight-blue lace corset top with a matching mesh skirt that flared over a pair of black boy shorts. She wore a lace choker and fingerless gloves. A matching set of Victorian skeleton keys hung from her earlobes.

I held the mascara wand aside and raised both eyebrows at Noel in the mirror.

"What's with the Goth revival?"

Noel sighed. "Total Goth scene on the eastside."

I looked Noel over again. Boy, were we headed to different parties. "Well, be safe," I said.

Noel stared back at me through the mirror. "I'll be the safest one tonight."

Couldn't argue with that. Give me a bunch of crackheads and drug dealing vamps any day of the week over cold, calculating wine snobs or a jealous ex.

Noel looked away when she pulled a tube of lipstick out of the medicine cabinet and applied it to her lips. Bright red. Even so, she resembled nothing of the sickly creature she'd been when I first met her. Her skin glowed, and her hair had an impossible amount of bounce and shine to it.

Noel nodded. "That's a nice dress. You look like you're going to prom."

"Right." I snorted. "Carrie's prom."

Noel flashed me a blood red smile in the mirror. "Wish I could stick around for moral support."

"Believe me, you're better off not meeting my new teammates, Levi and Mason." I scrunched my nose. "Complete douche bags."

"Are they at least hot?" Noel asked.

I frowned. "Most definitely not."

The only thing I saw when I pictured Levi's face was a sleaze bucket slime. Mason wasn't much better. He stood aside and let bad things happen without blinking an eye. Total tool.

After applying lip gloss, I set the tube on the counter beside my phone, a switchblade, and the silver clutch I planned to carry with me.

Noel followed my hand with her eyes.

"What's that? The hunter's survival kit?"

I looked down. "Hardly. I only have room for lip gloss and either the phone or knife."

"I'd go for the switchblade. Much quicker than 911."

No argument there. I unsnapped the clutch and stuck the switchblade inside. There was just enough room to nestle the tube of lip gloss in with the knife.

"Besides," Noel said. "The signal on the hillside sucks."

Who would I call anyway? Noel, Fane, and I would be on opposite ends of the city. Nope, it was just me and Mr. Blade.

Noel smacked her lips before turning away from the mirror. "Don't wait up for me."

I huffed. "I'll probably be out later than you."

"Sure about that?" she asked, flashing me a cheeky smile before ducking out of the bathroom.

I envied her and Dante's ability to make light of missions. My stomach always twisted up before an assignment, as though I were about to give a speech in front of a thousand people and had lost my index cards.

Noel called out a "goodbye" as she headed for the stairs.

"Be safe," I called after her.

"You, too."

The front door opened and closed. As I made my way downstairs, I heard Noel's car start up and pull out of the driveway. Once she'd zipped away, I went for the blood bags in the fridge. I didn't know where Noel had gotten them, and I didn't care.

Tonight demanded liquid courage and super strength.

I stuck a mug filled with blood into the microwave and hit the "re-heat" button. The metal box lit up and vented a slightly metallic smell.

The microwave beeped. I pulled the mug out and dipped my pinky into the thick red blood to test the temperature. Perfect. I was getting good at reheating blood just right. I lifted the mug to my nose, it was like inhaling a handful of coins. The aroma was far from my favorite, but the euphoria blood gave me was worth the coppery zing going down.

Maybe now I could get through the night.

✳ ✳ ✳

At ten fourteen, the doorbell rang.

I opened the door to find Levi, dressed in clean jeans and a long sleeved tee, leaning in the frame, holding up a bottle of Merlot. He looked me up and down, grinning from ear to ear.

"Hello, beautiful. I brought you a bottle of wine," he said.

I frowned. "I hope you came armed with more than that."

Levi reached around his back and pulled out a gun. "Like my piece?" His eyebrows jumped.

"Guns are too loud," I said.

"That's why I brought this," Levi said, bending down and pulling up his pant leg. There was a hunting knife holstered and wrapped above his ankle.

"And this," Mason said touching a knife holstered around his belt on one hip. There was another gun on his opposite hip.

"What's with the guns?" I asked.

"Back up," Levi said. "House full of vamps. We gotta go in armed to the teeth." He glanced sideways at Mason then back at me. "Aren't you going to invite us in?"

"Shouldn't we be going?" I countered.

"Not yet."

I blocked the entrance. "Why not?"

"Because Jared is meeting us here."

My heart skipped a beat. "I thought he wanted us to go in first."

"He decided we're all going to caravan to the hillside. Now are you going to let us in? It's cold out here."

Vampires don't mind the cold, I nearly snapped.

"Wait in your car," I said. "Tommy doesn't want you in here, and neither do I."

Levi's face darkened. "Is this how you treated your other partner? What's his name? Socrates?" He looked at Mason and laughed. "Must have been a new recruit to get himself kidnapped by a she-vamp."

"I'd like to see you go up against Giselle," I said.

Levi smirked. "Any time. Any day."

"Easy to say when you haven't met her."

Jerk!

Before Levi could respond, a sporty red car with a black stripe down the hood zoomed down the street and screeched to a halt along the curb. I winced. Good thing it was late and there weren't any kids playing outdoors.

Speaking of scumbag vampires... the door of the vehicle opened and Jared exited. A black SUV pulled up behind him, but no one got out.

As he strode up the driveway, I locked the door behind me.

Jared walked up to Levi and yanked the bottle of Merlot from his hands. "Is this a mission or a date?"

Without waiting for a response, he unscrewed the top and lifted the bottle like a salutation. When the opening reached his lips, Jared paused and smiled. Rather than take a sip, he held the bottle out to me.

"Pass," I said.

"Drink it, Raven."

My fingers dug into the silver clutch.

"I said, 'pass.'"

Levi leaned toward me. "You're going in as a wine girl. Drink up."

My heart pounded hard against my chest. Jared could force me to kill, but he couldn't make me drink.

"I don't need to drink," I said. "The vamps are going to die after they taste my blood."

"Come on, Raven," Levi said. "Give the poor suckers a little taste of the good stuff before they go."

I shot him a maximum strength glare. Talk about a clone! What a well-trained little sidekick Levi had proved to be. I always found peer pressure a major turn off. More than anything, it made me more determined to dig in my heels. I wasn't some weakling. I wasn't "Raven." I was Aurora Sky: Vampire Hunter. Bite me and die. They could all suck it.

"Bite me," I said.

Jared wagged his finger at me. "Watch the attitude."

I stared at his waving finger a moment, wishing I had the brute strength required to take down that mother sucker with my bare hands. The injustice of it all was that I could do boot camp ten times over and still not possess the power to go head-to-head with Jared. I needed more than lipstick and a switchblade. I needed a loaded gun.

"I'll have a swig," Levi said.

Jared stared at him for several beats before handing over the bottle. Levi took a large gulp and passed it to Mason who took a small sip and handed it to Jared who passed it directly back to Levi.

He took a sip and another. All of a sudden, he tilted the bottle and chugged it down, which had to be really hard to do with red wine.

"Easy does it," Jared said suddenly. "I need you functional."

"What's the plan, boss?" Mason asked.

"The four of us lead the cavalry inside," Jared said. "My team can handle things below. Someone needs to keep an eye on the three of you." Jared glanced my way. "You, especially. Things didn't work out so well the last time I left you alone upstairs. Now let's go." Jared yanked the bottle of wine from Levi's hands, took a long swig and set it on the porch. He pushed me toward Mason. "Take her. Me and Jeans will follow you."

Mason wasn't the smiling type. He was more like an ox who could knock a person down in two seconds flat if he wanted.

"Let's go," Mason said to me.

"What kind of name is Levi, anyway?" I heard Jared ask behind us. "Is your mamma valley trash or something?"

"Why you asking about my mamma?" Levi responded in a phony yokel accent.

"I sucked her last weekend," Jared said.

"She taste any good?"

"Lot better than your nasty ass blood."

I stormed off the porch, Mason on my heels.

"How can you work with those two?" I asked.

Mason's eyebrows knit. "What do you mean?"

I sighed in exasperation. If he had to ask, it wasn't worth trying to explain. "Never mind."

I shook my head and walked toward the Hummer parked in the driveway. And I thought the Jeep was big. What kind of missions did Melcher send this guy on? Up mountain passes? Across the tundra?

Or maybe it made Mason feel like a badass brute, not that he needed a Hummer for that.

A light went off inside a house across the street. Further down, a car started up. My neighbors were turning in or headed out for the night, going about their business. Here I was, smack dab in the middle of suburbia, but my life was nothing like theirs. I was off to hunt vampires. I was a vampire. A freak of nature. Destined by blood to live forever.

Levi's laughter hit my back. The high-pitched raucous made me glower even when I wasn't looking at him.

I hoisted myself into the Hummer, quickly slamming the door over Levi's chuckling voice.

Mason got in and started the beast up. He waited for Jared to pull into the road behind us before leading the two vehicle convey to the hillside.

11

Vamp Bait

The Hummer gripped the dirt road once we reached the hillside and zigzagged up the mountain. The corners of Mason's lips lifted ever so slightly. Guys and their machines. Behind us Jared kept pace. Maybe if I envisioned his car plunging off the cliff's edge enough times, it would come true. Poetic justice. Giselle would simply have to accept his mangled body and move on. It wouldn't be my fault if he had an accident.

All too soon, the stone pillars marking the drive of the lodge appeared behind the Hummer's headlights. Oh, joy.

Our small convey drove in.

Mason came to a stop behind a Mercedes-Benz. A man in his mid-thirties, dressed in a black suit, stepped out and handed his keys to the valet before proceeding to the front door. When the car pulled away, Mason took its spot and waited wordlessly.

The valet appeared three minutes later, striding up the drive towards Mason's door. Before he reached it, Mason stepped out. He left his door open. I listened for the valet to ask his name, but before he could say anything, Mason reached for the old man's head and twisted it so fast not one word was ever exchanged.

My breath caught in my throat. I knew it was coming, but it didn't make it any easier to witness.

The valet fell out of my line of view, and all I could do is stare at the space he'd occupied seconds before.

Jared cut off his engine behind us. A door, followed by another, quickly opened and closed.

Jared walked up to Mason and said, "Good work."

Mason made no expression. His lips puffed out, neither in a smile nor frown. "Help me move him," he said to Levi.

The two of them bent down, straightening slowly. Together they walked sideways toward the bushes lining the driveway, just beyond the glow of the lighted entry. As they receded, I was able to make out the limp body of the valet.

I faced forward and shook my head slowly from side to side. I'd just witnessed the murder of a human. There wasn't a thing I could do for him or the butler.

My door opened, and I gave a little start. I hadn't noticed Jared come around to my side.

"My lady," he said, sweeping into a mock bow. "Allow me the honor of escorting you into the party." He held his hand out.

I was too sick to glare at him. I stepped down numbly, ignoring his outstretched arm.

"The big guy did him a favor," Jared said. "The old man was on his last legs, anyway."

I made no response. Reason was lost on Jared. Saying anything was a waste of breath.

Mason and Levi strode over to rejoin us once their hands were empty.

"Nice little workout before the main event," Levi said.

Mason looked between us before resuming his way up the cold, stone steps. The red wine couldn't come close to numbing me from what he was about to do. He moved ahead of us. Jared held me back as I followed.

"Let Mason clear the way first," he said.

Mason pounded on the front door. When it opened, I shut my eyes. I couldn't watch. Nausea gripped me. In high school I'd been one of the few students who turned and walked away from the crowds that gathered around hall fights. I hated violence. It made my insides ill. And here I was in the thick of it. Blood on my hands. Fighting. Killing. Watching innocent people die.

"I think I'm going to throw up," I said, turning suddenly to the edge of the stairway.

As I curled over, Jared gripped me by my upper arms and straightened me up, scowl on his lips.

"Don't you dare," he said. "I don't want your barf breath turning our targets off."

This time, I managed to glare at him. "You make me sick."

"Just so long as you keep it inside," he said.

I pulled out of his grasp.

"Clear," Mason called out.

Jared gave me a pointed stare. "After you."

I climbed the last of the stairs and walked into the lodge. There was no sign of the butler inside the entry. Mason was as quick as he was ruthless. And Levi got an obvious kick out of anything deranged. Quite the dream team Jared had here.

163

The living room was empty, thank god.

We passed the staircase leading downstairs. Soft chatter and music drifted from below. The four of us passed by in silence. We circled around and came across a wider open staircase leading up. A burgundy carpet runner ran up the middle of the dark wooden stairs.

As we ascended, I willed my body and mind to go numb. I needed to get through tonight unscathed.

At the top of the stairs, we entered a wide hallway lined with windows. The lights of downtown Anchorage glowed in the distance below. The hallway led into a high-ceilinged open area with an antique rug centered in front of a leather sofa and chairs.

A young man in a suit sat on one of the chairs, one leg crossed over the other, a brown leather book in his lap. A thin set of printed sheets were stacked on an oak coffee table.

"Good evening and welcome," he said in a voice that sounded like it belonged to someone much older. "May I have your names, please?" He opened the book as he spoke.

"The von Trapps," Levi said with a grin. "Party of four."

The guy stared down at his book, forehead wrinkling a moment later. "I don't see any of those. Did you register under different names?"

His head was still bent as Mason approached. The guy didn't look up until Mason stood directly in front of him. He reached his hands forward. I closed my eyes in the nick of time, but couldn't block out the sickening crack that followed.

If I was going to walk out of there tonight with my sanity in check, I couldn't have the image of Mason snapping necks left and right festering inside my brain.

I wondered if the guy had been human or vampire. A weird mix of horror and relief rushed over me. Despite screwing our plan up, I was relieved Jared had come to the lodge rather than the palace. If he or one of his partners had gotten his hands anywhere near Fane's neck, I didn't know how I would have continued to live. And for me, living could end up being a very long time... or short, depending on how the evening went.

There was movement. I kept my eyes tightly closed until Jared said, "Haul his carcass out of sight."

While Jared's sidekicks disappeared down the hall with the body, I moved to the coffee table to read the printout. It was a list of wine types by room number. Or, more to the point, human wine girls by room number.

When the guys returned, Jared said, "Time to rock and roll."

Levi chuckled. "I'm ready to rock if you're ready to roll."

Jared handed the thin leather book to Levi. He pointed to where the now dead guy had been sitting. "Take his place," he said to Levi, "and see to it that all our esteemed guests don't leave before visiting room eight."

Levi's smile drooped for a second, before lifting back up. "Aye aye captain."

"Now let's get setup," Jared said to Mason and me. He led the way into a second hallway off the small open living area. The whole hallway was lined with doors. Each had a brass number nailed to it at eye-level. Some were closed, and some were ajar. From Melcher's comment earlier, closed meant occupied and ajar meant unoccupied. No silver bats in this joint.

Jared marched down to the last room, number eight. It was open about half a foot. Jared held the door open while Mason and I went in. He followed behind us and closed the door.

A young brunette woman in a short red dress with spaghetti straps lay on top of a queen-sized four poster bed. The satin bedspread was black—probably to help mask any blood splotches. There was an antique ceramic washbasin and stack of small neatly folded towels on top of an oak stand. Beside the stand, a wicker hamper had several bloodied towels tossed in.

The room had been dimmed. A lamp on either side of the bed glowed over the woman. Her eyes were closed as though she were asleep or passed out. There was an open wound on her neck and wrist. Jared walked to the edge of the bed and studied the woman. He turned and stared at me. The way he looked from my neck to my arm put me instantly on edge. He didn't have to say anything for me to know he'd have to cut me the same way as the wine girl. At least it was better than being bitten. A cut was much cleaner than teeth.

Jared turned back to the woman and snapped his fingers twice in front of her face. She didn't respond. "This one's juiced."

"They're all juiced," I said. "They're wine girls."

Jared looked me up and down. "Yeah, and you're not juiced enough."

I lifted my nose. "There isn't enough wine in the world to make your company tolerable."

Jared's eyes narrowed. "Enjoy taunting me while you can, Raven. One of these days I'm going to rip your wings right off."

Was that his cryptic way of saying my arms? I shuttered. At least Melcher's informant had come through and knocked out the girls. I wouldn't want to see Mason's hands on their necks even if they were selling their bodies and blood to vamps.

Jared turned to Mason. "Take the girl to another room and close the door. Close the door on any room that's not in use."

Mason pulled the unconscious woman off the bed and hoisted her over his broad shoulder.

Jared pointed at me. "You, on the bed. Keep your mouth shut and let the animals feed. Once they're convulsing, I'll kill them. Hold up," Jared said to Mason. "After I've made the kill, you'll drag the bodies out and stash them in an empty room. I'll signal you when we're ready."

Mason nodded before heading out of the room with the woman.

"One last thing," Jared said, pulling out a pocketknife. He flicked open a blade and smiled as he approached me. "Try not to scream."

As if I'd give him the pleasure. I turned my chin sideways to give him access to my neck.

"Just don't slit my throat," I said.

I tried not to flinch as Jared looked over my skin. The jerk was taking his sweet time—probably trying to make me more nervous than I already was. I was almost relieved when he made the first cut in my neck.

I cried out, despite myself. The cool blade sliced through my skin with an ease that sent sick chills through my body.

I met Jared's eye. "Aren't you going to cut my arm?"

Jared glanced at my arm briefly. "The neck is enough."

I sighed heavily before walking over to the bed. There was room behind the lamp on the nightstand to set my clutch. Having the switchblade within reach was a small comfort.

I lowered myself onto the edge of the bed first, scooted into the middle and lay down. My neck ached as I lifted my head to keep an eye on Jared's movements.

"Good," he said. "Now follow the example of the wine girl. Eyes closed. Mouth shut."

"Got it," I said, not masking my irritation.

Jared hid himself inside the bathroom. Luckily he kept his trap shut after that, too. I laid my head back, waiting.

All you have to do is lie here, I told myself. What we were doing was hideous, and I hated it, but it was easy. Focus on easy. I stared at the ceiling, unable to close my eyes. Easy didn't equal relaxing. My stomach was tied into knots as if I was waiting for the gynecologist to walk in. Hmm, this actually didn't seem as bad as that. My little joke cheered me for half a heartbeat.

Time ticked by slowly. I looked around, but there were no clocks. I was starting to feel bored when footsteps entered the room. A young man in his late twenties sauntered in holding a glass of red wine by the stem. He wore a fitted suit and held himself up as though he were someone of great importance.

Get over yourself, guy. I'd help him with that in about three minutes, give or take.

"Well, hello there," he said, noticing me staring at him.

"Hi."

He came around the bed, stopping a couple feet away, and stared at me. His eyes didn't go anywhere else, even when he lifted the glass to his lips and took a sip.

Okay, was he just going to stand there sipping wine, watching me? No, not creepy or annoying in the least bit.

I raised my eyebrows.

"Would you care for a sip?" he asked.

"No, thanks." What the hell? He was supposed to do the sipping, not me.

"Oh, right," he said with a chuckle. "You're not supposed to mix wines. My apologies." He pulled his eyes off me to glance around the room, after which he set his glass on top of a dresser. He turned back to me, stopping two feet away. "Do you taste as good as you look?"

I lifted my head. "I don't know. Why don't you tell me?"

He grinned. "You're a lot spunkier than the girl in room five."

"Not everyone can hold their liquor," I said.

The guy's grin widened. "I happen to enjoy a little conversation over drinks."

"Lucky you."

He took a step closer. My body tensed.

"Are you nervous?" he asked.

I turned my head sideways to look him in the eyes. "Actually, I'm bored."

The man's chest rose. His lips twitched as though unsure of whether to smile or frown. Finally he smiled and said, "Allow me to alleviate your boredom."

With that, he eased onto the bed and leaned into my neck. I waited for his wet tongue to touch my skin, but he took his sweet time breathing me in. At least he was well-groomed and hygienic opposed to some of the less savory characters I'd had to deal with.

While I was waiting for him to suck on my skin, I didn't notice his hand at my side until he ran it over my breast. I immediately sat up and slapped his hand. "What the hell do you think you're doing?"

He smiled and shrugged. "You're a beautiful woman. Can you blame me?"

Was this how he treated all wine girls? I wanted to spew. Suddenly I didn't mind killing this pervert.

"You're here to taste, not touch," I snapped.

He held his hands up in mock surrender. "Beg your pardon, darling. I thought you might enjoy a more personal connection."

Yetch! Was that the fancy term for groping? I despised this guy more with every passing second.

"Think again."

The guy looked side to side and leaned in, whispering as though conspiring with me. "Let's not mention this little misunderstanding to Diederick. I swear I've never done anything like that before. I've never felt drawn to a woman until I saw you. There's this magnetism surrounding you that's nearly impossible to resist."

Someone hand me my switchblade! I was ready to stab this sucker myself convulsions be damned. My jaw ached as I ground my teeth together.

The man cleared his throat dramatically. "Let's start over, shall we?"

"Better yet, why don't you shut up and suck my blood already," I said, turning my neck for emphasis.

"I like talking."

"This is a tasting."

Asshole.

His face lit up like this was all a fun game or some kind of foreplay in his sick mind. I was ready to end it.

I scooted closer to him and flashed my first smile before leaning in. "Suck my blood, and I might let you touch the other one."

When I pulled back, his grin stretched wide.

"I knew I liked you best," he said.

He wouldn't feel that way in a few seconds. He leaned forward. No more chit-chat. He pressed his tongue against my wound roughly, licked, and swallowed.

His eyebrows jumped. That was the last time he smiled. His body shuddered and jerked from his waist up, as though the poison hadn't worked its way down to his legs quite yet.

He tried reaching for me, but I scooted back as his fingers narrowly missed my leg. Instead, his fingers slid over the satin sheets as he tumbled off the side of the bed onto the floor.

I swung my legs to the ground. Once standing, I folded my arms as I watched him shake on the floor.

My heart held no sympathy for a groper who took advantage of drunk women. I wondered if this was how lives of crime began—this slippery slope of justification.

"You can come out now," I called, not taking my eyes off my victim.

Although the creeper was convulsing all over the floor, his eyes widened at my booming voice. Jared appeared by my side a moment later.

"What's with the slapping?" he asked.

"That vamp touched me." I pointed at the man shuddering on the floor.

Jared looked me up and down. "Wearing that dress? Can you blame him?"

"Bite me."

"Can't, I'd convulse."

Wouldn't that be a beautiful sight?

Unlike Valerie, Jared didn't lift the dagger for dramatic effect. He jabbed it into the vamp's heart in a quick, succinct motion, much like Giselle's maneuver when she stabbed Valerie.

Like father, like daughter. I shuddered.

There was something soulless about Jared's stance, as though the kill gave him neither pleasure nor pain. As though he could do it a hundred times and feel nothing.

I looked at the vamp's now-lifeless body, feeling nothing other than a nagging sense of doom that with him the last traces of my humanity had died a dark, cold death.

❋ ❋ ❋

After Mason disposed of the groper, we killed four more vampires. Fortunately, the other four didn't want to touch or talk.

I didn't want to talk, either. I wanted all of this to be over. Until then, I shut my emotions off as much as possible. My mind wandered away, down the mountain to Bootlegger's Cove. To the palace. To Fane.

Everything going on around me was like a bad dream. Nightmare or not, when I woke up in the morning it would be over. That's what I concentrated on most—the over part.

Jared had his timing down to a science, leaving the bathroom almost as soon as my victim experienced his first twitch. He stabbed them quickly. Once finished, he signaled

Mason who dragged the bodies out one-by-one like bags of rice. They had something of a factory line going on.

The steps that entered the room next were lighter than any of the previous vampires. I propped myself onto one elbow, suddenly curious.

A woman about twice my age approached the bed. She wore a tunic, slacks, and tortoise shell glasses. Curly brown hair framed her face and touched her shoulder blades.

Well, this wasn't awkward.

She pointed her nose down and stared at me over the rims of her glasses. "Finally, someone who isn't asleep on the job. Oh, but there's a smear of blood on your neck." She sounded more disgusted than concerned. The woman tapped her chin, frowning at me with disapproval.

Anger rekindled inside my belly. Who did this she-vamp think she was?

"What are you? The tasting police?"

The woman's jaw moved from side to side. "I am a high-paying customer, and I expect my needs to be met."

"I guarantee you've never tasted blood like mine."

The woman's pupil's moved when she looked at my neck. She cleared her throat. "I'll be the judge of that. Now lay down."

I did as she said. Once in place, the woman sat beside me, leaned down, took a quick lick of my neck and sat back up. She moved her lips from side to side as though swishing around wine rather than one lick of blood.

She swallowed. A second later, she dropped to the floor with a thud.

"Well?" I heard Jared ask. "How did she taste?"

I lifted my chin to look at him standing at the foot of the bed. My eyes shifted to the floor where the woman stared wide-eyed through her glasses at the ceiling as wave after wave of spasms overtook her body.

I followed her gaze to the ceiling.

"I've been told I taste like death," I said to the space overhead.

"I wouldn't know," Jared answered.

I sat up and swung my legs to the floor.

"Are you AB negative or positive?" I asked.

His eyes latched onto mine before answering abruptly, "Positive."

A grin spread over my lips. "So you're an informant."

Jared moved around the bedposts stealthily. As he knelt beside the woman's twitching body, he lifted the dagger.

"No, I'm a killer."

With that, he plunged the dagger into the woman's heart. I winced, instantly wishing I'd closed my eyes or looked away. Blood seeped through her tunic around the edges of Jared's blade.

Half a dozen vampires in one night. How many more would we have to kill?

Jared pulled his dagger out of the she-vamp's lifeless body. He moved across the room and opened the door. A moment later, Mason entered and made his way to the latest body without comment.

He bent down and hooked his arms under hers. The woman gaped, eyes wide behind her glasses. Mason had her halfway off the floor when a gunshot rang out from what sounded like the next room.

The sound of it blasted through the entire house like a cannon going off. A man screamed.

"What the bloody hell?" Jared roared.

Mason dropped the woman. Her body whacked against the floor.

Apparently, there wasn't any reason to stay quiet any longer.

As Jared and Mason stormed out of the room, I snatched my clutch off the nightstand and followed quickly—just as eager to see what the hell was going on.

We charged down the hallway. The moment we entered the open waiting area, flaming red hair caught my eye.

Hot lava! What the hell was Valerie doing at the lodge?

She'd dressed entirely in black. Not dressy black—as had been requested at the tribute party for Marcus—but ninja black in form-fitting leggings and a halter top. She held a pistol at her side. The barrel pointed down to the ground and the body on the floor.

Levi.

He lay face down, unmoving.

Time froze. Or so it seemed.

My body ceased briefly to function while my thoughts ran wild.

Mason's face contorted in rage. He charged Valerie without bothering to draw a weapon. He might very well have succeeded in taking her down if all that muscle had been bullet proof. Valerie lifted the gun and fired. A second shot rang out. My eardrums screamed in protest.

Mason's body smashed against the floor.

I'd seen so many bodies drop that evening that it was all beginning to splatter together like graphics across the pages of a comic book.

Levi and Mason dead. Alive a minute ago. Dead now.

It didn't quite compute.

Now was not the time to shut down. Damned if I'd let Valerie gun me down, too. Apparently, hurling rocks had only been the beginning. She'd clearly gone insane.

I jumped back into the hallway, out of the line of fire. The whole house felt like it had tilted—the walls slanting irregularly. The hall suddenly stretched a mile long. There was no way out from here.

Valerie had a gun. All I had was a switchblade and lip gloss. We'd learned all kinds of combat skills at boot camp. Knife throwing wasn't one of them.

After the ear splintering gunshots, the following silence magnified the off-kilter space around me.

"I'm not here to kill you, Aurora," Valerie called out in a sickie sweet voice. "I'm here to kill him."

12

Standoff

emerged slowly from the cover of the hall. Both Valerie's arms were raised, pistol aimed at Jared.

"Jared?" a man's voice called from below stairs.

I expected to hear footsteps running upstairs any second. For his part, Jared remained calm. He had his eyes on Valerie as though she were the one being held at gunpoint, not him.

Jared squared his shoulders. "Everything's fine," he called back.

I stared at Levi's and Mason's bodies on the floor. Everything was not fine.

"All clear down there?" Jared asked in a booming voice.

"Clear. Do you need us up there?"

Jared shot Valerie a smug smile. "I've got everything under control. Round up your team and head out."

"Yes, sir."

In the silence that followed, I heard footsteps below, followed by the slam of a door and engine rumbling to life then fading into the distance. Team two cleared out quick... leaving me behind with Evil Red, Jared, and two dead agents.

"I thought you were going after Henry tonight. What are you doing here?" I asked, still shocked to see Valerie at the lodge.

Valerie lifted her chin. "Why would I go after Henry when I heard Jared would be here?"

I shook my head slightly, still processing what had just happened.

Valerie's eyes narrowed. "You called me back. Unfinished business, remember? I'm here to finish it."

My chest constricted. That would have been a lot more helpful if the plans hadn't changed. Now I was stuck dealing with a loose cannon.

Jared, who had stopped roughly eight feet away from Valerie, resumed his advance.

Valerie pointed her pistol at Jared's face.

He stopped and smiled. "You can't kill me."

Valerie smirked. "Why? Because you're a vampire?" Her eyes narrowed. "Watch me."

Jared took another step.

"I'll do it," Valerie said. "I shot you before, and I'll shoot you again. I'm on a roll tonight, asshole."

Jared stopped. "You can't shoot me, because I'm your maker."

Valerie snorted. "Is that what you call attempted murder?" This time she took a step closer. "Before I put a bullet in you, I want you to beg for forgiveness."

Jared lifted his chin. "Really, Red? Is that any way to treat the man who gave you everlasting life?"

Valerie lowered the gun a fraction. "What are you talking about?"

I didn't like the conversation's direction one bit. Valerie so did not need to know she was undead. She already acted as though she was indestructible.

"Don't listen to him. He's trying to distract you," I said.

Valerie's head jerked. Her irises flared when she looked at me. "Shut up, you backstabbing, fang-banging whore."

My mouth dropped open. Backstabbing? She had me confused with herself. For some reason, her words made Jared smile. Not me.

"You don't give a damn about me or Dante or anyone else— not when you're too busy spreading your skinny legs for Fane Donado even after I warned you to stay away from him."

Blind rage shot through me like a thunderbolt. My fingers tightened to fists. "Quit making shit up!"

"I saw Fane's car in front of your house again," Valerie said.

"He came by to talk, and it's none of your damn business anyway."

More to the point, it wasn't any of Jared's business, and he was listening a little too intently for my liking.

Jared smirked. "Men don't just come by to talk."

Valerie's forehead wrinkled as she glared and snapped her attention back to him.

"Why are you speaking?" she demanded.

Jared lifted his hands. "Hey, I'm not the one dicking around behind your back."

Valerie scowled. She'd already killed two agents without a moment's hesitation. I had to defuse the situation before I ended up as another casualty.

Before I could speak, Jared said, "Wake up and smell the blood. You're a vampire. Both of you are, thanks to me."

Jared's smile was the ugliest I'd ever seen, and all the more so when accompanied by his smug attitude.

"Liar," Valerie said.

"You know what makes a vampire," Jared said. "AB positive or negative blood activated by disease. The agency brought you in and shot you up with all kinds of fatal viruses. Put two and two together."

"I'm a vampire?" Valerie repeated in a faraway voice. Her lashes fluttered. She stared down the hallway as though the walls had suddenly dissolved into an infinite horizon.

"Congratulations, ladies. You get to live forever." Jared's eyebrows jumped. His shoulders relaxed, and he showed teeth when he smiled as though he'd suddenly turned into some kind of game show host.

And Valerie played right into his hands. Her pistol arm lowered until the gun rested limply at her side.

"No growing old and ugly. I get to stay this way forever." Her voice rose in excitement.

"Quite the extra perk, isn't it?" Jared jut his chin out. "You've killed two agents, but Melcher doesn't have to know. I'll tell him it was one of Diederick's employees."

The hell he would. Jared had no right to negotiate.

Valerie lifted the gun slightly, but not high enough to kill. From that angle, she'd be lucky to hit Jared's thigh.

"And why would I continue working for a vampire hunting agency?" she asked.

"Money. Protection. Housing," Jared fired off quickly.

"I hate my housing situation."

Jared waved his hand in the air. "I'll have Melcher change it."

Valerie lowered the gun. "I want my own house. No roommates and no staff members."

"I can make it happen... if you promise not to kill any more agents." Jared glanced at Levi's lifeless body. "I was growing fond of Blue Jeans."

"He drew his weapon first," Valerie said.

"What's done is done," Jared said, lifting his head. "It's not as if we can bring him back from the dead."

"How can I trust you won't report me to Melcher if I let you walk out?" Valerie asked.

Jared stared at Valerie, suddenly all serious. "I give you my word. Consider yourself fortunate because I don't give it often, and I never rescind."

Jared's word of honor. This was too much.

"He stabbed you! He strangled you!" I said.

Jared waved it off. "I'm required to make it look like an accident."

"Accident?" I challenged. "You attacked her." I turned to Valerie. "He attacked you."

Valerie shot me a cold stare as though I were raining on her parade. "At least I got to keep my organs."

Jared chuckled. "And I thought I liked Raven best. Ginger takes the lead."

"Yeah? Well, she can have it so long as you keep your promise to go after Giselle."

Valerie's eyes narrowed. "That bitch stabbed me. If anyone's going after her it's me."

"You see?" Jared said, smiling. "We have a common enemy."

"I want in on the mission to take her down," Valerie said.

Jared straightened his back. "You already had your chance."

Valerie walked over to the coffee table and set her gun down. Jared's eyes locked on the weapon, but he was too far to get to it. One wrong move, and Valerie could have it back in her hand in a millisecond.

"Bring me on this mission, and you and I are square," Valerie said. "I'll continue undercover work—so long as I am compensated to my satisfaction—and I won't retaliate later down the road."

Jared stared at her, considering a moment. "Very well," he said. "You, me, and Raven. Together again for one last encore. Think you can get it right this time?"

"She's the one who let the bitch live," Valerie said, nodding at me.

Jared's eyes narrowed. "And you shot me."

Valerie glared back. "You stabbed me first."

Jared's shoulders relaxed. He laughed suddenly. "Like you said, we're square."

Valerie grabbed her gun. "When do we go after the blonde bitch?"

"It will be better if Melcher never knows you were here tonight. I suggest you complete your original mission."

Henry. The Palace. Fane.

I did not like the sounds of that one bit. Valerie was way too trigger happy tonight. And I doubted that discovering she was undead would make her any less merciless when it came to Fane.

Jared turned to me. "Raven, call in the cleaners." The corner of his lips lifted. "Tell them to bring in the whole crew."

"I didn't bring my phone." The words tumbled out. I turned quickly to Valerie. "Can I borrow yours?"

Valerie scowled. "Why didn't you bring your own phone?"

I lifted my clutch. "Didn't fit."

"Why bring that stupid thing at all then?"

"Where else would I store my switchblade? In here?" I leaned forward and pointed between my breasts.

Jared snorted. "You wish."

I ignored him and kept my focus on Valerie.

She huffed and pulled her phone out of her tight black pant pocket. "I want this right back," she said, holding it up.

I walked over and snatched it. "Thanks." I lifted the screen and saw one service bar. Remote locations had their advantages. "Damn, no signal. I'll see if I can get one from outside."

"You're kidding me," Valerie said.

"It's the hillside," I said nonchalantly. "The signal sucks. I'll try from the driveway."

I started for the staircase, not waiting for an answer. Jared swiftly stepped into my path.

"Don't go calling someone 'just to talk.'" Jared made air quotes.

"The only call I'm making is to the cleaners," I shot back. "You can check call history after I'm done. Do you want to clean this mess up? Because I certainly don't?"

Jared stepped aside. "Make it quick."

"Yeah, I want my phone back. Next time bring a bigger purse," Valerie called after me as I hurried down the stairs.

I rushed through the living room and out the front door. Valerie's red Honda Civic was parked behind Mason's Hummer.

I ran over and crouched beside the passenger's rear tire. As soon as I was out of sight, I snapped open my clutch and pulled out the switchblade.

Once the tip of the blade was positioned on the rubber, I pushed in carefully. I only wanted to poke a small hole in the tire, not slash it.

It needed to be enough to flatten her tire, but not too soon. If the tire leaked air too quickly, Valerie could always turn around and grab the keys to one of the many vehicles parked around back.

I'd had good car karma that week.

Here's hoping I was still on a roll.

Once I'd backed away from Valerie's car, I brought up the cleaners on her contact list and lifted the phone above my chin. Now I really did need a signal. Two bars appeared in the screen's upper corner. I pressed "call" just as Jared and Valerie appeared behind me on the front porch.

A soft crackle eventually turned to ringing and a voice answered, "Sal's dry cleaning."

"This is Agent Sky, and we're going to need your whole crew."

I ended the call and met Jared's eye.

He spun his key ring around his finger. "Raven, you're with me."

Jared barreled down the stone stairs without waiting for a response and headed for his vehicle.

Valerie descended and stopped in front of me. She snatched her phone from me. "I'll take that."

"You're really going to let him walk away?" I asked, more curious than anything else.

"He can get me what I want. He better get me what I want. He owes me for life." Valerie looked into the distance, a smile spreading across her cheeks.

"That makes you happy?"

It wasn't the reaction I'd had.

"Of course it makes me happy! I'm a vampire. I'll never get old and wrinkly. I get to live forever."

"For that you're willing to forgive Jared?"

Valerie's eyes narrowed. "If I were you, I'd worry more about earning my forgiveness for what you did with Fane. You better hope he's not at the palace tonight."

The clutch tightened in my fist.

"For the last time, nothing happened between Fane and me. He's helping us get Dante and Gavin back—your boyfriend."

Valerie rolled her eyes. "Gavin can rot for all I care."

"If you care so little for ex-boyfriends, why worry about Fane?"

"Fane needs to be taught a lesson," Valerie said with a manic gleam in her eyes. "I warned him not to hurt me. No one dumps Valerie Ward, especially not some bleached blond, ugly ass vampire. Not without consequences."

Yeah, she was insane, all right.

An insane stalker. As long as she lived, Fane wasn't safe.

Jared honked his horn, and I gave a startled jump. My heart sped off in all directions. The abrupt sound didn't jolt me the way the gunshots had earlier, but it had come close.

Fane and Noel were right, there was no reasoning with Valerie. She was beyond hope and even more now that she knew she was a vampire.

Valerie glanced at Jared's car. "If Fane is at the palace and he gets in my way... no guarantees." She tossed her hair over one shoulder, teeth gleaming in the dark.

Once Valerie turned, and started walking away, I snapped open my clutch and reached inside for the switchblade. If I truly wanted to stop her from harming Fane, I'd have to do more than puncture her tire.

Valerie Ward had to die.

She was a vampire and she knew it. That made her more dangerous than before. As long as she breathed, she was a threat.

The horn blasted a second time. I dropped my clutch, and with it the switchblade. By the time I'd scooped the items back up, I was too late. Too much distance stood between Valerie and me. A surprise attack was all I'd had. Jared had ruined my chance—like everything else.

Without another moment's hesitation, I walked up to Jared's car and let myself in.

There was no way I could let Valerie accompany Jared and me to the swap. It would all go wrong and further jeopardize Dante. I couldn't risk his life or Fane's.

For that matter, I couldn't allow Jared to go to the exchange armed. He was too erratic and would only end up getting us all killed.

Giselle was the most rational out of the three—the best of the worst. I believed that if I handed over Jared, she'd let Dante walk. She wanted revenge, and she needed Dante and me if she had any hope of getting to Melcher.

Jared was taking me home. This was my window of opportunity, and I had to take it. As much as I wanted him out of my sight, this was my chance to drug him. I just needed to figure out a way to get him inside my house and a drink in his hand.

Valerie appeared in the review mirror, holstering her gun and checking her phone. The vixen probably still thought I'd called Fane.

Good thing I'd gotten to her tire. All I needed was to slow her down enough to neutralize Jared and call Fane over immediately to help with the exchange. Even if the tire held— or Valerie was able to exchange vehicles quickly—she still had an extra fifteen to twenty minutes to drive across town to Bootlegger's Cove.

Once Jared pulled up to my house, I'd have to be lightening quick and strike hard.

The car roared to life all around me, and Jared zipped out of the driveway well ahead of Valerie.

He peeled out onto the pitch-black dirt road, gravel spraying, rat-a-tat-tat like gunfire behind us. There wasn't a single streetlight on the mountain road, nothing but infinite darkness similar to a black hole sucking us in as Jared barreled down the mountain.

I thought I'd overcome my fear of driving, but terror rushed back at me faster than the trees that flashed past the car's headlights.

My arms shot out for something to hold onto.

"Are you trying to kill us?" I screamed.

"We're already dead," Jared answered as he careened around the next bend.

The tires slid over the rocks, unstoppable even with the weight of Jared's foot on the brake. He cranked the steering wheel toward me, held firm, then cranked it back and straightened the car out, narrowly avoiding the ledge.

That had been a close call. I couldn't believe we hadn't flown off the side of the mountain. Not that it slowed Jared down any. The car shot forward as he gunned it toward the next curve.

"Slow down!" I yelled.

"What was that?" Jared said, cupping a hand over his ear—a hand that would have been better left on the steering wheel. "Did you say speed up?" He jammed his foot against the gas pedal harder.

"Please slow down!"

Jared grinned and let up on the gas, not entirely, but enough to make it down the mountain alive. Once we hit pavement, my breath began to stabilize.

"Can't wait to do that again," Jared said smugly.

Icy hostility filled me, like a damp chill penetrating through flesh and bone. Boy was I looking forward to knocking him out.

"I hate you," I confessed.

Jared leaned back, one hand on the wheel. "Relax. You're riding with a pro. The car goes where I want it to go. Take our collision. I planned that down to the millimeter."

I whipped my head around to scowl at Jared so fast I nearly gave myself whiplash.

He kept his eyes on the road. "You should have seen yourself. Crash test dummy." He jerked forward against the wheel, laughed, and leaned back.

My fingers curled. He was baiting me, I knew it. I could be stupid and react, or play it smart and try to get more information out of Jared while he was in confession mode.

I took a deep breath. "Did Melcher help plan my accident?"

Jared didn't answer. Silence filled the car for so long I began counting in my head. Either this was one hell of a dramatic pause, or Jared was keeping tight-lipped.

"Melcher's not that creative," Jared finally said.

"But he did know you were going to harm me?"

"Raven," Jared said, followed by yet another dramatic pause. "I may have to start calling you Feather Brain. In case you haven't gathered, Melcher is running the show. He has a quota to fill. He had his doctors prepped and ready for you before your head ever hit the dashboard."

Bile rose to my throat.

"And you do his bidding."

"I get what I want out of it," Jared said. "Melcher wants to rid the world of vampires even if that means creating more in the process. I, on the other hand, believe in the continuation of our race. I cannot father more of our kind, but I can turn people. I can bring them to the brink of death and gift them with everlasting life."

"What happens when Melcher has no more use for you?" I asked. Or the rest of us for that matter.

Jared gave an exasperated sigh as though I'd asked the dumbest of questions. "He will always have a use for me. Civilizations crumble and fall, but no one can stop vampirism. Consider it job security. Not all of us get to create and kill. That's my job. I can't turn just anyone, but I can help candidates with the right blood type." Jared looked at me. "Real vampires don't have masters like they do in the movies, but if they did, I'd be yours. Just remember I made you what you are."

I took a deep breath. Might as well ask the million dollar question.

"Is Melcher a vampire?"

Jared tapped the steering wheel and began humming to himself.

"Is he?" I asked louder.

"Why don't you ask him yourself?" Jared glanced from the road to me, holding my stare for longer than I would have liked given his position behind the wheel.

Fine, he didn't want to tell me. Next question.

"If you didn't kill Agent Crist, then who did?"

"Who do you think?"

I bit down gently on the inside of my lip. "It couldn't have been Melcher," I said, looking at Jared for a reaction.

His face remained neutral. At the next curve in the road, he cranked the wheel with one hand.

"Not possible," I said, as though he'd answered in the affirmative.

I had no trouble imagining Melcher pulling all the strings—he'd always been a sneaky son of a bitch—but I couldn't picture him killing Crist. Melcher was the mastermind, not the brute force. A fanatic obsessed with his cause, but one who sent out his minions to do his dirty work.

I shook my head. "Agent Crist was Melcher's partner. What motivation would he have to end her life?"

Jared snorted. "Her blood."

Thanks to Giselle, I had my suspicions about Melcher, Mr. High and Mighty, being one of the undead. Now it was confirmed. "Melcher hates vampires," I said.

"This is true." Jared lowered his chin. "According to Gabriel—that's Melcher to you—God never intended for man to live forever."

"What? So the Almighty made a mistake?" I asked in bitter disbelief.

Jared shook his head from side-to-side slowly. "God doesn't make mistakes. The lifecycle of a human is a delicate progression. Age completes that cycle. Disease controls population. We are finishing what nature could not. Any human who cannot age and craves blood is damned."

"If Melcher truly believes he's fighting evil with evil, why would he kill a human—or was Crist a vampire, too?"

"She was human," Jared answered simply.

"But he wants to protect humans," I said. I wanted something to make sense. "How could he do it?"

Jared shrugged. "He was thirsty."

With each new revelation, my heart jumped up as though someone was hitting it as hard as they could with a mallet like the ones used on high strikers at old carnivals. Next it dropped... more like plunged. Down, down, down.

"No," I said. "There has to be another explanation. Crist was on to him. She knew what he was, so he silenced her."

And here I'd thought Melcher had been covering for Jared. What if it was the other way around?

Jared chuckled. "You think that was the first time Melcher offed an associate? Who do you think always cleans up his mess? I even suggested he hire another vampire as his partner to avoid temptation, but he insisted the person be 'pure of soul.'"

No. This was getting too crazy.

"I don't believe you. Even if Melcher's a vampire, he wouldn't kill anyone—especially not Crist."

Jared straightened. "Frankly, I don't care what you believe."

Goosebumps rose over my bare arms. I had to be the first vampire in history who dreamed of retiring in Hawaii. I shivered and wrapped my arms around my chest—not that Jared would notice or care that I had no coat, and he had the heat turned off in his car.

I leaned forward in my seat. "What's Melcher going to say when he discovers you spilled the beans to me and Valerie?"

"Nothing because no one's going to tell him a thing about tonight. Not unless you want it known that you've been sleeping with the enemy."

I scowled, but held my tongue. Let Jared think what he wanted, especially if it made him believe he had something to hold over me—something to keep me in line. The less he suspected me of plotting against him, the bigger edge I'd have once we reached home.

Jared issued a sharp whistle. "Francesco Donado. He's been around in more ways than one."

Jared shot me a sly glance. I kept my mouth clamped tight.

When he saw I wasn't going to take the bait, Jared continued. "We've had our eyes on him for some time. He hasn't slipped up... yet. Sociable guy. Melcher's going to want to put another agent on him, and it's not going to be you."

"What? Melcher has no plans to recruit him? He's not agency material?" I asked half-pissed and half-digging for as much information as possible.

Jared rubbed his chin against his shoulder, keeping one eye on the road. "Some animals are better kept out in the wild."

We were back on 36th Avenue. In another few minutes, we'd turn onto my road. I needed to figure out a way to drug Jared. First, I had to get him inside my house. It was hard to think when his loose lips were telling me things I wanted to know. This might be my last opportunity to glean information off him.

Any attempt at seduction would fail miserably. Even if I thought that sort of thing might work on Jared, there was no way I could pull it off. My face would give it away instantly. Plus, he was convinced Fane and I were doing the dirty.

I leaned back in my chair. "Is Melcher really going to allow Valerie to have her own house?"

"If she can follow orders and behave, then the agency will provide her with housing of her choice."

I clicked my tongue. "I have something at home I think you should see."

"And what's that?" Jared didn't sound nearly as interest as I wanted him to be.

"Some security footage recorded at my house."

"Of?" Jared asked, still sounding disinterested.

"Valerie. Before you consider bringing her along to the exchange I think you ought to see how unpredictable she is."

Jared lifted his chin. "She'll step in line now that she knows what a bright future she has ahead of her."

"You're still going to want to see it."

"I'll be the judge of that," Jared said. "I'll look at it and decide if it's anything to worry about."

"Fine."

Jared wouldn't be deciding anything. Soon, he'd be asleep. Soon, I'd get Dante back.

13

Ambush

While Jared sat in front of my laptop at the kitchen table, I rummaged around the kitchen cupboards, setting the tea tin with the sleeping powder onto the counter. I couldn't offer Jared blood—supposedly I hadn't known that I was a vampire until tonight and would have no reason to stock it.

Tommy lay curled up asleep on the carpet in the living room. When Jared first walked in, he'd run to the door and barked. Some quick soothing words and several pats had stopped that. Under normal circumstances, I would have loved nothing more than for Tommy to take a bite out of Jared, but right then I needed Jared inside the house.

Jared huffed. "All I see is a whole lot of nothing."

"It should be coming up any time. Can I offer you a wine cooler or something?"

Jared's head shot up. "Do I look like someone who drinks wine coolers?"

I shrugged. "The only other alcohol we have is rum."

Rum that Gavin had brought over for Valerie and left at our place despite Valerie's attempts to get me to help her finish the bottle.

"Rum? That's it? What kind of party headquarters are you running?"

"We aren't," I said. "We follow orders and stay out of trouble."

Jared snorted. "Yeah, I believe that one. Make me a rum and Coke—two parts soda and one part rum."

"Two parts soda and one part rum. Got it," I said, turning so Jared wouldn't catch my smile.

My heart sped up with excitement and nerves as I pulled first the bottle of rum from the cupboard followed by a two liter bottle of Coke from the fridge. Once I'd selected a clear glass, I poured the rum in first to a little over a fourth of the glass.

The cap on the Coke bottle made a phish sound when I loosened it. With a steady hand, I filled the glass with two parts soda. That done, I positioned my body so I was blocking the tea tin from Jared's line of view should he turn around. I removed the lid gently and reached for the bag of powder. It was the first time my hand shook.

I should have asked Noel how much of this stuff went into one drink. I never thought I'd have an actual use for the drug and here I was attempting to take down one of the baddest mother suckers on the face of the planet.

One part rum. Two parts soda. Three parts sleeping powder? Maybe a tablespoon would do the trick.

I dumped the powder in quickly and stirred the drink.

"I still don't see anything," Jared said.

The time on the stove clock showed that it was 12:05 a.m. I'd made it to Saturday. More than anything, I wanted to run up to my room and call Fane. There was no going anywhere until Jared took the drink.

I walked over and set it beside Jared. "Don't spill any on my laptop."

Jared looked from the glass to me. "What are you drinking?"

I shrugged. "It's been a long night."

He nodded to his drink. "Exactly. Have a sip."

My eyes dropped to the glass on the table. A shiver of unease ran through me. Was Jared suspicious? No. There's no way he'd know or even suspect I'd try anything that rash. He was just being a jackass.

I breathed out. Once I was sure that my voice would come out neutral, I said, "I'll grab a wine cooler. Rum tastes gross."

"It's a lot better than Kool-Aid wine," Jared said to my back.

Speaking of Kool-Aid, I wished he'd hurry up and drink his Aurora Surprise... and I hoped to hell it worked.

The cool air from the fridge felt nice against my flushed skin. Adrenaline pumped through me like heat in a furnace. When I turned around with a wine cooler, Jared was drinking down the rum and Coke. Not sipping—drinking.

He polished off half the drink before setting it down. The chair under him groaned as he leaned back.

"If I don't see something interesting soon, I'm leaving."

I tilted the bottle back and took a sip before answering. "Jeez, sorry. I can't remember the exact time when she appears."

"This better be good." Jared lifted the glass and downed the rest. After he set the glass down with a smack, he looked from my laptop screen to me. "I've finished my drink and I still haven't seen anything."

I twisted my lips to the side. How long did the sleeping powder take to work? How long had it taken when Henry gave it to me? Not long, but it didn't ever take full effect. But I hadn't finished my drink, either.

I refocused on Jared rather than his empty drinking glass.

Jared raised his eyebrows expectantly.

"Valerie came by and broke out the front window. You watched her kill two agents tonight. If she comes along, one of us could end up hurt when she loses her cool, which is guaranteed to happen. Giselle came in here and stabbed her because she did exactly that once already."

Jared leaned into the laptop. His nose practically touched the screen. At first I thought the footage had come up, but the same static door frame appeared on the monitor.

I folded my arms across my chest. I was more than ready to ditch the dress and take a shower. I felt like I needed to wash all the death off myself. Even though I hadn't stabbed anyone, I'd watched seven vampires die, two humans and two agents— eleven souls gone before my eyes. Six of them had sucked my blood. Drinking me had been the last thing they'd done.

I blinked several times. Jared sat in the same position staring at the screen. From where I stood, I could only see the back of his head. I wished he'd go to sleep already. Maybe if I droned on long enough, the sleeping drug would have time to take effect.

"What I'm saying is she's going to walk in pissed, and Valerie doesn't think rationally when she's angry. Or at all, really. Is it really worth jeopardizing the whole operation to bring her along? Jared?"

I leaned onto my tiptoes trying to get a better look at him.

He didn't answer, but he was still sitting up.

I inched in closer. As I neared, Jared slumped forward, face landing on my keyboard. I cringed at the thought of his stubbly chin on my laptop. No time to worry about that. No time to jump for joy, either. I had to call Fane immediately.

Seeing Jared slumped over the table looked surreal. I didn't quite believe it. My heart sped up as much from excited energy as nerves.

I did it! I freaking did it!

I ditched the wine cooler on the kitchen counter and hauled ass down the hall.

I'd feel a heck of a lot better once I restrained Jared in case he woke up before Fane arrived. But I wanted to call Fane first. Then I'd see what kind of rope or duct tape I could dig up. I had experience with duct tape.

A car horn blasted outside. I jumped in place.

I'd had it up to here with car horns.

It sounded like it came from the driveway. I leaned against the door and looked out the peephole. Couldn't see anything on the street.

The horn blasted two more times. Tommy trotted to the entry growling. Goosebumps rose over my flesh.

"What is it, boy? What's going on out there?" I patted his head, never more grateful to have the golden retriever by my side.

I'd done the impossible. I'd gotten Jared alone and drugged him. But something weird was happening in the driveway, and I was all alone except for Tommy.

I needed Fane right away. I raced up the stairs, losing one of my flats as I charged up the steps. Tommy ran up after me as though we were chasing something through the house. Not pausing for breath, I raced inside my room and lunged for my phone.

I touched Fane's number and the phone began to ring.

And ring and ring and ring until his death message played.

I ended the call.

No, not right now. I need you Fane.

I tried again and again.

Tommy sat on his hind legs staring up at me.

At least the honking had stopped. But who could I call for help?

Noel. That was the only other person who knew what was going on. The only other person I could count on.

I lifted my phone and called her.

After three rings she picked up. Before Noel answered, I heard techno music pumping in the background.

"Hey, how did it go?" she asked.

Relief surged through me.

"It was a blood bath and now Jared's at the house. I drugged him," I rushed to say.

"What?" Noel practically screeched.

"He's in the dining room unconscious right now, but I can't get ahold of Fane. His phone keeps going to voice mail."

The music on Noel's end faded and eventually stopped. Either she'd relocated or I'd lost the call. Luckily, her voice came through clear an instant later.

"Maybe Fane's got his hands full with Valerie."

My lip curled back involuntarily. "She didn't go to the palace. She showed up unannounced at the lodge."

"What the hell? Why?"

"It's a long story. Right now I need to do something about Jared before he wakes up."

"Okay, I'll leave now."

Thank goodness. I wanted to hug Noel the moment I saw her. I was so relieved to hear her voice and have help.

"One more thing," I said. "I think there's someone in our driveway and I have no idea who."

A brief moment of silence passed before Noel said, "I'll hurry."

Tommy laid down on the carpet, resting his head on his paws. I wished I could feel half that relaxed.

I tried Fane again, but again, there was no answer.

Damn it!

There was no time to waste.

I set the phone on my desk while I pulled open the bottom drawer. Inside, I grabbed a roll of duct tape. Suddenly, my phone rang and set my heartbeat racing. I grasped it in my hand. Fane's name displayed on the screen. Thank god.

"Fane, I've been trying to reach you!" Captain Obvious, I know, but who hasn't said something stupid when they're overdosing on adrenaline?

"It's Henry."

"Henry?" I frowned. What was Henry doing answering Fane's phone? "Where's Fane?"

"He's here and he's safe for now."

Anger quickly replaced confusion. "What do you mean, 'he's safe for now?'"

I'd give Henry more than a black eye if he'd done anything to Fane. We'd saved Henry from the agency and put him into protective care. Somehow I doubted he appreciated our efforts.

"Like I said, he's fine, but you need to go outside."

My breathing came out shallow. "Who's outside?"

"Just go outside. They'll bring you to the palace."

My heart stopped briefly. It was the kind of terror I imagined when confronting a poltergeist. What did you do in that case? What could you do? Where did you go?

The answer was nothing and nowhere.

There was nothing I could do and nowhere I could go except outside because nothing in the world was more important to me than Fane Donado.

"See you soon, Aurora," Henry said before ending the call.

� � �

I performed the world's quickest wardrobe change. Dress off. Dark jeans and tank top on. Securing a dagger above my ankle took a little longer, but no way was I stepping outside unarmed.

"Come on, Tommy," I said, clutching my phone and the roll of duct tape. "We have one last task to complete before I go."

The golden retriever followed me downstairs.

Light seeped into the hallway from the kitchen.

Dang and double dang.

I felt like a pit bull being dragged away from a meaty bone. I had half a mind to attack whoever was outside, but that wouldn't do Fane any good.

After tonight, I wanted my own gun. A knife just wasn't cutting it. Ha, ha. Excuse the pun—a sure sign that I was wired.

I called Noel again. After several rings she answered. "Hey, I'm on my way."

"Good because I have to go. Henry's holding Fane hostage."

"What the hell?"

"Listen, Noel, I have to go now. I'll be back with Fane as soon as I can, but just in case, I'm writing down Giselle's phone number. If something happens to me, make the swap. Get Dante back."

"Wait, Aurora—"

I ended the call. Before facing whoever waited outside, I walked swiftly to the kitchen and wrote down Giselle's name and number on a pad of paper by the wall on the kitchen counter.

Jared remained slumped over the table, breathing from his nose on my laptop.

My nose wrinkled in disgust.

It was a laptop. It could be replaced. Dante couldn't.

My fingernails dug into the tape's seam. I yanked back. The duct tape made a thundering rip. If Jared hadn't been drugged, this was the moment he would have woken up. Thank God he remained unconscious.

I crouched beside his chair and taped his wrists together first. My work was quick, but tight. The tape better hold up if

Jared happened to stir before Noel or I made it back. It would have to do. I'd used as much extra time as I dared to change and call Noel. I kept expecting a knock at the door, a blast of a horn, a call on my phone—or all three.

I sat on the floor to tape Jared's calves to the chair legs.

Tommy panted in rhythmic bursts. I looked over at him and he stopped.

Once straightened out, I set the duct tape on the table, went over to Tommy, and stroked his head.

"You have to stay here, Tommy. Guard Jared until Noel gets home. Can you do that for me?"

His ears perked up.

"Whatever you do, don't get hurt and don't leave the house. Okay?"

Tommy wagged his tail.

Tears gathered into my eyes. I hoped this wouldn't be the last time I saw Tommy. He seemed safe enough. I wasn't so sure about myself.

I put on my jacket, stuffed my phone in the pocket and headed for the door.

Time to face the music—or whatever awaited me outside.

When I first stepped out, I was alone on the porch. A big black SUV idled inside the driveway.

Oh god, what if it's one of Melcher's? What if he's on to me? No. Couldn't be. I'd only discovered his secret within the last half hour.

I turned and locked the door. By the time I turned back around, a large muscled man dressed in dark jeans and a loose black T-shirt stood, arms folded on the porch.

"Diederick is waiting for you in the car," he said.

Sick shivers ran through me. Diederick?

"What is he doing here?"

The man in black had me by the arm before I even saw his arms uncross.

"There's no time to explain," he hissed inside my ear. "My job was to help him escape and get him out of town, but he insisted on waiting at the bottom of the mountain. He recognized the Mustang and ordered me to follow it."

This had to be Melcher's informant. In that case, why was he gripping me so tight?

The informant glanced quickly at the striped Mustang parked on the road before returning to my ear. "Where's Jared?"

My heart flipped. I couldn't have an informant knowing I'd drugged the agency's top recruiter.

"He escaped out the back way," I answered quickly.

Liar, liar, blood on fire.

The informant gave a slight nod. "Good. I'll do what I can for you, but for now you have to come with us."

Without waiting for a response, he hauled me over to the waiting SUV. The informant pulled open the back door with one hand and shoved me inside with the other.

Real gentlemanly.

I threw my hands out to catch myself on the cold leather seats and right myself into a sitting position. There was only a second to get my bearings before the informant leaned over me. As he did, I noticed Diederick sitting in front of me in the passenger's seat. He didn't turn around.

The informant pulled out a zip tie and grabbed my wrist.

"Hey!" I said as he groped around for my second wrist. I lifted it out of reach.

"Give me your other wrist," the informant said.

"No. I've come out willingly. Why do you need to tie my wrists?"

"So you don't cause any problems. Now give me your other wrist."

"I won't cause any problems... as long as you back off," I said, pulling my wrist out of the informant's hold.

He tightened his grip. "It wasn't a suggestion."

I glared at him. I wanted to get to Fane, but not with my arms bound.

Diederick turned his head. Immediately, his blood-shot eyes latched onto mine. His arm lifted, and with it came a gun. Diederick aimed it at my temple and pulled the safety back.

My heart stopped.

It was as though everything around me froze.

Gun aimed at head. Gonna die. Good bye, Aurora Sky.

"Give him your wrist," Diederick said, slow and menacing, enunciating each word.

My throat dried. I didn't move right away, as though I'd gone into a trance and wouldn't snap out of it even if my life depended on it.

"Your wrist," the informant repeated.

I blinked once and lowered my arm. The informant reached over and grabbed it. This time, I didn't resist.

"Check her for weapons," Diederick said gruffly.

The informant looked me in the eye then went straight to my pant leg like he'd known I had a knife there all along. He removed my blade with quick, deft fingers.

"Dagger," he said, holding it up for Diederick to see. Diederick nodded. "Let's go."

The informant shut my door and walked swiftly around the SUV to the driver's seat. Soon we were on the road headed downtown.

I kept expecting Diederick to rage at me, but once my wrists were secure, he said nothing, not even to the informant.

Maybe I should have felt more stressed, but I found the car ride oddly lulling. Perhaps I was simply tired from a night of slaughter. I'd finally got the best of Jared. Even if something happened to me, Noel could arrange the swap and reunite Dante and Tommy.

Soon I'd be with Fane.

I set my bound hands in my lap. For the remainder of the ride, I stared out the window, heartbeat increasing the closer we got to Bootlegger's Cove and the palace. The last time I'd been there, I'd killed Marcus. Melcher and Jared had showed up right afterwards. Jared had stormed in wearing the same blue bandana as the dude driving the car that hit me. That's when I knew bandana man and Jared were one and the same.

I'd thought I'd walked out of the palace for good that night.

I still remembered that evening as crisp and clear in my memory as the dark, cold outdoors enfolded me on my walk home. I'd taken the Coastal Trail to Earthquake Park. From there I walked along Lake Hood Drive, passing the airport's fenced perimeter, finishing the last leg of the route along a bike trail that passed our street and old house. It had taken me an hour and a half to walk home.

The cold hadn't bothered me at all. I thought I'd gone numb from seeing Noel with Fane, from killing Marcus, from finding out that Jared had taken my life away.

But I'd been a walking corpse. A creature of the night. A bloodsucker. A killer.

If only I'd known sooner.

What then?

It wasn't likely I would have escaped all this and be sitting on a beach in Hawaii sipping chi-chis.

But maybe, just maybe, I wouldn't be in the position I was in now—wrists bound, Dante and now Fane held prisoner in separate locations.

"We're almost there," the informant announced as we passed Westchester Lagoon.

As if I wasn't already well aware.

14

Trapped

No one spoke, not even when we parked against the curb outside the palace. There wasn't much to say. Soon enough, Diederick would do the talking or shooting. The informant had promised he'd do what he could for me, but I had no doubt his first priority was to keep his own identity safe.

Fane's car was parked in front of the palace. Seeing the old beater gave me a surge of comfort. As long as we were together, everything would be okay.

The informant parked the car then came around for me. He led me by the arm up to the set of double-doors with their custom stained glass windows.

The informant released my arm to open the door. I walked in first, glancing sideways as I passed the kitchen. It felt like a lifetime ago that I'd sipped champagne during my first appearance with Noel.

The step-down living room wasn't far away. The informant passed me and stopped on the edge. Someone had redecorated. There was less furniture and statues—more open space.

Fane sat in a leather armchair facing us, an arm slung over the arm rest. Two muscular men stood on either side of him. Our eyes met briefly before Fane's gaze moved beyond me and turned cold. It surprised me to next lay eyes on Joss, sitting on the far end of a sofa. Maybe he hadn't wanted to be left alone. Henry sat on the opposite end of the sofa from Joss, facing away from us. When he turned and saw me, he scowled. The little snitch. I knew he couldn't be trusted.

Diederick stepped into the living room. "Hello, Francesco. Hello, Josslyn."

Fane lifted his chin. "Diederick."

"Good evening," Joss said, looking every bit as calm as Fane.

Diederick stopped five feet in front of Fane. "Do you know this woman?"

Fane's gaze settled over my bound wrists for several seconds before returning to Diederick. "I hired her."

"Hired her for what exactly?" Diederick asked.

The leather chair squeaked when Fane leaned forward. "To keep her eyes open for vampire hunters. They've been infiltrating our social gatherings for at least the past year. We have the name of one who was supposed to show up here tonight, but it sounds to me like he went to your place, instead."

Fane's eyes flicked over Diederick as though he were responsible for screwing things up. If my hands weren't bound, I might have been tempted to applaud Fane's performance.

Too bad the informant was listening to every word spoken. On one hand, we needed Diederick and Henry to think I was on their side. On the other, I couldn't have Melcher's man running back with stories about me being a double-agent. Somehow we had to smooth all this over.

At the moment, I was coming up blank.

There wasn't much time to brainstorm. Diederick suddenly turned, whipping out his gun as he did. He pulled me against his chest and pressed the cold barrel against my temple.

I cried out in surprise.

Fane jumped up from the chair, but the two muscled men were on him before he could make it another step.

Dressed all in black, Fane and I looked like a pair of matching bookends. It reminded me of Sandy at the end of Grease—good girl gone bad—my Olivia Newton-John to Fane's John Travolta.

If only we could break out into song and dance rather than combat.

"Who killed my employees and guests?" Diederick asked.

Speaking was difficult with my heart lodged inside my throat.

"They told me it was a man named Jared," Henry said. "They claim he killed Marcus, too."

Diederick's grip tightened on me. "One man couldn't have slaughtered my people single-handedly. Who else did this?" Diederick dug the barrel of the gun into my temple.

"He had help," I said, barely above a whisper.

"Who?"

"I don't know," I lied.

Diederick's fingers dug into my arm. The pressure against my temple increased. "Do you value you your life? Because I'm five seconds away from blowing your brains out over this nice hardwood floor."

"Wait a minute," Henry cried.

Without a doubt it was in concern for the floor, not me.

Fane struggled against the men gripping his arms. His lips curled back. "Do that, and you're dead."

"I'm the one holding the gun." Diederick yanked me sideways. "Now give me their names."

I couldn't swallow, let alone speak.

"I bet it was Valerie," Joss said.

The pale husk of a man tapped his finger to his lower lip in thought. Out of everyone in the room, he looked the least stressed.

I stared at him. Everyone stared at him. In Fane's case, it was a full on glare. He probably wished Joss had stayed home.

Diederick's jaw relaxed as his frown softened. "Who is Valerie?" he asked Joss.

"No one you need to concern yourself with," Fane said, glaring harder at Joss.

The pressure on my temple subsided, though the gun remained beside my head.

"Tell me more about Valerie," Diederick said.

"She's a dangerous vampire hunter," Joss said, wrinkling his long, pale nose. "She attempted to attack us in our own home."

"How do you know her?" Diederick asked.

"This wasn't the first time she targeted Francesco," Joss said. "They were lovers."

"Joss," Fane said in a warning tone.

The informant's head must be spinning. First Jared's name and now Valerie's was being bandied about, not to mention

Fane claiming I worked for him. Sorting that out wasn't going to be pretty, but it trumped having my head blown off.

Diederick leaned forward, his grip on me lessening. "Continue, Josslyn."

"She used her feminine charms to draw Francesco in while he was a student at Denali High School."

"What about her blood?" Diederick asked Fane. "It didn't poison you?"

"She's not that kind of hunter," Fane said.

I was surprised he could speak at all with the way he ground his teeth together.

"I have to warn Gavin," Henry said suddenly. "We've hardly spoken since he started going out with her. I thought he had fallen in love, but she seduced him, didn't she? The same way she seduced you?" He looked at Fane, who scowled in response.

"Valerie Ward did not seduce me."

"She most certainly did," Joss said.

Diederick looked around the room at everyone. "This is why I stick to wine, not women," he said. "Much safer and more satisfying."

"Tell that to the guests who attended your tasting last night," Fane said.

Diederick's eyes narrowed. The men holding Fane's arms straightened their backs.

"You better get your hands off me now," Fane snarled at them.

But they didn't.

My heart raced. Good. I might need that adrenaline in a second.

"I'd say we've all had a rough night," Joss said. He still didn't appear alarmed in the least. "Wouldn't it be more sensible if we all worked together?"

Since when did Joss become the negotiator?

"My team and I can handle this," Fane said. "Valerie Ward is none of your concern."

Diederick's fingers left my arm and tightened into a fist. "Oh, but she is. This woman, this Valerie, and this man, Jared, have cost me everything. I want to know where they are right now."

I knew exactly where they were, and it didn't bode well. There was no way in hell I'd put Noel at risk or lose Jared by giving up his current location at my house. Then there was Valerie. Obviously she hadn't made it yet, which meant she was on her way.

Let the blood bath begin.

Out of all the side effects of being a vampire, I was beginning to wonder if breathing, or lack thereof, was one of them. It seemed like I hadn't taken a breath since walking in, yet I was still standing.

Diederick lowered his gun. He stared at Fane. "You dated her. You know where she lives."

Fane's jaw tightened. "I told you, my team and I will handle this."

"This isn't open for negotiation. In fact, given your past history with this woman, I think it's best you stay here."

"The hell we will," Fane said, jaw tightening. He broke away from the men at his side, walked forward and took me gently by the arm. "We're going."

My heart fluttered as his fingers pressed through my coat. Fane shot Joss a look that said, "Get your bony ass off that sofa right now."

I walked with him out of the living room, not looking to see if Joss followed.

The two men who had held Fane circled around us and blocked the entry leading to the front door. Fane dropped my arm. His fingers balled into fists.

"Move. Now," he said.

They held their positions, saying nothing back.

My breath hitched. Did Diederick really mean to imprison us at the palace? We needed to get out of there—back home to Noel and Jared. If only I could get Diederick, Henry, and their goons to suck my blood.

As my thoughts circled around my head, searching for a ready solution, Fane pulled his arm back and socked one of the men in the jaw. The big brute grasped his chin in surprise. Fane twisted quickly, aiming his fist at the second guard, but this one had more time to react. He grabbed Fane's wrist and wrenched his arm around.

"No!" I screamed.

What could I do? The informant had bound my hands and confiscated my knife. That didn't prevent me from beating at the guard nearest me with both hands.

Fane ground his teeth together. "I am giving you three seconds to unhand me," he said.

Diederick walked toward us. "Please understand I mean no disrespect, but your personal involvement with Valerie makes you a loose cannon. I have to look out for my safety and that of my allies here. I am sure we will all feel better once this woman is dealt with."

"If you do not release me at once you will regret it," Fane said. "I promise you that."

Diederick's eyebrows furrowed. "I do apologize, Francesco, but I'm afraid we're going to have to hold you in the music room."

My heart dropped.

The music room. Marcus' soundproof torture chamber.

No way. They couldn't throw him in there, not Fane Donado. He wasn't some vamp to be snatched and tossed inside a cell.

My face heated. My entire body shook in outrage.

"Diederick. How could you suggest such a thing?" Joss cried out. "Francesco has been nothing but forthcoming. He's been trying to help."

Diederick stared at Joss, seeming to consider this. The guards waited with iron grips—at least mine had an iron grip. I couldn't imagine Fane's guard was holding on gently.

Fane quit trying to twist free, focusing a chilling glare on Diederick instead.

"I truly am sorry," Diederick said. "But this is for Francesco's protection as well as our own. I cannot take risks, not after tonight's massacre." He nodded at the men.

The guard gripped me with one hand as his other frisked me from shoulder to ankle. He snatched my phone from my pocket.

The guard with Fane pushed him from behind past the living room. Fane narrowed his eyes to slits as he passed Diederick.

"Big mistake," he said in a low, menacing voice.

Diederick watched with detachment. If I were him, I'd be a lot more concerned. Fane might not be malicious or cruel, but he was fearless, and pride was a lethal weapon.

"And the woman?" the guard holding me asked.

"Put her in with Francesco," Diederick said. "We'll question her more later."

My stomach churned. On one hand, I was happy to stay with Fane as long as possible. On the other... I was returning to the music room. It's where Marcus had tried to kill me before I killed him.

I did not want to go back in there.

My feet cemented themselves to the stone entry—stones imported from Jerusalem. Henry had given me the lowdown on that when he and Gavin gave me the palace tour the first time I stepped foot at Marcus'.

Henry looked at me now, searching my face quizzically. He probably still suspected me in Marcus' murder.

I stopped resisting and allowed my guard to escort me past the living room. We entered a narrow hallway off the far side of the townhouse. It wasn't far to the music room. The door was open. Fane's guard pushed him inside. Mine was right behind them. He gave me a shove in behind Fane, who had whirled around and stood arms crossed tightly over his chest. He glared with venom through the entry. I'd barely regained my footing when my guard closed the door on us. The lock clicked into place from the other side. Fane and I were trapped inside the music room.

I'd failed Dante yet again. How was I supposed to free him when I was now a prisoner locked securely inside the palace?

✳ ✳ ✳

The door of the music room wasn't budging, no matter how hard I stared at the hunk of wood. I pivoted, turning my back in frustration.

"God, I hate this room."

My eyes darted from one wall to the next. I didn't want to remember what happened here nearly seven months ago. I continued gazing at the door even knowing I couldn't stare at it all night. Locked inside the music room, wrists bound. How was I supposed to stay calm?

Fane kicked the wall. "Way to go, Henry."

"What happened, anyway?" I asked. "When did he turn on us?"

Fane pulled on the hair at the top of his head. "Everything was going fine. Joss and I picked Henry up and met his friends here before the party started. I didn't mention the change in plan. I figured Henry was on edge enough already. In the end it didn't matter, anyway. Valerie never showed up. We opened the doors and had ourselves a tribute party. Then, about an hour ago, I saw Henry take a call. He started acting funny after that. He went around whispering to his friends. When I confronted him, he said he needed to talk to me in private right away." Fane flicked his fingers in the air. "We went upstairs into a room. They pulled a gun on me." Fane snorted. "Like I was going anywhere. They took my phone and here we are."

The last place I wanted to be.

Fane crossed his arms over his chest. "I take it your mission was a success if all Diederick's guests and associates are now dead."

"Getting caught doesn't quite count as a success. But I did get Jared." My teeth jammed together when I smiled. Despite being trapped, fooling the mighty vamp still made me smile.

Fane inclined his head. "What do you mean you 'got Jared?'"

My smile widened. "I invited him in for a drink after he drove me home. He came in, and I drugged his rum and Coke."

Fane didn't smile back. If anything, his frown deepened. "That was reckless even for you."

My smile dropped. Way to put a damper on my moment of triumph. "Well it worked, didn't it?"

Fane's arms dropped to his sides. "No, it didn't. Look where we are." He groaned. His frustration echoed off the walls.

My eyes narrowed. "You don't need to remind me. I'm very familiar with this room."

I turned away from Fane and looked around. The room was the size of a small office and empty besides one massive stereo system and two giant speakers. The walls were covered in grayish white padding. Nothing had changed. It was exactly as I remembered it.

My gaze drifted down to the floor, the exact spot where Marcus had fallen to his death after I stabbed him. I stared so long my eyes went out of focus.

I lifted both hands and pointed at the floor. "There. That's where Marcus died."

Fane glanced down.

"He bit me first, but it did no good. I mean, he got the shakes, but it didn't knock him out. He came after me." I nodded at the speakers. "He played Alice in Chains. 'We Die Young.'"

I never wanted to hear that song again. I circled the center of the room. "He grabbed me by the neck. He squeezed so hard I thought the end had come, but then I took out my knife and stabbed him in the thigh. After that, the heart. Then he went down. There," I said nodding once more at the spot on the floor. "Strangulation isn't pleasant," I continued. "I had to strangle a vampire to death for my final test at boot camp."

I looked at Fane, searching his face for a reaction. His eyebrows furrowed. He frowned.

"Your hand was forced," Fane said.

"Not anymore," I said. "I completed Melcher's mission like he wanted. He said we'd get Dante back afterwards. I'm making sure that happens. I called Noel before I left the house. She was on her way. She'll secure Jared." I nodded my head. "She will."

Fane's eyes flicked toward the door. "Why didn't you tell Diederick you had Jared?"

I inclined my head. "The man you saw with him is an agency informant."

Fane's eyes expanded. "Oh, shit."

I nodded. "When he showed up at my house he wanted to know where Jared was. They followed his car to my place from the hillside. I said he'd escaped out back."

"Good thinking," Fane said.

And good to hear he agreed with one thing I'd done that night.

"It was at the time, but God knows what he's thinking now." My wrists chaffed where the informant had bound them. First duct tape, and now zip ties. The glamorous life of a vampire hunter.

Fane looked paler than usual. "What's he going to think of my story about hiring you to spy at parties?"

A calm wave washed over me. "It doesn't matter what he thinks. Valerie's on her way to the palace to get Henry as we speak. If he attempts to stop her, he's dead. And in order to maintain his cover, he'll have to take action."

"How do you know Valerie's coming?" Fane asked, taking a step toward me.

"She made an unscheduled appearance at the lodge. She's already shot two agents tonight. She would have shot Jared, but then he told her she's a vampire."

Fane sucked in a breath. "Valerie knows she's undead?"

I met his eye. "She does now."

"Porca vacca! Cazzo!" Fane yelled, suddenly sounding very Italian... and very angry. His jaw tightened, and his shoulders tensed. Fane rushed to the door and pounded on it.

"What are you doing?" I cried, coming up behind him.

"We have to warn them. She could kill Joss." Fane beat at the door with his fist.

I fought to free my own wrists, straining against the ties. They cut into my skin and stung. How could such a thin piece of plastic hold firm?

When no one answered Fane's incessant pounding, he threw his shoulder into the door. It smacked hard, but still no one came.

"Dammit," Fane said, jamming his back against the door. "Why didn't you say something earlier?"

I frowned. "Everything happened so quickly. I had no idea they'd throw us in here."

Everything had happened so fast and now, thanks to me, we were locked inside the music room. No, not me, the agency. Once more they'd screwed me over. They'd been screwing with Fane before I was ever turned into a vampire hunter.

Valerie never would have set her sights on Fane if Melcher hadn't assigned her to get close to him. I hadn't required any such instruction. I'd been drawn to Fane's darkness all on my own. The more I got to know him, the more I saw his dark exterior for what it was: a disguise hiding the goodness inside.

"She has no reason to kill him," I said, hoping to ease Fane's mind. "Those other two agents tried to attack her. Somehow I have trouble picturing Joss charging her."

"No, he wouldn't," Fane said. "But if she sees Joss, she'll know I'm here somewhere, and she'll want to know where."

My heart jerked like a football being dropkicked. I hadn't thought about that part. Joss might hold out, but Henry wouldn't. He had no loyalty toward us. And when Valerie found us, we'd be like sitting ducks.

15

The Chewing Dead

I fought the plastic tie, attempting to pull my wrists apart and break it in the process. It bit into my wrists. The right one stung. A trickle of blood inked its way down the inside of my arm. With a cry of pain, I stopped. The only thing I'd broken through was skin.

Fane moved to me swiftly. He lifted my hands and inspected the tie. "It's not coming off without scissors or a knife."

Fane released my hands, walked to the stereo, and stopped in front of it.

I stared at his tall, dark, lean form. Fane stayed that way, back to me, taking keen interest in the giant speaker.

"Are you thinking we should blow out her eardrums when she walks in?" I asked. At this point, the only thing I had to work with was humor.

"Actually, I was thinking I could throw this speaker at her when she opens the door." Fane turned around and grinned for one brief second. "There are two of us and one of her."

"More like one and a half," I said lifting my wrists. "And she's got a gun."

Fane's eyes roved the room. "Never underestimate a cornered animal. When will she be here?"

"I don't know. I punctured her tire on the hillside to slow her down."

Fane's lips twitched right before he laughed. It was the best sound I'd heard all night.

"You slashed her tires?" he asked, voice lifting.

A smile broke over my lips. "One of them."

Fane smirked. "The princess doesn't know how to change a tire. We could be waiting all night." He paced the wall by the door.

"Maybe they'll leave before then," I said nodding at the door. "Maybe one of Henry's friends will drive Joss home."

Fane stopped pacing and frowned. "They won't leave until they've made a decision about us."

"Are you sure?" I asked. "Maybe they'll sleep on it."

Fane shook his head. "Diederick isn't going into a peaceful slumber anytime soon—not after what happened tonight."

"Well, maybe he'll come in to question us, at which time we can warn him about Valerie."

"And tell him what exactly?" Fane asked.

"That if he hadn't tied my hands, threatened me, and thrown me in here, I might have had a chance to warn him sooner." My shoulder jerked. "I don't know."

Fane's jaw tightened. "And if it's Valerie?"

"Like you said, there are two of us. Whoever opens that door has to answer to us both. Together until the end." I lifted my chin.

Fane smiled briefly. "Together until the end," he repeated. He took a step toward me. "This won't be our ending, Aurora

Sky. We have the whole world outside that door waiting to be explored. We have each other."

Tears swam in my eyes. I never felt them coming. Fane blurred before me. A warm wet line drew down my cheek. I swallowed.

Fane didn't step closer; his words and voice were comfort enough. It wasn't as if I could hug him back if he embraced me, anyway.

Fane wrapped his thumbs around his belt loops. "When this is all over, I think we should get out of town."

"Oh, yeah?" I asked, blinking back my tears. I lifted both wrists to swipe the wet trail on my cheek.

Fane's eyes shone when I looked into them. "Wherever you want to go. I'll take you there."

I raised my eyebrows. "The Eiffel Tower?"

"Done."

"Taj Mahal?"

"Why not?"

"How about the Pyramids?"

"I hope you like camels."

I laughed. "It would be nice to see something other than moose."

Fane stared into my eyes. "Just say the word."

"You're telling me Joss won't mind funding our world tour?"

Fane's chest expanded as he arched back. "I've got my own money."

"So long as you didn't make it robbing graves," I said. That's how Giselle and her family got their start. It completely creeped me out.

"I didn't make a dime of it," he said. "Been in the family for generations. I've just gotten to enjoy it longer than my ancestors." He laughed without humor.

I squinted at Fane. This was something he hadn't mentioned before. He'd led me to believe that Joss paid their bills with his online rare books business.

"Do you come from a wealthy family or something?" I asked.

Fane removed his thumbs from his belt loop and folded his arms. "Something like that," he answered cryptically.

"So you inherited everything and, being unable to produce an heir, kept it for yourself?"

No wonder Fane handled vampirism so well. It would be a lot easier to come and go as he pleased if he was financially set for life.

"Not everything," Fane said. "I had a younger brother. I've made sure to take care of each generation of his family."

"Anonymously?"

"They know about me."

My jaw dropped. "What? They know you're a vampire?"

Fane nodded once. "That's right."

There was a lot I didn't know about Fane, but I hadn't expected this. Not only did he have a lot of friends, he had family—actual family, as opposed to a vampire family.

"And that doesn't freak them out?" I asked.

"Did Santa Claus freak you out when you were a kid?"

I tilted my head, not sure where he was going with this. "What do you mean?"

"Each new generation of Donados tells their children about me while they are still young. They believe in vampires the same way kids believe in Santa when their parents tell them he exists. Only in my case, it's true."

"And they don't go running off to tell their friends?" I asked. It seemed way too risky to share with kids.

Fane shook his head. "They are sworn to secrecy. It's the Donado family secret."

"Still seems like it would be tempting to brag to a friend," I said.

"Family comes first."

"Okay, so do you have a Christmas reunion or something with them every year?"

Fane's shoulders sagged. He broke eye contact, staring to the side of me.

"I haven't been back home in a while, but we keep in touch."

Interesting. So he considered Italy home. I supposed it made sense—he was born there, but I'd sorta thought he'd made America his home. My insides ached at the thought of Fane jetting off to join his family in Europe. I didn't want him to leave me behind. He said he'd take me wherever I wanted to go, but until the exchange was made and Melcher was dealt with, I wasn't going anywhere. How long would Fane wait for me?

I swallowed. "I hope I can meet them some day."

Just as long as we lived through the night. It was ironic thinking about staying alive when we were undead.

Fane crouched beside the stereo and looked over every square inch before straightening. He moved to the door and studied the hinges. He'd looked much more relaxed moments before when we were talking. At the moment we were trapped, but maybe I could distract him while we waited for the door to open.

"What was your life like before you turned? I asked.

Fane looked over his shoulder at me. "Let's save that story for another day."

"Come on," I said, looking around the room. "How else are we going to fill the time?" Not to mention if we waited, I might never get to hear it. I wanted to know about Fane before Alaska, before America, before vampirism. "I bet you were a troublemaker even back then." I lifted my eyebrows in challenge.

Fane moved away from the door, past the stereo, and leaned against a speaker. "There's not much to tell," he said slowly. "I was born into the nobili, an elite caste in Venice, kind of like the one percent as you call it in the states. I was privileged, but my entire future was planned out from the moment I was born, right down to the woman I would marry."

My nose wrinkled. "Thank God for the plague."

Fane shook his head solemnly. "You wouldn't say that if you'd seen the lives it claimed."

I lowered my chin. Bad attempt at humor, but I was still grateful time had persevered Francesco Donado and led him to me.

"Tell me about your life before the plague," I said. "What did children of the ruling class do for kicks back in the day?"

Fane stared at his combat boots.

"It's not particularly exciting."

Then why didn't he want to share? Now I really had to know.

"Come on," I coaxed. "I want to know all about your past."

Fane walked back to the door and tried the handle. His fist moved from one side to the next, but the knob stayed in place. There was no escaping the past, not inside the music room.

My feet covered the ground. Within seconds I was beside Fane. It didn't take long in a room that small.

"Did you have to go off to battle?" I asked softly.

My knowledge of history was sadly lacking, but history and war went together like cigarettes and smoke. What atrocities had Fane witnessed in his time? What battles had he been forced into by duty and honor?

Fane turned suddenly, his face grim.

"You can tell me," I said. "I know I'm a new vampire, but I've seen plenty—done plenty—already."

Fane shook his head. "You have it all wrong. I was too young to be sent into battle or hold civic duty." He pressed his lips together.

I leaned to one side. "Then what?"

Fane released a loud breath. "I was part of a stocking club, okay?"

"A what?"

Fane straightened. "You heard me. A stocking club."

That didn't really help. I still had no idea what he was talking about. I'd heard the term blue stockings once, but I was pretty sure it referred to women readers in Britain. Fane wasn't a woman. I wasn't even sure he was bookish.

"I heard you," I said, "but what's a stocking club? I assume you didn't hang out with a bunch of guys in tights."

Fane closed his eyes briefly. "Well, sorta. They were theater clubs."

I nearly laughed. On one hand it sounded impossibly funny, but on the other, yeah, I could see Fane in a theater club. He'd always had a dramatic flair about him even in the way he stood. Fane cleared his throat. "We arranged banquets, plays, and mock battles for members, diplomatic embassies, and noble weddings."

Mock battles. He really had been sheltered—merely playing at fight, not actually engaging in it. Thank God.

"The clubs all had different names. Mine was called the Eternal." Fane turned his wrists up and looked at his pale arms. "At the time, I had no idea how fitting that word would become for me."

No kidding. Now we were both members of the eternal club.

"We were patrons of the less dignified arts," Fane continued. "Or so our fathers' believed. They preferred marble busts and gilded paintings to musicians and actors."

"Thank goodness for the youth of Italy," I said.

Fane leaned forward. "Thank God for the youth of today." He paced the far side of the room. "I'm glad I didn't get old and oppressive, donning a black robe like my father in service to the republic. He was nothing more than a political monk sworn to duty."

The black robe I could picture, but not the obedience that went with the position.

"I'm glad you didn't age," I said. "Aside from the obvious reasons, I can't imagine you in some stuffy political chamber following strict rules. I'm sorry about the plague, though. I imagine some of your friends died."

Well, all his friends died at some point, but it would have felt different back then.

"The plague killed nearly a third of the population," Fane said.

I covered my mouth with both hands in dismay.

"Venice being a warm, humid seaport made it an ideal location for the disease's spread." Fane sniffed. "Most people thought it was punishment from God."

"When it didn't kill you, did you think it was an act of God?" I asked, more curious than ever.

Fane shook his head. "I never expected to survive. I can still hear the despair in my mother's sobs as she cried at my bedside. My body began shutting down, and the end was nigh. Everything came to a stop." Fane stomped on the floor for emphasis.

We stared at each other during his lingering pause. After everything he'd been through, Fane had a right to be dramatic—especially since his early life had been encircled by theatrics.

Fane slapped a hand over his heart. "Then I felt it, the slow murmurs of my life returning, blood rushing, heart pumping, my limbs trembling."

My fingers twitched as he spoke.

"At first I was a numb shell of a person. Death clung to me like a shroud. My mother considered it a miracle I even survived. Then I had my first taste of blood—nothing devious. I found it in the kitchen inside a pail used to collect blood when our cook slaughtered one of the pigs for supper. I drank it when no one was looking, the first time anyway. Not only did I recover fully, but I felt stronger, my senses keener. At first we believed I'd dodged a bullet, until our cook caught me drinking blood."

I grimaced. Fane was lucky he'd lived in a time of do-it-yourself at home butchery. It wasn't like they had blood bags back then.

"Blood cravings?" I asked.

Fane nodded. "I lost my appetite for food, but I was as thirsty as a newborn babe. The moment I saw the blood, I knew I needed to drink it the way all mammals know they must drink water. It filled me instantly with life and vitality."

"I imagine the cook found that odd."

"She thought I was a vampire."

"What?" I cried. Odd as it was, I hadn't been expecting Fane's cook to actually get it right.

"You have to remember that people were much more superstitious back then," Fane said. "There were many myths circulating through Europe about vampirism. They were known as the chewing dead. Corpses suspected of being vampires were buried with a brick lodged between their jaws to prevent them from gnawing on neighboring cadavers or going after surviving family members." Fane squeezed his thigh. "Our poor cook thought I was going to prey on my family and everyone in their employ while they were sleeping. She took off one night, but not before sharing her suspicions with the rest of the staff." Fane smirked.

"What did your family say?" I asked.

"Oh, they thought it was lunacy, naturally. Donados have always had steady heads on their shoulders. Of course, things got interesting when it became apparent I wasn't aging." Fane patted his pocket. "Had to leave my smokes in the car, didn't I?"

Forget cigarettes!

"What happened next?" I asked.

Fane hooked a thumb in the pocket he'd been patting.

"My mom feared I'd be decapitated. She and Father decided I must leave Venice and never stay in one place too long. They plotted with my brother that we should stay in contact for as long as they lived. I saw them again before they died. They passed me off as their grandson, the spitting image of his father." Fane snorted. "It was on my mother's deathbed that she made my brother and me promise to keep the family together as long as my life continued. And so I returned to Venice every couple decades to check in with my brother's children then their children and their children's children and so on down the Donado family line."

I shook my head. "It's just so wild. And Joss? How did you meet up with him?"

"Our paths didn't cross for another few centuries."

"Life without Joss, imagine that?" My eyebrows jumped.

Fane hooked his second thumb in his other pocket. "Joss wasn't as fortunate as I. He lived in a small village in England during a cholera outbreak. By this time, I'd lived and traveled enough to figure out I was immune to disease of any kind. I always had my eyes open for others like me. All I knew at that time was it had something to do with disease, but what made it trigger vampirism in a few random souls was a mystery to me—one I was hell bent on getting to the bottom of. When news of an outbreak reached my ears, I headed straight into the thick of things in search of answers, drawn to contagion like a soldier to war. By the time I arrived in England, the cholera outbreak had reached a fever pitch, killing nearly a thousand souls a day."

"My god."

Fane frowned.

"In some places the victims were buried so soon after being declared dead that premature burial occurred regularly."

"Holy shit."

Fane met my eye. "Josslyn was one of those unfortunate souls buried alive in a mass grave."

I shook my head. I'd seen plenty of terrifying things in the past year, but the image of bodies being dumped into mass graves, while some of the people were still alive, horrified me. Maybe I'd been too hard on Joss.

"I pulled several poor souls from the pit after hearing their miserable groans." Fane removed his thumbs from his pockets and mimed lifting a body. "I thought they might go through the transformation like me—weak at first before making a full recovery. I even tried feeding them blood, but eventually they all died."

"Until Joss," I said. I was beginning to appreciate their friendship more, especially after all the trouble Fane went to hauling half-dead humans out of a mass grave looking for others like him.

"Joss pulled himself out of the body pit. I saw him crawl out on his hands and knees. Once he made it out, he collapsed onto his back. He just lay there staring wide-eyed at the sky with this dazed look on his face." Fane turned to me. "I saw the same look on you that day in gym class."

I lifted my wrists and pressed them against my chest. "Yeah, you called it. Dead girl walking. I didn't even know vampires were real at that point, let alone that I was one of them."

"Your employer must have given you blood," Fane said.

I looked down at my wrists. "Transfusion, direct to the veins."

Fane frowned. "I don't understand why he's creating vampires."

"Creating vampires to kill other vampires," I said. "That's Melcher. He believes they're a threat to humanity, God's mistake."

Fane raised an eyebrow. "And who is he to decide?"

"He's the one with the military backing," I answered.

"And who would replace him if he died? Does he have a second in command?"

"He had a partner, but he killed her. I suspect he and Jared have been working together a long time. Fortunately, Jared won't be a problem for much longer."

"I'll help you. After we get out of here." Fane glanced up at the ceiling. It was as solid as the floor. Fane's eyes found their way to mine. "You won't ever have to kill again," he said.

A life free of killing. Imagine that. I hadn't even been at this a year, and I was more than ready to retire. The sooner the better. It wasn't my job to police the underworld. Why couldn't Melcher have recruited willing agents? There were candidates out there like Dante and Noel who actually enjoyed what they did. Surely there were more where they came from—without having to force people into it.

The agency might not have all the AB negative recruits they wanted for blood poisoning, but that didn't mean they couldn't train any blood type to battle the unruly undead. As corrupt as they were, someone needed to stop murderous vampires from preying on the public. It wasn't as though the police were monitoring the undead. They didn't even know they existed.

Would Dante wish to continue on with the agency after he found out they'd turned him? If Jared and Melcher were removed, he just might. What else would he do? Finish his degree in Environmental studies? Become a consultant?

I had a difficult time picturing Dante driving to the occasional on-site survey or looking over reports in an office. And that wouldn't work out very well if he never aged.

Where was his place in the world? Where was mine? Noel's?

Maybe I should worry less about the distant future and more about the immediate future.

I dropped my arms, kicked at the ground, and shook my head in agitation. Fane had survived the plague and centuries on the move only to end up trapped inside a padded room. I supposed it could have been worse. It could have been one of Melcher's locked cells.

That thought was hardly comforting.

"When all this is over, the first thing I'm going to do is visit my family," Fane said as though aware of my thoughts. He straightened his spine. "I want you to come with me."

My heart fluttered. Fane wanted me to meet his family. "How long has it been since you were home?"

Fane held up his fingers. "I've lived in Anchorage eight years, New York before that. Just before we made the cross-country move from the Big Apple to the Far North, I went home for a visit, but it was very brief."

Eight wasn't much in vampire years, but Fane's family might feel different.

"Do you get homesick?" I asked.

"The homesickness never goes away. You'll understand once you leave Alaska."

I lifted my chin. "If you buy me a villa in Tuscany I think I'll manage."

Fane chuckled. He stepped in front of me, arms relaxing. He tucked my hair behind one ear gently. My neck tingled where he brushed the exposed skin below my ear.

"Sure you can handle something as mundane as life in the country?"

I looked into his devilish brown eyes. "I don't plan on staying in one place for long. You did just promise to take me to the Eiffel Tower, Taj Mahal, and the Pyramids. Obviously we have a lot of traveling to do."

Fane's gaze dropped to my lips. "Among other things."

I swallowed.

Why did I have to go all school-girl nervous whenever I got within an inch of Fane? We'd made out before. That time of my life seemed like decades rather than months ago.

I wanted to begin fresh, to clear my conscience.

Recovering Dante was more than a rescue mission. If Fane and I were going to have any change of a long-lasting future together, I had to set things straight with Dante. I had to be guilt free.

I backed away from Fane slowly until I reached the big speaker.

Once in front of it, I leaned back as much as I dared without losing my balance.

Fane followed me over, planting a foot on either side of me. His hand slid down my thigh, his lashes lifting as he smiled.

"If only they'd locked us in more comfortable quarters."

I shook my head. "You left your cigarettes in the car. I left my Trojans at home."

Fane's lips split open when he laughed. His hand left my thigh as he took a step back. He and I both knew I had no need of contraceptives. I hadn't needed one with Scott Stevens, but I was glad he'd used one, glad there'd been rubber between me and that jock's dick.

I wanted Fane more than ever. I wanted a real man, a vampire. Just not in here, like caged animals with my wrists bound.

"When we get out of here..." Fane said, letting his sentence hang like a lingering look.

When we get out of here, we're going to kick some serious ass, I thought as the door to the music room flew open.

16

Big Game

Valerie stood in the doorframe, straightening to her full height as though anticipating an attack. She had her gun at her side, slightly lifted.

"And here you are, just like Henry said." Valerie took one step inside and glared venom at Fane.

"Where's Josslyn?" Fane demanded.

Valerie tsked. "Don't worry about your mopey friend, Fane. I'm sure the agency has an extra cell they can put him in."

Fane lurched forward. Valerie's arm lifted at the same time. She leveled her gun at his chest.

Fane stopped in place, hands balled into fists. "He has nothing to do with any of this."

Valerie's eyes narrowed. "Then he should have stayed home. Instead, I bagged me two for the price of one."

"What happened to Diederick? And the other guys?" I asked.

Valerie's lips twisted into a smile. "Dead, dead, dead—and dead."

I winced. There went another informant.

"Melcher isn't expecting Joss. Just let him go," I said.

Valerie ground her teeth together and swung her head slowly, pointing her heated gaze on me. "How many time do I have to tell you to SHUT UP?"

I scowled.

Valerie turned to Fane. Her shoulders relaxed. "Did she tell you what we are?" Valerie smiled and answered before Fane could. "Vampires." Valerie looked Fane up and down with a sneer. "You see, Fane? You're nothing special. I don't need to be with a vampire. I am a vampire."

"Take me, instead of Joss," Fane said.

My heart slammed against my ribcage. No. God, no.

Valerie stared at Fane a moment. Her lips formed a smirk. "I don't think so. No. I'm going to leave you two love bats right where I found you. This is what you want, isn't it?" Valerie tilted her head to the side and batted her eyelashes. "Privacy? Alone time? No interruptions." Her tinkling laughter filled the room, but stopped just as suddenly. Valerie's eyes narrowed to slits. "I'll give you all the privacy in the world." She took a step back.

"Valerie, wait," I said, stepping forward.

"The good news is you're a vampire," Valerie said, cutting me off. "If you get hungry you have a snack." Her eyes flicked to Fane. "Unfortunately for our libertine here, he can't drink your blood unless he's up for an epileptic fit." Valerie's lower lip pouted. "You never should have left me for a vampire hunter, Fane. Enjoy sucking your own blood."

Valerie jumped back as Fane lunged, but he was too late. The door slammed just as he reached it.

"Dammit!" Fane yelled. His bellow filled the room. "We have to get out of here."

I did a full circle in place. The square walls spun around me. There was no getting out of the music room. Not a chance in holy hell. Not even sound escaped those padded walls.

Fane's combat boots smacked the hardwood floors. He raked a hand through his hair. "I should have insisted Joss stay home."

"We'll get him back," I said in the calmest voice I could muster.

He stopped in place. His eyes narrowed when he looked at me as though I was someone he didn't recognize. The flirtatious smile had long since disappeared. Did this mean he wasn't taking me to see the Taj Mahal any longer? Okay, not the best time for humor—not even when it was locked tight inside my mind.

"How do you propose we do that from in here?" Fane asked.

"Once we get out, we'll get him back," I clarified.

My words sounded ridiculous, even to me. We were trapped. We were all trapped. Everyone except Noel. Our fate rested in her hands.

Come on, Noel. You know where we are. Now come let us out.

First she had to get home to Jared and make sure he remained secure. That might take a while. I had to have faith. The alternative—that Jared had woken up, broken through his restraints, and killed or captured Noel—was unacceptable.

I leaned my back against the far wall. Fane stayed by the door as though guarding it. What I really wanted to do was sink to the ground and rest my tired legs and feet, but doing so felt like giving up.

As time wore on, my hope of rescue turned into thoughts of blood.

"If you get hungry you have a snack." Valerie's words taunted me.

Blood would give me the strength to get through this ordeal. Unfortunately, the only accessible blood, other than my own, was Fane's. And honestly, it didn't sound so bad despite what most seasoned vamps said about our blood type tasting off.

At some point, Fane stopped pacing and took to staring at the door as though his glare could splinter wood. The silence was unbearable.

Then I heard it. A light knock.

Fane's shoulders straightened. He positioned himself at the edge of the door frame.

The dead bolt clicked, and the door opened. Noel stood on the other side still dressed in her Goth garb.

"Noel!" I cried. I'd never been happier to see her in all my life.

Fane exited the room in a blur, breezing right past her like a dark cloud. I rushed forward. If my hands weren't bound, I would have hugged Noel. "Thank God!"

Her eyes immediately dropped to my wrists.

"Shit," Noel said. "Let me help you with that."

While she pulled a dagger from the inside of her coat, I lifted my wrists—more than ready to be freed from the plastic confine. Noel slipped the blade beneath the plastic tie and sliced through it in one upward heave. Once my wrists were free, she replaced the dagger inside her coat.

Free! Free from the music room and free from the zip tie. I threw my arms around Noel.

She sucked in a breath when I squeezed her. So maybe it was more of a crush than a light hug. I released Noel. She glanced beyond my shoulder into the now-vacated music room. Her eyebrows furrowed.

"What the hell happened?"

I started down the hall toward the living room, talking as I went. "Diederick followed me home from the hillside. He called Henry and the two of them collaborated to capture Fane and me, but then Valerie showed up for Henry. She found us inside the music room and left us there locked up." I stopped and pivoted abruptly to face Noel. She almost ran into me. "Where's Jared?"

Noel's frown quickly shifted into a smile. "Bound, gagged, and stuffed inside the trunk of his car. I had to un-tape his legs from the chair and tie them together with rope. I tied his wrists while I was at it... double-knotted. Harder to chew through than tape."

Despite the ordeal of the last few hours, the biggest smile stretched over my face. Gleeful laughter bubbled inside me.

I reached forward, grabbed Noel and pulled her against me for another bone-crushing hug. I seriously loved this chick.

I stepped back. "You are a life saver in more ways than one. How did you know we were in the music room?"

"I didn't," Noel said. "The place was so quiet I was afraid you might not be here anymore, but I wasn't leaving until I checked every room."

We joined Fane inside the living room. He looked around, a tight frown on his lips. There weren't any signs of the previous group. No bodies. No blood.

"The cleaners must have been here," I said.

Noel's eyebrows shot up. "Good thing I didn't walk in on them." She looked from Fane to me, a question on her face.

Time to update Noel on the part of the evening that didn't have a happy ending.

I released a long breath before filling her in. "Valerie said she was taking Henry and Joss in to Melcher."

Noel's hand flew to her heart. "She got Henry and Joss?"

Fane looked over.

"That's not all," I said. "Valerie knows she's a vampire. Jared told her."

Noel lowered her hand. "If Henry spills the beans, we're in deep shit." She shook her head. "Deep, deep, deep shit."

I straightened my shoulders. "If Henry says anything, we'll tell Melcher he's lying. Melcher already knows that Henry was onto me at the lodge. And we're friends and roommates. He could easily jump to the conclusion that you're in on the hunting business, too."

Noel sighed. "It's not ideal, but it's something. Melcher should take our word over his."

"Maybe he'll toss him to a new recruit before he has a chance to talk," I said.

Noel rolled her eyes. "Wishful thinking. Okay, so I understand why Valerie grabbed Henry, but why Joss?"

"She's Valerie," I said. "She's a vindictive bitch."

Noel looked from me to Fane. "We'll get Joss back," she said.

Fane's jaw tightened. "How?"

"I don't know. I'll figure something out."

"We'll figure something out," I said.

Noel shook her head. "Take Jared. Get Dante and Gavin back."

"Jared?" Fane asked as though suddenly remembering him.

Noel pushed her hair back. "He was unconscious when I got home. I chloroformed him just to be certain he wouldn't wake while I tied him up. I backed his car into the garage and called Daren and Reece over to put him inside the trunk."

Those guys were turning out to be more useful than I would have guessed.

"The good news is he didn't see me or the boys," Noel said. "But you need to get him out of our garage as soon as possible."

Fane crossed the living room and joined us. "We can use him to get Joss back."

My breath caught in my throat. I stared at Fane for several seconds while the full weight of his suggestion registered.

"If we trade Jared into Melcher now, Dante's as good as gone."

Fane's jaw tightened. He moved away from me.

"As am I," I continued. "Jared will know I drugged him. If we return him to the agency... I'm done for," I finished, voice cracking.

Obviously Fane cared more about Joss than me. Even though they'd been companions for the past hundred plus years, I wished he would have chosen me first.

Tears threatened the corners of my eyes.

"Aurora's right," Noel said. "We can't give Jared back."

Fane's shoulders sagged. "I know," he said. "But the thought of Joss locked up in a cell..." Fane's voice faded with his words. He cleared his throat. "He's my responsibility."

Noel straightened. "We'll get Joss back. I promise. Dante and Gavin, too. We'll get them all back. Don't forget that Aurora and I are able to get on and off base. We'll come up with a plan."

Fane nodded slightly, looking unconvinced.

"First, we need to take care of the immediate threat, and that's Jared." Noel looked at me.

I smiled grimly. "I'll leave with Jared once we get home. I'm going to need a phone. They took mine."

Fane's head snapped up. "I'm going with you."

Our eyes met. In his look, I saw concern. Hope fluttered inside my stomach. As long as Fane still cared—still had the capacity to love me—the world around us could crumble like ash, and I would rise above it again and again.

※ ※ ※

Outside the palace, Fane crossed the street with us and stopped beside Noel's convertible. "I'll follow you two home."

I nodded before slipping inside the passenger's seat. Before I had a chance to click in my seatbelt, Noel tore off onto the road, zipping out of the neighborhood in a flash.

"You in some kind of hurry?" I asked.

The convertible climbed the hill beside Elderberry Park.

"Every second that Jared is in our garage is a second too long," Noel said. She braked at the light at the top of the hill and turned right once verifying there was no oncoming traffic.

A yawn slipped through my lips.

Noel chewed on her lower lip. "I wish you could get a few hours of sleep before you leave. It's already been a rough night. Not the ideal time to make the exchange, but keeping Jared around is too risky."

I shook my head. "I don't want to wait another hour to turn that slime bucket over to Giselle and get Dante back."

"Don't forget Gavin," Noel said.

"Don't worry. I'll get as much out of Giselle as I can."

Noel's phone rang. She pulled it from her coat pocket and glanced at the screen. "I don't recognize this number. Hello?" she asked, cradling the phone between her neck and ear. "Hang on a sec, okay?" Noel handed her phone to me. "It's Fane. Can you find out what's going on?"

Once I took Noel's phone, she returned her hand to the steering wheel.

"Hi," I said answering. "Where are you calling from?" The last person to have Fane's phone was Henry, which meant it was probably now property of the agency. Wonderful. Fane struck me as the type who would delete incoming and outgoing calls, but who knew what kind of information could be pulled from the gadget? We both needed to get out of Alaska as soon as possible, but in an ironic twist of fate, Fane might end up being the hold up. Just as I wouldn't leave until Dante was free, Fane wasn't going anywhere until he had Joss back.

"I'm on a landline inside the palace," Fane said. "Noel needs to turn around and come pick me up."

I sat up in the chair. "What happened?"

"Valerie slashed all four of my tires."

I squeezed the phone in my hand. That bitch! It wasn't enough that she went on a killing spree, kidnapped Joss, and left Fane and me to rot. She had to go and slash the man's tires, too.

"Hang tight," I said. "We'll be right back."

"See you soon," Fane said, ending the call.

Noel's fists tightened around the steering wheel. "What's happened now?" she asked.

"Valerie slashed Fane's tires."

"Dammit," Noel said. "The sun's going to rise soon."

Outside our windows, grey light hovered over the edges of the darkened houses, surrounding everything in a lambent haze. Time was running out.

"Don't turn around," I said.

They could have been someone else's words. I didn't remember thinking them or even feel my lips move, but it was my voice that spoke.

"What?" Noel asked, whipping her head my way.

"I wasn't sure if we were going to make it out of that room," I said. "I can't put Fane's life in danger a second time. Drop me off at home then go back and pick him up. I'll be gone by the time you get back."

As the next intersection approached, I waited to see if Noel would listen to me or turn around. She went straight through the light.

"You can't go alone," she said.

"I'll take Tommy with me."

Noel zipped down the middle lane, blasting through the next light.

"Fane's going to be furious," she said.

She was right. He was going to be pissed, but at least Noel wasn't turning around.

"He's already upset," I said. "I'll talk to him soon. If everything goes the way it should, I'll rescue Dante and be back soon. Then there will be four of us to take down Melcher and get Joss back."

Noel chewed on her lower lip. "And if something goes wrong?"

"Then it's even more important he stays out of it."

"What's to stop Giselle from killing both you and Dante after she gets Jared?" Noel asked.

"Melcher," I said. "She wants us to go after him."

Noel stopped chewing on her lip and squared her shoulders. "In that case, I'll see you and Dante soon, and then the four of us can discuss phase two of the plan."

I couldn't decipher if her vote of confidence was for her own benefit or mine, but the conviction with which she said it made me want to hug Noel a third time. A surge of hope came over me—the belief that we might actually make it through this—that soon I would be face to face with Dante, bringing him home.

Which was another reason I didn't want to involve Fane in the exchange. It would be better if I could speak to Dante alone first. How would he feel if I showed up to rescue him with my vampire ex-lover?

The one I'd never stopped loving.

Dante didn't know he was undead yet. That was a conversation that required delicacy. Besides which, Giselle might pull out a gun and use it if I brought backup.

No, it was safer for everyone involved if I brought Jared to Giselle alone.

As we neared our house, Noel turned to me and asked, "What should I tell Fane?"

I sunk into the chair. "Tell him I'm sorry about tonight. Tell him I'll be back soon. Tell him..." I inhaled through my nose.

Part of me wanted her to tell Fane I loved him, but that wasn't for Noel to say.

"Tell him we'll get Joss back," I said instead.

"Okay."

Once she'd pulled into our neighborhood, Noel slowed the car. One by one, the houses passed until we reached ours. Noel stopped on the road and put the convertible in park. "See you soon," she said grimly.

"Where are Jared's keys?"

"In the ignition. We found a gun and ammo in the trunk. I moved them in the glove compartment."

I forced a smile onto my lips. "Well, we wanted to capture Jared tonight, and we did. Mission accomplished."

"Yeah, let's toast once Dante, Gavin, and Joss are back."

"It's a plan," I said.

I loosened my grip on Noel's phone and held it out to her.

"Keep it," Noel said.

"Are you sure?"

"You need to contact Giselle, don't you?"

I glanced from the phone to Noel. "Thanks. I'll bring it right back."

"You do that," Noel said, her lips forming something that resembled a smile.

I reached for the door handle. "Don't let Fane do anything stupid while I'm away."

This was beginning to sound like goodbye.

Noel flicked her wrist at me. "Go already. Get that asshole out of our house and bring Dante home... and my phone."

I forced a smile over my lips. "Will do."

With that, I got out of the convertible.

Adrenaline kicked in the moment my feet hit the pavement. As soon as I slammed the door shut, Noel took off down the road. With swift steps, I hurried to the front door. When I walked in, Tommy sat on the other side of the door, waiting. His tail thumped against the floor.

I crouched in front of him and held his head gently in my free hand. "You ready to get Dante back, boy?"

This set Tommy's tail wagging.

"All right," I said, straightening. "Let's go get him."

Noel's phone rang inside my hand, startling me. The last number to call appeared over the screen. Fane was probably wondering what was taking so long. I contemplated answering and telling him we were on our way, but I'd already lied once.

I'd do everything in my power to make it up to him. I wouldn't stop until both Dante and Joss were back. Then we'd go from there.

I no longer cared about seeing the Pyramids or the Eiffel Tower or the Taj Mahal. So long as I got to see Fane again, I'd consider myself the luckiest woman in the world.

I ran upstairs and turned over my backpack above my desk. A textbook smacked the surface, followed by the soft plop of a spiral notebook and the tapping of pens, pencils, and highlighters. I grabbed a spare dagger from my sock drawer and tossed it inside the backpack. Next, I hurried to the kitchen, pulled out a blood bag from the fridge and tossed it inside my pack just in case I needed a boost later on.

I lifted Noel's phone and jammed my finger across the number pad.

"Here goes nothing," I said aloud.

It rang three times before Giselle answered.

"What now?" she asked by way of greeting.

"I have him," I said.

"Xavier?" Giselle asked, her voice perking up.

"Yes."

"Where is he?"

"Inside the trunk of his car."

"Restrained?"

"Yes."

"Conscious?"

"Not at the moment." Not unless the chloroform and sleeping drugs had worn off. I wasn't going to worry about that yet.

"How did you manage to capture him?" Giselle asked.

If I didn't know any better, I'd say she was suspicious.

"He drove me home from a mission. I invited him in for a drink and drugged him," I said.

Now let's get this show on the road.

Once I finished talking, the line went quiet.

Please tell me Giselle believed what I'd said. What if she didn't? What if she hung up on me and killed Dante? We were playing Russian roulette with his life.

Finally, Giselle spoke. "I will contact you at this number in ten minutes. In the meantime, I suggest you put on a pair of hiking shoes and have your car keys ready." With that she ended the call.

I stared at the phone. Did that mean the exchange was a go? That I'd soon see Dante?

I glanced down at my tennis shoes. They would have to do. What did she mean by hiking shoes anyway? Where was she keeping Dante? The top of Mount McKinley?

Whatever her plans, I wasn't sticking around for another ten minutes. I had to get out of there before Noel returned with Fane.

I whistled. "Come on, Tommy. We're going."

Tommy trotted behind me to the door connecting the kitchen to the garage. My heart lurched at the sight of Jared's car. There wasn't any noise coming from it. No banging or shouting, which was a good sign. The Aurora Surprise had really done the trick.

I opened the passenger door, pushed the seat forward and coaxed Tommy into the back seat. There wasn't a lot of room for the golden retriever, but he managed to fit. Once he was inside, I pressed the garage door opener against the wall and hurried around to the driver's side. With a twist of the keys, the car roared to life.

My heart ricocheted off my ribcage. I half-expected the sound of the ignition to wake Jared and set him to kicking the door of the trunk. There wasn't time to worry about it. I backed into the driveway and put the car in park. Without a clicker, I had to close the garage manually. I jumped out of the car and raced back into the garage to close the door. I smacked the button and raced back out as the door lowered.

Daylight crept faintly through the neighborhood. It was definitely time to get going. I headed toward campus to wait for Giselle's call in the university's parking lot.

17

Into The Wild

The campus parking lot was deserted. The gas tank was three quarters full, but I turned the ignition off while I waited to hear back from Giselle. Thankfully, no sound emerged from the trunk. The thought of double-checking that Jared was still tied up in back sent waves of nausea through my body. He could be waiting quietly for me to pop the trunk then leap out and attack me. Nope, I was keeping that door firmly closed.

Noel's phone rang, startling me even though I'd been expecting the call.

"Hello?" I answered.

"Head south on the Seward Highway," Giselle said. "I will call back with further instructions." With that, the call disconnected.

I set the phone on the passenger's seat and started the ignition.

South. Okay. Guess I wouldn't have to climb McKinley after all. But just how far did she plan on making me drive?

Hopefully not too far. There was plenty of wilderness between Anchorage and Girdwood.

Soon I was passing Potter Marsh, driving alongside the boardwalk. A tall man in a puffy green vest stood at the end with binoculars. A paranoid part of me wondered if Giselle had hired him as a lookout. This man didn't appear to be in cohorts with her as he pointed the binoculars skyward at an eagle soaring overhead.

I rounded the next bend, the yellow line at the edge of my vision as I followed each curve. The Kenai Peninsula was to my right, the Chugach Mountains to my left.

The last time I traveled this road had been with Fane when we skipped class to go to Portage Glacier. That seemed like an ice age ago. Even though I was new to the whole immortality thing, my old life seemed like a distant memory.

It pained me to remember how upset he'd been about Joss and how mad he must be at this moment that I'd taken off without him.

He was always willing to help me and Noel. Now it was our turn to return the favor. Once I exchanged Jared for Dante, getting Joss back was priority number one. It would all work out in the end. It had to.

My eyes moved back and forth from the phone to the road. Where exactly did Giselle have me going? I never imagined a road trip would be part of the exchange. Then again, it wasn't like the suspicious vampire would give me her address or risk walking into a trap by returning to my house.

Still, driving without a destination put me on edge. I just wanted to get the exchange over with.

I passed three cars that had pulled off along the mountainside. A middle aged couple stood precariously close to the road, staring up. They were looking at Dall Sheep, no doubt. Tourists, I thought to myself. Unlike me. Resident vampire hunter turned hostage negotiator. They hadn't prepared us for this type of mission at boot camp.

Soon I passed Beluga Point. Viewing season was over. I'd been away at boot camp when the white whales were active, catching fish in the silty inlet waters during the months of July and August.

My mom and dad had taken me out here to watch them when I was younger. At some point, I lost interest. At some point, it became a "tourist thing."

Since when did whale watching become something only a visitor could enjoy?

If I managed to take down Melcher and leave the state with Fane, I'd most likely never return.

Suddenly I felt bereft at all the opportunities I'd missed to drive out and see the belugas. I'd never once pulled over to check out a Dall sheep. They were just another thing I took for granted—another tourist attraction.

How could I lack such interest in life? The sad truth of the matter was that even without being vampires, most people were already half-dead to the world.

I passed Girdwood and the railway to Whittier.

Noel's phone rang after I passed the turn off to Portage Glacier.

"Drive to Exit Glacier," Giselle said. "Once inside the parking lot, look for the green Subaru with a moose crossing bumper sticker below the trunk. The keys to the car are buried beneath some loose gravel behind the left front tire. I want you to switch vehicles. Once you've moved Jared, call me from the phone inside the glove box. Do you understand everything I've said?"

I sat up in my seat. "Move Jared? Are you mad? What if he tries to escape?"

"If he attempts to attack you or run, shoot him in the leg," Giselle said evenly. "Just make sure he's still able to walk."

Why did he need to be able to walk, and why had Giselle suggested I wear hiking shoes? I didn't like the sounds of this one bit, especially not the part about exchanging cars and moving Jared. Suddenly I regretted not bringing Fane along.

Too late now.

"Now roll down your window and toss your phone out."

My eyes bulged. "What?"

"Do not end this call," Giselle said. "Roll down your window."

I cradled the phone between my ear and neck, one hand on the steering wheel, one hand pushing down the control for the driver's window. Wind blew inside the car. Tommy leaned forward, sticking his nose toward the open window.

"The window's down," I said.

"Toss it. Now."

I took hold of my phone and chucked it out the window. It clacked against the pavement. In the mirror, I saw it fall flat.

There went all contact and communication with the outside world. Not to mention contact with Noel and Fane. We'd all lost our phones in the last twelve hours. I'd never felt more cut off as I entered the Chugach National Forest.

I was tired of Giselle's games. She had me driving all the way to Seward.

And that wasn't even the final destination.

What next? A scenic tour of the Kenai Fjords?

I caught myself spacing out as Sitka spruce, mountain hemlocks, and alpine lakes whooshed past the windshield. Ice edged the lakes. Fall had come and gone. Soon snow would blanket the land, tucking it in for the long, cold winter.

I took a left at the fork around Tern Lake, continuing south on the Seward Highway. I passed Upper Trail Lake through Moose Pass, Kenai Lake and Bear Lake. Just outside Seward's city limits, I turned right to get to Exit Glacier.

Gravel pinged off the bottom of the car. The Jeep would have handled the dirt road much better, though I was glad it was Jared's car I was ditching and not Dante's. I had his dog back and his Jeep. Now I just needed Dante.

The green Subaru was easy to find given the parking lot was practically deserted. Alaska's tourist season was as short as the summers. From the parking lot, I couldn't actually see the glacier. It had receded over time and required a short walk to view. I might be around long enough to see it disappear altogether. What kind of world would that be?

On one hand, such a thought was depressingly pessimistic. On the other, highly optimistic to assume I'd outlast a glacier, to say nothing of the exchange or attempt to take down a government-backed agency.

I pulled up beside the car with its "Moose Xing" bumper sticker.

I turned the ignition off and pulled out the keys. Once I'd stuffed the keys in my pocket, I reached for the revolver on the passenger's seat. Four of the chambers were loaded. I dug two bullets out of the ammo box and slipped them into the empty compartments. Then I snapped the chamber into place.

One foot then the other touched the gravel as I stepped outside and took a look around the deserted lot. A small group of cottonwood trees was all the audience I had. I went around the front of the car to the Subaru, crouched beside the front tire and set the gun down momentarily. Unearthing the key wasn't difficult. Giselle had tossed just enough dirt and gravel to cover the key. I straightened out and unlocked the doors of the Subaru.

Then I turned back to Jared's car. Tommy pressed his nose against the back window, breath fogging up the glass. I opened the passenger door, tossed the box of ammo inside my backpack and slung it over one shoulder before scooting the chair forward to let Tommy out. He ran happily to the nearest tree and lifted his leg.

While Tommy took care of business, I walked slowly to the trunk of the car. There was no noise, nothing to indicate a hostage in back. Heart in my throat, I stuck the key into the lock of the trunk, turned and lifted. As the trunk flew up, I stepped back and aimed the gun.

In my mind, I pictured Jared popping up like a demonic Jack in the Box, but he stayed down. I took a tentative step toward the trunk and leaned forward. Jared lay on his side, back to me—legs folded and tied with rope at the ankles. Was he still unconscious?

It's a trick, my mind screamed.

Damn Giselle. Moving Jared was a terrible idea.

"You need to get out of the trunk now," I said in a surprisingly firm voice.

Too bad there was no answer.

"Jared? Get out," I said louder.

There was still no movement. I sighed. "I'm taking you to Giselle, like you wanted," I said, trying a new tactic. "I know this isn't what you had in mind, but I had to make it look real."

Jared turned suddenly onto his back, a malicious smile carved over his lips. I jumped in place.

"You are so dead," Jared said. His smile widened.

Having moved past the anxiety of opening the trunk, I squared my shoulders and glared into Jared's eyes. "Too late. You already made me undead, and I'll unmake you if you don't help me get Dante back."

Jared all but snarled. "You're lucky I need you, Raven." He sat up and thrust his arms forward, shoving his wrists—duct taped and tied in rope—toward me. "Get this shit off of me."

I didn't move a muscle.

Jared's eyes narrowed. "The longer you make me wait, the more you'll regret it later."

The only thing I regretted was not being able to pop him in the head right there. I would have liked nothing more than to leave his corpse to rot in the back of his trunk.

"I told you, I need to make this look real," I said.

"Where's Giselle?" Jared demanded. He squinted as he looked around the lot. I realized he wasn't glaring. He was adjusting to the light.

"I don't know where she is," I admitted. "She had me drive to Exit Glacier to swap cars. I'm supposed to call from a cell phone inside the other vehicle for further instructions."

Jared leaned forward, smiling almost gleefully. The promise of a hunt appeared to thrill him. "My cautious little puppet. Too clever for her own good. She thinks your phone's being tracked."

"Is it?" I asked, a flare of alarm shooting through me. Considering all the conversations I'd had with Fane on my phone, I'd be screwed if the answer was yes.

"Technology is a necessary evil in terms of recruitment. But when it comes to tracking down enemies, we're old school."

"How very sportsmanly of you," I said. "Now can we get going before your paranoid daughter becomes even more suspicious?"

Jared was far from honorable. He would have killed Giselle while she was unconscious in Sitka. Andre was the only member of his family who'd had a fighting chance. Too bad he hadn't taken Jared down once and for all.

Jared smirked. "Untie me and we'll go now."

"What if she has someone watching us?"

Jared's eyes narrowed. "You're the one holding the gun. How do you plan to get me to the other vehicle? Carry me?"

"Fine," I said, stepping forward. "But just your feet."

I took a step toward the trunk and stopped. "Lift your legs in the air."

Jared didn't move a muscle.

I pulled out my dagger. "I'm waiting."

Jared's lips pulled back into a snarl. "What do you think I'm going to do with my hands taped and tied together?"

Finally, he lifted his legs into the air. Without a gun holster, I had to set the revolver on the ground. It was too big for my pocket. Placing it at my feet was far from ideal, but at least I had the dagger and plenty of practice using it.

Cursing Giselle silently inside my head, I sawed at the rope around Jared's ankles. Noel had done a masterful job tying the knots. I didn't want to waste time attempting to loosen them with my hands. Cutting through rope wasn't exactly a quick process, either. Luckily Jared kept his legs up and stayed still as I worked the blade back and forth. I slowed my movements as I reached the last threads of rope and prepared to swoop down for the revolver. Only a couple strings of fiber remained.

Before I could finish cutting him loose, the soles of Jared's shoes flew at my face. I screamed. Pain exploded over my skull. The dagger fell from my hand.

The world went momentarily dark. Nearby, Tommy barked. The noise increased, turning into a snarl as he closed in.

I blinked the spots away in time to see that Jared had leapt out of the trunk. As Tommy bounded toward him, Jared kicked the revolver then dagger under his car. Tommy grabbed him by the pant leg, teeth bared, snarling like a maniac. The friendly retriever suddenly sounded like Cujo.

"Call off the animal," Jared yelled.

The whole front side of my face throbbed and my heart raced. I sucked in a deep breath, pulling oxygen into my brain.

My heart beat like a jackhammer against my ribcage. I couldn't have called Tommy off even if I wanted to. Speech escaped me. Jared better not have caused brain damage. He'd already killed off hundreds of brain cells for sure.

My head hurt, my heart was all over the place, and my weapons were now beneath Jared's car.

Jared tried to move. Tommy snarled with renewed rigor, his jaw not easing up. Jared screeched.

"Raven!"

I breathed in and out evenly, giving my heart and head a moment to ease up.

"Good boy, Tommy," I said, taking my time. "Now drop it."

I still had to get Jared to the exchange. The sooner he was out of my life, the better.

Tommy didn't let go. If only Dante could see his loyal companion—the golden retriever did him proud. Maybe when we returned to town, Dante could start a K-9 division of the agency. Right, since Melcher was so pet friendly.

I patted my hand against my leg. "Tommy, come here."

Tommy released Jared's leg and trotted over to my side, eyes still on Jared. He smacked his lips.

Jared leaned over and inspected his leg.

There was no way to tell if Tommy had bitten through flesh. It wasn't like Jared could get rabies. He probably already had it.

Jared straightened and scowled. "Did you have that dog inside my car?" he demanded.

"You can send me the cleaning bill later." Like never. "We're moving over to the Subaru, anyway."

With the tips of my fingers, I massaged my forehead. Jared kept his eyes on Tommy.

"You're not winning any points here, Raven."

"I just want to get Dante back. You were going to let Valerie come. She would have put his life at risk."

Jared pursed his lips. "Maybe, but you're still not off the hook."

"Let's just get going," I said.

"What about weapons?" Jared asked, eyes moving to the back tire of his car.

Yeah, right. Like I would turn my back to him and crawl under there.

"Take my pistol," Jared said, nodding his head at his car. "It's in the trunk, already loaded."

Jared had a loaded gun with him inside the trunk? Wonderful. I thought Noel had done a thorough search of the trunk before dumping him inside. She'd found the revolver and ammo and left them on the passenger's side. How did she miss a pistol?

"I prefer the revolver," I said.

"Do you want to keep wasting time or do you want to get going?" Jared asked impatiently.

Now who was eager to get to Giselle?

Giving myself a wide berth as I passed Jared, I peeked inside—one eye on my captive the entire time.

"There's nothing in there," I said, quickly stepping away from the trunk.

No way was I leaning over the trunk where Jared could push me inside and slam the door. Fool me once.

"Hidden beneath the lining," Jared said impatiently.

I looked from the trunk to his condescending sneer.

"Step away from the trunk," I said.

Jared smirked and backed away slowly. "Now who has trust issues?"

"Can you blame me?"

Once he was a fair distance away, I found the loose section of fabric in the trunk and pulled back. In a compartment beneath there was a pistol just as Jared had said there'd be. A quick scan didn't come up with anything other than the gun. I snatched it and turned to Jared.

"Okay, I see the gun, but got any ammo?"

"I told you it's already fully loaded."

"What if I need to load it again?"

"It only takes one bullet to kill. Tick-tock, Raven."

More like a ticking time bomb.

Tommy's ears perked up as though awaiting my decision. I took a deep breath.

"Let's go get Dante."

I opened the passenger's door of the Subaru for Jared. He shook his head.

"She could have eyes on us as we approach the final destination. I'll sit in back as though I were your captive."

You are my captive, I thought.

After I opened the back door, Jared slipped in—his lips pressed together tight. I shut the door behind him and moved around to the other side.

"Come on, Tommy."

My golden wingman could keep an eye in back on Jared while I drove. He trotted around the car, following me to the rear door behind the driver's seat. When I opened it, Jared scowled. "I don't want that animal anywhere near me."

"Too bad." I turned to Tommy. "Inside, boy."

As he jumped in, Jared said, "Keep your teeth to yourself."

Once we were all inside the car, I leaned over and opened the glove box. There was a cell phone inside, just as Giselle said there'd be. It was an old-fashioned flip phone. A note was taped to it with a number and the words CALL THIS NUMBER in the same neat block writing she'd used to pen my name on the envelope she left at mom's French class.

I settled back into the driver's seat, flipped the phone open, and dialed.

Once she picked up, I asked, "What's next?"

"Now head back to Anchorage."

I squeezed the phone in my hand wishing it was Giselle's neck.

Drive back to Anchorage! She had to be kidding.

I refrained from spouting profanity into the phone. She was playing it cool, and so would I.

"Got a particular location for me?" I asked.

"I'll call when you get closer. Make sure to answer the phone." With that Giselle ended the call.

I slammed the phone shut. "Damnit!"

Jared chuckled from the backseat. Glad he found all this so amusing. It wasn't as if he had to worry about rescuing a friend. All this was just a game to him. A hunt. The more difficult Giselle made things, the more he probably liked it.

I started the car, threw it into reverse, and zoomed backwards in a tight arch. Once pointed forward, I pressed the pedal and gunned it forward. I was sick of dragging this thing out. I was tired of games.

Jared chuckled louder. "I see my darling little demon daughter is getting under your skin."

"She has me driving back to Anchorage," I said, waving one hand at the windshield. "Five hours of driving for nothing. Why would she do that?"

"Her attempt to throw me off," Jared said. "She knows I'll be trying to figure out her next move and is hoping to turn me around."

"Have you figured out her next move?"

"I know my next move, and that's all that matters," Jared said. "It doesn't matter where she takes us. Today she dies."

Wrong. Today Jared died, and before he did, I wanted to get as much information out of him as I could.

"Why didn't Melcher tell me I was a vampire from the beginning?" I asked. "I mean, obviously agents have to figure it out at some point when they notice they're not aging."

Jared folded his arms. "You're awfully curious. You know what they say about curiosity, don't you?"

"Yeah, well, I'm not a cat."

"No, Raven, you're not," Jared said solemnly. "You won't age, but don't forget, you only get one life."

I thought that was the end, that Jared wouldn't answer my question, but a few minutes later he spoke.

"All recruits are on probation for the first couple years. It gives the agency time to evaluate your performance. If it doesn't go well, there's no sense telling you what you are."

"What do you mean 'if it doesn't go well'? What happens to recruits who don't perform?"

"Oh, them. Into the slammer," Jared said in a tone that instantly conveyed how little he cared.

"You mean into a cell to be used during initiation?" I demanded. My stomach twisted. That could have been me, or Noel, or Dante locked away if we hadn't performed to Melcher's satisfaction. Right now, that was Josslyn and Henry.

"Not at first," Jared said. "First we get them hooked on blood. A week before a new recruit's initiation, we deny them that blood—get them good and thirsty until they're desperate enough to attack."

Psychos!

"What happens if an agent freaks out when you tell them what they are?" I asked.

Jared sniffed. "Rarely happens. If agents make it that far, they've already seen and done enough to numb them down. By then I think they know deep down that they're a vampire."

"But what if they don't want to work for the agency anymore? Maybe they don't want to hunt their own kind."

Jared snorted. "Retirement is not an option."

"What if they make a run for it? Did Melcher implant a tracking device inside us? A kill switch?"

My grip on the wheel tightened. My heart beat wildly with anticipation. At the moment, I felt fortunate for the opportunity to get answers. I dreaded them at the same time.

There was no answer from the backseat. I could feel Jared's eyes boring a hole into the back of my head. Maybe I'd pushed it too far—made him suspicious. It didn't matter. If Giselle was truly clever, she'd take him out. I may have dangled the bait, but she was the one setting the trap. I had no idea what we were walking into. Before it all went down, I needed to get as much information out of Jared as I could.

I risked glancing in the rearview mirror. Jared's teeth gleamed when I did.

"Thinking of making a run for it, Raven?"

"Yeah, right," I said without a second thought. "Where would I go? What would I do? How would I support myself?"

"At least you're a rationalist."

"So, is there a tracking device in me? In you?" I pushed. Jared claimed there weren't any in our phones, but the agency had all the resources they needed to implant one inside agents.

"Gabriel doesn't use tracking devices," Jared said. "He doesn't need to. Besides, what fun is there in a tracking device? That kind of technology is for humans. If Gabriel wants to find someone, he'll find them. His tracking skills are as good as mine. Not that he needs to use them. He has me."

I fought back a shiver by grinding my teeth together instead.

"You enjoy the hunt," I said.

"Even more than the kill." Jared's eyes gleamed in the rearview mirror.

Tommy's head had disappeared the moment we got back on the highway. Nothing like taking a snooze after nearly biting a vamp's leg off.

"What about the antidote?" I asked. "What happens if I stop taking it? Obviously I won't turn into a vampire since I already am one."

"Nothing happens. It means your blood will no longer poison other vampires."

I thought maybe it was just a placebo, but it was worse: poison.

"It also prevents you from being poisoned by another vampire hunter," Jared said. "If you were to bite another hunter you'd go into temporary paralysis without your injection."

"Why would I bite another vampire hunter?" I asked.

"By accident. It's very rare, but we did have an informant once bite a hunter unwittingly. They were unaware of each other. The informant was posing as a vampire and the hunter as a human. Nearly got each other killed. Now informants are injected with an anti-poison every month to counterbalance the toxin if they're idiotic enough to bite a hunter. We can't have our own people dropping down."

The same anti-poison went into my injection. I remembered Melcher telling me that. Otherwise the poison I carried in my blood would attack my entire body. It would make the convulsions my victims experienced look like massage therapy in comparison to what I would experience from a full dosage of poison working its way from the inside.

Having that in my body couldn't be good for me. I couldn't wait to get off the injections. I wouldn't have to worry about biting a hunter. I didn't plan on biting anyone. I'd get my blood from blood bags—the civilized way.

"Does Melcher ever allow recruits to retire?" I asked. "He can't expect them to serve him indefinitely."

"Of course he can. He gave you everlasting life. You're a solider in a never-ending war. The sooner you accept that, the better."

"And what about our families? What do we tell them, or do we have to fake our own deaths at some point?"

My question was met with silence. So far Jared had been forthcoming, which meant one thing. He didn't see me as a threat. I was just a teenage girl, another soldier he could order around for all eternity.

"Can you stop talking for one minute?" Jared snapped. "Women and their blah, blah, blah. Can't leave a guy in peace. No more questions."

I lowered one hand and flipped him off. He couldn't see it, but it made me feel better.

Jerk.

I wasn't just thinking about my family, but Dante's. He'd mentioned he was close with his folks. How did Melcher handle that one? My mom had been entrusted with information about vampires, but she didn't know I was one. If Melcher was so hell bent against Selene telling her family, I couldn't imagine he'd want Dante informing his family or me telling my mom. Valerie said he'd told her family she was dead. She could never see them again.

My heart squeezed into a fist. An ache of sadness filled me at the thought of never seeing my mom again. My family would be safe. We would see each other soon.

I said these things over and over to myself all along the drive.

My stomach gurgled. The digital clock on the dashboard read 11:06. Having been up all night, my stomach thought it was much later. The blood bag sounded good, but not with Jared conscious. I might have to share.

In the distance, an SUV was parked within a couple inches of the highway, and a man crouched in front of a camera propped on a tripod just off the shoulder.

My eyes searched for the source of his interest and found a beautiful pair of trumpeter swans in the center of Tern Lake.

"Tourist," Jared said with disgust.

"And you're a resident?" I challenged.

"Of Alaska? Not a chance."

"I hear Paris is a beautiful city," I said, fishing.

Jared looked up, meeting my eye in the rearview mirror.

"Beautiful," he intoned as if the opposite were true. "You should have seen it during the French Revolution. They locked me up for killing an imbecile, but thirty years prior to that the streets of Paris ran red with the blood of aristocrats and anyone even suspected of being sympathetic to the monarchy. People used it as an excuse to kill anyone who practiced a religion other than their own or had so much as ever looked at them cross-eyed. Whether you want to admit it or not, we live in a rotten world."

"Is that what Melcher wants you to believe?"

"I've always known humans are sinners. I was, too. But not anymore."

"Not anymore?" I asked incredulously.

Jared leaned forward. I didn't like that his head was close to mine.

"I am a true crusader, chosen by God. Faith doesn't matter. I have been blessed with immortality."

My fingers tightened around the steering wheel. "I thought you said our kind was a mistake."

"Some of our kind. Not me."

No, not Jared. Of course not. The way he talked, he probably considered himself an avenging angel rather than a vampire. And then there was Melcher. No doubt he considered himself the messiah.

What came first? The recruiter or the commander? If Giselle was correct, Melcher had been around longer—recruited the recruiter.

"I have a hard time believing you're one of the good guys," I said.

Jared's forehead lowered as he leaned toward me. "Vampires suck life from the weak. I should know. Some of us are tasked with balancing the scale. Nature requires every predator be kept in check. Since the vampire is at the top of the food chain, god-like in his immortality—not even time can touch him—only one worthy predator remains and that is a vampire's only equal. One of his own."

My heart sped up. I shook my head.

"Yes, you," Jared said. "You're a killer, and like it or not, you and I are the same."

"We're nothing alike."

Jared chuckled. "Deny it all you want. It doesn't change a thing. You need me, Raven. Giselle needed me, too."

Right. Giselle needed Jared the way a human needed a blood clot. I snorted.

"Don't be fooled by my daughter's cold demeanor. Inside she's a lonely child who has lost her family. She won't last long on her own. I wouldn't be surprised if she's attempted to lure Dante to her side."

"Not in a million years," I said, gripping the wheel. Jared was delusional. Dante was the last person in the world who would ever succumb to Stockholm syndrome.

Jared stretched his still-bound hands over his head and back down to his sides. "I'm sure my imprisonment caused her great distress. We used to work together, you know? Grave robbers." Jared's nose wrinkled. "Nasty business that. The others never had the stomach for it."

Giselle had told me they did more than rob graves. She'd said that Jared began killing victims so that he could sell their bodies to medical labs.

"I thought you said she didn't know how to follow orders." Jared turned his head. "She did what she was told right up until a week before my imprisonment. Robbing graves is a rough way to make a living, so we started a new venture." Jared's eyes shined.

I wanted to cover my ears.

"We killed people and sold their corpses to doctors for dissection."

I shook my head. "I don't want to know."

"It didn't bother Giselle, not until Simple Seymour. He was a half-wit, you understand." Jared's fingers tightened into a fist. "I did him a favor, but Giselle chose that moment to develop a conscious—over an imbecile, no less. The irony. She kept his pocket watch—thing didn't even work—and would just stare at it for hours on end. Refused to accompany me after that, which is how she escaped capture while I was left to rot alone."

"Poor you," I said sarcastically.

Jared's eyes narrowed. "Do not bait me, Raven. There is nothing as hellacious as an eighteenth century prison. The miscreants caged inside those dungeons are the foulest smelling creatures you can possibly imagine. I wouldn't want to be a flea inside that hellhole."

"Well, you got out."

"Eight months later," Jared said. "Eight months."

So what? Now he was traumatized for life? Hard to believe.

"Time does not erase memories," Jared continued. "If anything, it brings the past closer. I remember that time of my life like it was yesterday."

I cleared my throat. "Why did you kill your family if they weren't to blame?"

Jared's jaw tightened. "They did nothing to try and get me out."

"Are you sure? Maybe they couldn't get past the guards."

I knew from Giselle that this wasn't the case, but Jared didn't know that. The way he glowered indicated that he knew perfectly well no such attempt had been made on his behalf.

"They left me to die."

I didn't like the way Jared's eyes narrowed on me as though I'd been part of the family who'd forsaken him over a century ago.

Time to ask the million dollar question.

"So Melcher rescued you from prison and you've been hunting vampires for him ever since?"

"At first," Jared said. "As science and technology evolved, so did our understanding of vampirism. Melcher has studied the phenomena for centuries. He traveled the world investigating the origin of our condition until he put it all together. Disease triggers immortality in people with our blood type."

"How did he manage to get his own government agency?"

"Easy. Gabriel comes from one of the world's oldest and most powerful families. Who do you think is really in charge? Your president?" Jared snorted.

The mountains beyond the windshield blurred out of focus. A sense of hopelessness overcame me. I couldn't let it. There had to be a way to beat Melcher no matter how powerful he was.

In the review mirror, I saw Jared lean his back against the car door and close his eyes.

I turned my attention back to the road. All fear of driving had left me. I drove ten miles over the speed limit. I wanted to get back to Anchorage as quickly as possible. I wanted to get to Dante.

Right before the turn-off to Portage Glacier, the phone rang. I pulled onto the highway's shoulder, answering after I threw the car into park.

"Yes?" I answered impatiently.

"When you reach Girdwood, turn right and head to the Alyeska Resort. Park in the far lot and walk up to the tram. When you reach the tram, call me and I will give you your next set of instructions. Bring Jared with you."

I flipped the phone shut and put the car back into drive. There was no traffic in either direction as I pulled back onto the highway.

"Where next?" Jared asked, voice slightly muffled through the backseat.

How nice that he could nap, relax, or whatever he was doing back there at a time like this.

"We're going to Girdwood, Alyeska Resort tram."

Jared sat up. "Does she want us to go up the mountain?"

"She didn't say. I'm supposed to call when we reach the tram."

Jared leaned forward, staring through the windshield wide-eyed. He rested his arms on top of the seat back, wrists still tied and way too close to my face. Jared claimed to not care where she was taking us, but he suddenly appeared very interested—excited, even.

"She's taking us to our final destination," Jared said.

"Maybe she's having us switch vehicles again."

Jared shook his head. "No, she has us getting out this time."

He was right. It felt different. I was beginning to wish she had made me drive all the way back to Anchorage. I didn't fancy heading off into the wilderness to witness two killer vampires face off.

Three, I reminded myself. I counted as a killer vampire. It was my duty to take down both Jared and Giselle. If I got Dante back, I had no more use for her. He could lead me back to Gavin. Even if he couldn't, I might have to chalk it up to collateral damage. Noel wouldn't like that, but she wasn't the one in the middle of a hostage situation. There was no telling what would happen.

"She's going to draw us into the open," Jared said, grinning. "Very mistrustful, that one. Did you pack any mosquito repellent, or better yet, bear spray?"

"You afraid of bears or something?" I asked.

Jared leaned against the seat back. "Those things will bite a person's head off. Show a little respect."

Bears didn't worry me. Biters like Jared and Giselle were another story.

My grip on the steering wheel tightened when the Chevron gas station and Food Mart came into view. We'd reached Girdwood.

18

Trigger Happy

ared laced his fingers together as I turned right and drove down Girdwood's main drag. Soon, Mount Alyeska came into view. The chair lifts were suspended in mid-air, awaiting the first snow dump. The road came to an end at the old lodge. I took a left and headed for the Alyeska Resort.

Unlike the parking lot at Exit Glacier, the one at the resort was half-full. I found a spot at the end as Giselle had suggested, turned off the ignition and pocketed the key.

"This is it," Jared said, voice rising. "Doing this outdoors is a nice touch, don't you think?"

I grabbed the gun off the passenger's seat before stepping out of the vehicle and opening the back door.

Jared stepped out, eyeing the gun in my hand. "Keep that thing hidden," he hissed. "There are people around. Take off your jacket and ball it up inside."

Lips pressed together, I whistled for Tommy. He bounded out of the car.

Jared frowned. "You should leave him here."

"Not a chance."

"At least hide the gun before someone sees it and reports you. I am not missing an opportunity to get to Giselle because you were stupid enough to have the state troopers called on us."

My eyes narrowed. "Fine, but just remember, any sudden moves and Tommy will attack."

Upon hearing his name, Tommy sat beside me and stared at Jared.

What a good boy.

I set the gun on the hood of the car and covered it with my jacket.

Jared held his wrists out. "And remove these."

"Not a chance," I said. When he glared at me, I added, "What about Giselle?" I didn't care about her, honestly. I preferred Jared with his hands bound together.

"Holding me at gunpoint is enough. There's a switchblade in my left pocket."

I stared at Jared for two seconds before looking down at his crotch. I so didn't want to be fishing around anywhere near there.

He cleared his throat impatiently.

Crap. Like I wanted my fingers within an inch of his nasty bits.

I reached forward quickly, wanting to get it over with already.

"My left," Jared snapped.

I pulled my hand back and moved to the opposite pocket, shoving my fingers down until I touched something solid. I dug out a thin black handle and snapped the blade open. Jared held his hands higher.

I sucked in a deep breath, pulling oxygen into my brain before slipping the blade beneath the rope tie and sawing through.

Jared shook his wrists at his sides while I kept a wary eye on him.

He stopped and reached a hand forward. "Give it here."

Tommy bared his teeth. A low growl rumbled through his sharp canines.

Jared leaned back, a frown about as friendly as Tommy's forming over his mouth.

I glanced at the switchblade, not wanting to let it go. "You shouldn't have any weapons on you. What if Giselle pats you down?"

Jared snorted. "The only way she'll touch me is if she's trying to kill me."

"What if she asks me to pat you down?"

Jared grinned slowly. His eyebrows jumped. "You'd like that, wouldn't you, Raven? Hands all over my body, giving me a rub down."

"Get over yourself," I said in disgust. "I'm keeping the knife." I closed the blade and stuffed it into my back pocket.

"You better not lose it," Jared said.

I took my jacket and gun off the hood of the car, keeping the coat draped over the pistol. I held it aimed at Jared. Had to get into the role. There was no telling what we were walking into, but at least I had the weapons. Giselle had to be armed to the teeth. I trusted her as much as Jared. If anyone was going to give me trouble, I expected it would be her. Dante better be with her, unharmed.

Jared walked in front of me to the tram. Tommy followed a few steps behind. The moment we left the parking lot, all conversation stopped. We reached the tram landing, but it must have been at the top of the mountain—it wasn't waiting below.

I flipped open the phone and called Giselle.

"We're at the tram."

"Good," she said. "Now walk to the Winner Creek Trailhead. Keep me on the line."

I looked at Jared and nodded to the left. "Winner Creek Trailhead. Let's go."

We walked up the hill to the signed trail. Below the sign, a piece of paper had been tacked to the post.

DANGER
Due to bear activity, area beyond this sign
CLOSED
To all travel

Jared looked at the sign and frowned.

With the phone still pressed to my ear, I said, "The trail's closed."

"I posted that sign so no one would bother us," Giselle said.

"Oh," I said, stomach tightening. How very nice and isolated we'd all be. Goody gum drops.

"I want you to walk the trail until you reach the gorge. Keep the phone on at all times. If you disconnect and attempt to call for backup, I will push Dante over the edge."

I seized the phone against my ear. "If you hurt him I won't leave these woods until you're dead."

"I won't hurt him unless you give me a reason to," Giselle said evenly.

I breathed heavily through clenched teeth. "How far is the gorge?"

"Two and a half miles."

"What if the signal drops?" I demanded.

"It won't. I tested it."

"But what if it does?"

If she killed Dante over a lost signal, I'd never forgive the bitch—even after I killed her. It wouldn't be enough.

"Just get going and stay on the line."

I met Jared's eyes and nodded forward. He began walking, leading the way without comment. I cradled the phone between my shoulder and ear while I slipped my jacket on, setting the gun down briefly. There was no reason to hide it anymore. We were alone in the woods.

We stepped onto a boardwalk and followed it through Girdwood's rain forest. I kept the phone pressed against my left ear in case Giselle issued any more commands, but she remained silent as we walked over the boards, further into the forest.

Moist air settled over my face. Mosquitoes buzzed around my head. The little bloodsuckers hadn't gotten the memo that summer was over—time to drop dead and die. I couldn't do anything about the one biting the hand holding the phone as I gripped the gun in my right palm.

A second one bit the top of my head.

Jared set a brisk pace.

In two miles, I'd see Dante. He must be at the gorge for Giselle to threaten to push him over. The whole thing made me sick to my stomach. I didn't like it at all. An accident could happen. What was I thinking? Accident or not, something bad was about to go down. We weren't all walking out of here alive to go on our merry little ways.

I cursed under my breath.

Jared glanced back briefly before pushing ahead. Neither he nor Giselle asked what my problem was.

The boardwalk ended. We hiked a dirt trail deeper into the dark forest. Thick bright green moss clung to a third of the trees. Ferns covered the forest floor, lining the edges of the trail. From time to time, light filtered in before extinguishing itself in the next step.

I kept the phone to my ear until the trail narrowed along a steep edge. Until that point, the landscape had been relatively flat and level. This wasn't a mountain top, but the drop was enough to do bodily harm. I held both arms out for balance, pressing the phone back to my ear once we'd passed.

The deeper in we got, the more I could hear my heart pounding in my ears.

I'd never been religious, but I found myself making deals with God if only he'd keep Dante safe and allow us to walk out of here alive.

I'm here, Dante. I'm coming for you. Hang tight.

Jared continued leading the way, not stopping until he reached a trail sign.

Winner Creek Gorge Tram Ahead

"We're almost there," I said into the phone.

There was no answer.

"Giselle?" I asked, voice rising.

Oh god, had I lost connection at some point during the trek and not realized it? The tree coverage was thick in here.

The phone gave a slight *crackle* before Giselle said, "Continue to the hand tram."

For once, I was happy to hear her voice.

Jared folded his arms over his chest. I raised the gun, pointing it at his chest. "After you."

As we neared the gorge, the sound of rushing water filled my ears. I could see a platform up ahead. I gripped the gun. Giselle could be anywhere at this point.

Jared uncrossed his arms as he stepped onto the platform, walked to the ledge and yelled across the gorge. "Giselle! Je suis arrivé!"

There was no answer back.

I stepped onto the platform, gun aimed at Jared's back. I entertained a brief fantasy of Giselle instructing me to take the shot, but no such order came.

"I want you and Xavier to get inside the tram and cross the river," she said. "But first throw the phone into the gorge. I will see you on the other side."

My throat tightened. I walked up beside Jared, stared down into the deep, wide gorge with the river rushing by below, and chucked the phone.

I had to be setting a record for number of phones destroyed or lost in the last twelve hours.

Jared looked from the steel cage to me and grinned. "We're crossing the gorge, aren't we?"

I nodded, unable to take my eyes off the rapids below.

"Well? What are you waiting for? Let's go."

As Jared stepped into the tram, I swung around and stepped down to the dirt trail where Tommy sniffed at surrounding ferns. He trotted over, tail swishing when he saw me waiting. I held a hand up in front of him. "Tommy, wait here," I said. "I'll be right back with Dante."

Tommy sat, ears and nose dropping. The sad look he gave me tugged on my heart, but he needed to stay. There was only enough room on the hand tram for two people. If Dante and I had to make a quick getaway, we wouldn't have time to take turns crossing the gorge. That, and Tommy could easily attack Giselle if he perceived her to be holding Dante against his will. Unlike Jared, Giselle had weapons to use against him.

Tommy's head sagged. The fact that he minded so well increased my guilt. This way was safer. We'd be right back. I hoped.

Tommy didn't get up or follow me to the platform.

The tram wasn't much bigger than a phone booth. Real cozy standing against Jared in a steel cage, suspended over a deep gorge.

I hesitated outside the cage, glancing across the way. What if Giselle cut the cable while we were crossing? No, it was too thick, and she wanted to face Jared before she killed him. Otherwise she wouldn't have made a big deal about bringing the bastard to her alive.

I took a deep breath and stepped onto the tram, latching the door once I'd settled across from Jared.

He immediately grabbed the ropes and pulled us away from the platform. The tram gained momentum temporarily as it plunged down. Once we were dangling level from the ropes, the cage bounced several times in place. Jared pulled us steadily across. When we reached the midway point, I ventured a glance down. The river thundered beneath my feet, liquid blue with sprays of white visible through the bottom of the cage.

The second platform got closer with each pull of the rope. I gave up the charade of pointing the gun on Jared. If he really wanted to, he could snatch it from me in an instant. He obviously wanted to see Giselle as much as she wanted to see him.

I didn't care who the winner at Winner Creek was so long as Dante and I walked out alive. Once he was free, we could take out the last man—or woman—standing.

As we neared the platform on the opposite side, I moved my focus forward. There were no signs of Giselle or anyone else. The platform was empty. My body tensed. I looked all around the woods surrounding the platform on high alert.

"Don't worry," Jared said under his breath. "She's not going to jump out and surprise us. Mark my words, she'll wait until we've stepped off the platform and be waiting calmly in the woods on the other side."

"If you say so," I said, eyes trained forward.

Jared nudged me with his elbow. "Smile, Raven. You get to sit this one out. Giselle's all mine."

He pulled on the rope with renewed vigor, increasing our speed the closer we got to the other side. I unlatched the cage of the door as we pulled up to the platform and quickly stepped out, Jared right behind me.

We walked across the platform, taking the steps down to the forest floor. I did a quick scan of the forest, but didn't see anyone. Did she mean for us to hike in further?

Jared stopped not far from the platform and looked around.

I lifted the gun, not sure where to aim it.

"Oh, Giselle," he called. "Where's my warm welcome? Why don't you give daddy a kiss?"

I searched the trees for movement.

Giselle stepped out from behind a tree about twenty feet away. She wore a thin navy jacket over plaid pants and held a fencing sword in each hand. Her long wavy blonde hair tumbled loose over her shoulders.

"Hello, Xavier," she said calmly, eyes locked on Jared's.

Jared looked her up and down and grinned. "My dear, you haven't aged one bit. Still skin and bone, I see, but other than that, nature has been kind to you."

"And too kind to you," she said.

Jared's grin widened. He lifted his chin. "Alive and well as you can see. Escaped the hang man's noose."

"What a pity," Giselle said.

The grin shriveled from Jared's face.

"I brought you Jared. Where's Dante?" I demanded.

Giselle glanced at me briefly before returning a steady gaze on Jared.

"Well?" I said.

"I'm right here."

Dante! It was Dante's voice. My heart surged with relief. He stepped forward to the right of Giselle. His face was cleanly shaven, and he wore a clean pair of jeans and a hoodie. As far as I could tell, Dante was unharmed. I couldn't make out any restraints. Not only that, but he held a rifle against his side.

Relief was as fleeting as a butterfly flitting and floating away into the moss covered forest. Had Jared been right about Giselle recruiting Dante to her side? No way. Not possible.

"Dante?" I said slowly. "What are you doing?"

Jared chuckled. "You see, Raven? Can't trust anyone. Your partner has switched sides."

Dante lifted the rifle. He didn't aim it at anyone, but he had it ready. The question was, for what?

"I don't work for her," Dante said, nodding sideways at Giselle. "I'm returning home with Aurora."

My heart flipped. I lowered my arm and the gun to my side. The relief I felt was almost overwhelming. Dante was alive, unharmed, and on my side. Always on my side. I couldn't ask for a greater friend in all the world.

"I'm here for you," I said.

Dante's expression softened when our eyes met.

"Well, isn't this one big happy reunion?" Jared said sarcastically. He took a step forward, eyes on Giselle. "Unfortunately for you, those two work for me."

"I don't work for you," Dante said. "I know all about you. I know you ran Aurora's car off the road. I know you tried to kill her and Valerie in Sitka. I know the whole thing was a ruse to pin the murder of Agent Crist on Andre Morrel and his family when it was you who killed Crist. You murdered a member of our team then you killed off your old family to try and cover it up—everyone but her." Dante inclined his head in Giselle's direction without taking his eyes off Jared.

Jared ground his teeth together. "Quite the rumor that's going around about me and 'ol Crist." His eyes slid over Dante. He smirked and walked toward him. "Ease up, soldier boy. I didn't kill Agent Crist. Now hand over the rifle."

In a flash, Dante lifted the rifle against his shoulder and aimed at Jared's chest. "Stop right there."

Jared stopped. He ground his teeth together as he emitted a nasty snarl. "So you are on her side?"

Dante watched Jared over the barrel of the rifle.

"I'm on one side and one side only—humanity's."

Jared's jaw relaxed. He let out a bark of laughter. Dante kept his stance, rifle trained on Jared who continued to laugh.

"What's so funny?" Dante demanded.

Jared stopped laughing. He looked Dante up and down and made a sound of disgust in the back of his throat. "You're a vampire, fool." Jared looked at me. "Tell him, Raven. Tell your partner what he is."

Dante glanced sideways at me, keeping the rifle pointed at Jared.

"Quit stalling, Xavier," Giselle said. "This is between me and you. I even brought you a sword." She tossed one of the swords at Jared. It landed at his feet. "I don't do things the coward's way—the way you killed Etienne, Andre, and Henriette."

Wrinkles formed around Jared's cheeks when he glared. "I am no coward," Jared said. "You were the cowards leaving me behind to die after the police locked me away."

Giselle's lips stretched into a smile. If I didn't know any better, I'd say it looked almost sweet. She circled slowly around Jared, mirth in the gaze she leveled at him.

"Give me more credit than that, Xavier. Who do you think reported you to the authorities in the first place?"

My breath hitched.

She didn't?

Giselle's smile widened.

She so did! I stared at her, stunned. Then slowly, heart hammering, I looked at Jared.

His eyes bulged. His face turned red. His lips curled back so far I noticed his back molars had been filed to points. I'd never do that to my teeth. Gross. I didn't care if I was a vampire. Jared snatched the sword from the ground. "You're dead, bitch."

"You and I both know I never lose a sword fight," Giselle replied.

How could she act so calm? She might have been a calculating she-vamp, but she was a thin wisp of a thing, further dwarfed by Jared's rage.

He lunged. Giselle met him halfway, their blades clashing, steel grinding against steel as the edges slid apart.

Giselle's eyes seemed to light up at the sound.

I moved back as Jared and Giselle circled each other. Dante lowered the rifle as he joined my side. I wanted to throw my arms around him, but it didn't seem like the right time.

"Are you okay?" I asked.

"Fine," he said, watching the sword fight as closely as I. "You?"

"I'm okay. I'm so happy to see you. I can't believe she didn't tie you up."

Dante grimaced. "Yeah, well, after she told me what you said about Jared killing Agent Crist as an excuse to murder her family, I got pretty worked up. I already wanted him dead after he came at you twice. When I heard he'd killed Agent Crist, I said she needed to release me so I could go after him myself." Dante snorted. "I guess she found my anger convincing. She wouldn't let me go, but she said I could have a gun at the meet if I promised not to screw anything up."

My jaw dropped. "She trusted you?"

"Trust me?" Dante shook his head. "She doesn't trust anyone. Besides, I told her I'd let her have her chance at Jared. If she doesn't take him out, I will. If she manages to kill him, she has to deal with me next."

"And me," I said, lifting the pistol in my hand. "It doesn't matter who wins. They're both dangerous."

"I'm not leaving until I see Jared die," Dante said.

I knew how he felt. The trouble was that if Giselle killed him, she'd probably kill us next. I had a hard time believing she'd give Dante a loaded gun knowing he meant to go after her once she beat Jared. There had to be a firearm stuffed somewhere on her. I'd seen what she was capable of. She did not hesitate. Not for a second. Even now she went at Jared with her sword as though she'd trained for this moment her entire life.

Jared grunted, lunged, and slashed at Giselle. She jumped back, avoiding the tip of his blade. Whereas Jared looked diabolical in his rage, Giselle showed little emotion—only cool disdain.

Dante watched their actions closely. Even as he spoke to me, his eyes never left the duel. "For her sake, I hope she gets a chance to avenge her family before I put a bullet in her. It doesn't matter who wins this round, but at least she's not deceitful like Jared—still denying his part in Crist's death and calling us vampires. That's rich."

Right. About that. It wasn't the ideal place to have the "Dante, you're a vampire" talk, but now that he mentioned it, I felt obligated to comment. First things first.

"Jared didn't kill Crist."

Dante turned his head to me, eyes still on Jared and Giselle. "But you said—"

"I was wrong. I accused him to his face. He said Melcher killed her."

Dante snorted. "When hell freezes over."

"It has," I said somberly. "He's telling the truth."

Dante dropped his chin. "How do you know?"

I turned away from the fight. "Melcher's a vampire and so are we. We're all vampires. They turned us, Dante. They turned us the moment they brought us in for transfusions."

Dante shook his head. "But the antidote—"

"It's no antidote. It's the poison that makes vamps writhe when they bite us," I said. "It was all a lie. We're undead. Vampires. Recruited and turned to fight Melcher's war."

Jared screamed. I turned quickly and saw him clutch his shoulder. Giselle backed away and stopped, poised with her sword at her side, eyes shining and below them, a little smile on her lips. She was the first to draw blood.

Jared said something in French before charging forward. Giselle took two steps toward him. Their blades collided and broke apart. The pair circled each other around the forest floor, stepping over roots as they went. There wasn't much of a clearing, which kept them in close quarters.

I glanced back at Dante, who frowned. He straightened his spine.

"Someone's been messing with your mind, Sky. We are human. I know we are."

Stubborn vamp boy! And Noel had thought I couldn't handle the truth. Dante wouldn't accept that he was undead if the truth walked up and bit him in the neck.

Jared screamed again. He swiped a hand over his thigh and lifted bloody fingers.

Dante's brows rose. "Things aren't looking good for Jared."

This time, Giselle didn't wait. She lunged forward and knocked Jared's sword from his hands. The blade hit the hard packed soil. Jared took a step back, followed by another. Giselle stepped forward slowly.

Jared continued backing away then stopped. "You should have never reported me to the police."

Giselle lifted her sword. "You're right. I should have killed you myself."

She lunged, but before she could strike the fatal blow, Jared ducked at the last second. Giselle missed and passed him. As she did, Jared jumped back up and shoved her face-first into a tree.

Giselle's sword fell from her fingers when she hit the tree trunk. She fell, landing on her back.

Jared quickly snatched a mango-sized rock off the ground and leapt on top of her. He lifted the rock.

"I am going to bash in your skull, you backstabbing bitch!"

"Like you killed that boy?" Giselle lifted her head off the ground. A drop of blood ran down the side of her face like a tear.

The rock shook in Jared's hand.

Without saying a word, Dante and I crept in closer.

"What is it with you and that infernal boy?" Jared demanded. "He was an imbecile."

Giselle's eyes narrowed. "He was defenseless."

She ought to be worrying more about her defenselessness at the moment than a boy who died over a hundred years ago.

Jared straightened his back. "The world is better off without him, just like it will be better off without you."

Jared slammed the rock down. Giselle moved her head at the last second, but it wasn't enough to miss the blow altogether. She cried out as it struck one side of her head. She kneed Jared in the gut. He grunted as she twisted around and crawled toward her sword. Jared leapt to his feet and got to the sword before Giselle. He dropped the rock and scooped up the blade. Giselle was still on her hands and knees when he kicked her in the face so hard she fell onto her back, suddenly motionless.

Ouch. I knew from personal experience that had to hurt like hell.

"Game over," Jared said through gritted teeth. "Au revoir, Giselle."

"Jared, stop!" I screamed.

My voice didn't startle him for a second. The contorted expression on his face made him appear demonic as he stood over Giselle's body, sword raised. It was too sick. I couldn't let him, even knowing that saving Giselle was what had gotten me into this mess in the first place. This wasn't about saving her. This was about ending the vampire who had taken my life.

As Jared raised the hilt of the sword, I raised my gun and fired. The shot rang out through the forest, echoing across the gorge.

19

Survivalists

ared dropped the sword and stared at me in shock. He took a step forward, stopped, keeled over and fell to the ground on his stomach.

The gun shook in my hand. Oh my god, I'd shot him. I'd killed him. It was over. I stared at Jared's body in disbelief.

My heart hammered inside my ears, or maybe they were still ringing from the shot.

Jared and Giselle were laying on the ground. Dante and I were left standing.

A hysterical laugh burbled up my throat, but I held it in. A sickening sense of joy came over me. And relief. I'd never felt so much relief.

"You did it," Dante said. "You got him."

I nodded slowly. "It had to be done."

"Damn straight it had to be done," Dante said, walking over to Jared's body.

Dante stared down for a long while before turning to look at Giselle. Her eyes were closed, but her chest rose up and down slowly. I kept my ground.

"That one's still breathing," Dante said.

"Where's Gavin?" I asked.

"The vampire is still locked inside her basement."

"Do you know where that is?"

Dante shook his head. "She blindfolded me the entire way here. Doesn't matter. He's a vampire."

"So are we, and he's a friend of Noel's."

"I'd know if I was a vampire."

"Blood doesn't excite you?" I challenged.

Dante's frown deepened. "It's a side effect."

"It's a symptom."

"I don't believe it," Dante persisted. "The agency would never allow something like that. We kill vampires. She kidnapped an agent and stabbed another."

He took a step toward Giselle.

My eyes were on her. They should have been on Jared. By the time I noticed him rise onto his knees, it was too late. His hand shot out, grabbing Dante by the ankle.

I screamed as Jared yanked back. Dante fell to the ground beside Jared, who snatched the rifle out of Dante's hands by the barrel. Jared cracked the handle over Dante's head.

"No!" I screamed.

Dante slumped over, taking the spot Jared had occupied on the ground moments before.

Jared stood with the rifle, laughing hysterically. His lips pulled back, showing the whites of his teeth, when he looked at me.

"You think I'd trust you with a loaded gun? I filled it with blanks."

Oh. Shit.

I glanced at the pistol, no more helpful than a BB gun.

Jared cocked the rifle, lifted it to his shoulder and started toward me slowly. I lifted the pistol, both hands clasped around the handle as though in prayer. I might not be able to kill him, but I could slow him down.

Jared tsked. "What a pity, Raven. So much potential. We could have been a team. It just goes to show: Never trust a woman."

Jared headed straight for me.

I braced myself and aimed at his face. My trigger finger twitched. Jared lifted the rifle higher. I watched his finger on the trigger, waiting until he got closer.

As he closed in, Giselle appeared behind him. I'd never seen her get up. My eyes widened in surprise, which was enough to tip Jared off. He whirled around. Giselle's blade sliced through his side.

Jared screamed.

He swung the barrel of the rifle around, aiming for Giselle, and took a shot. She dropped to the ground just in time to avoid eating lead.

I ran to Dante, dropping to the ground beside him.

"Dante!" I cried, shaking him by the shoulders. "Dante?" I said, nudging him.

Another shot rang out.

"Dante, get up!" I yelled.

His eyes opened suddenly, as though he'd received an electric shock. I nearly cried out in relief.

"We have to get out of here now," I said.

I got to my feet and grabbed his hand. Dante pushed off the ground as I pulled him forward. I yanked his hand toward the platform. We made a run for it. Turning my back to the enemy was far from ideal, but to do otherwise could cost us our lives.

We scrambled up the platform stairs and sprinted to the metal cage. Dante ripped open the door.

"Get in!" he said.

I didn't need to be told twice. The cage bounced when I jumped in. Dante stepped in behind me. Before he could close the door, Giselle ran up the platform, sword in hand, and grabbed the door with her free hand.

"I'm coming with you," she said.

"Where's Jared?" I demanded.

"He's retreated into the woods."

"So why don't you go after him?" Dante asked.

Giselle glared at him. "Because he has the rifle. The rifle I entrusted you with."

Dante pulled the door closed. "You're not coming with us."

Giselle looked at me. "I'll take you to Gavin."

I chewed on my lower lip, thinking.

"Aurora, forget the vampire," Dante said. "We have to report this to Melcher."

My hands trembled. I stuffed the gun inside the back of my jeans and took Dante's hands in mine, squeezing gently. Dante turned his head slightly to the side, suddenly still. He searched my eyes.

"Dante, I can't go back to the agency," I said slowly. "Not after I tried to kill Jared. You know what Melcher would do to me."

Dante's grip on my hands tightened. He nodded and relaxed his hold.

"That means I can't go back, either."

Giselle shoved her way inside the cage with us.

"The two of you are going to need a benefactor and a place to stay," she said. "Unless, of course, you fancy getting yourselves killed."

The cage wasn't designed for more than two people—even if the third occupant was a skinny vampire. Dante and I had to squish together to make room for Giselle.

We were only inches apart. His chest heaved as his lungs pumped the cool air around us in and out. He grabbed ahold of the rope, arms flexing as he pulled the cage across the chasm. Halfway across, Giselle reached inside her pocket and tossed her phone into the raging river below.

As the cage neared the platform on the other side, Tommy appeared on top of the concrete block.

Dante leaned against the ledge, jolting the contraption along the way. "Tommy!"

Tommy barked and jumped onto his hind legs. His tail wagged like crazy.

Woof. Woof. Woof.

Each ecstatic bark became louder the closer we approached. Dante put his entire upper body in to pulling the rope.

Giselle craned her neck toward the approaching platform. "Is that a dog?"

No, it's a horse. I kept my sarcasm to myself.

Once the cage bounced over the platform, Dante jumped out. In an instant, he gathered Tommy into a hug.

"Tommy, boy! I'm back!"

Tommy barked happily.

I stepped out, followed by Giselle.

"That's nice, but we need to get going," she said.

Dante glared at her over his shoulder. "We're going." He stood and switched to a smile when he looked at his dog. "Ready for a road trip, boy?"

Tommy stared up at him and wagged his tail.

"Let's head out."

Dante led the way back to Alyeska. None of us spoke during the walk through the woods. It was as though nature had cast a spell of silence over us. We walked in silence, single file. I'd never felt more wired or exhausted in my entire life. My body and mind kept teetering from one extreme to the other.

"Are we taking the Subaru?" I asked when we reached the parking lot.

"The truck," Giselle said, nodding at a big-ass blue Ford truck parked at the front end of the parking lot.

It wasn't until we were inside Giselle's truck, headed out of Girdwood, that Dante cleared his throat and said, "Now would be a good time to bring me up to speed."

I took a deep breath and told him about the tasting, Valerie, Levi, and Mason, the human deaths at the agency's hands, and their recruitment of previous targets.

Dante shook his head. "Something is rotten in Denmark."

From the driver's seat, Giselle glanced over briefly before returning her attention to the road.

"So how do we make this right?" Dante mused, drumming his fingers over his thigh.

Staying alive was more my focus than making things right.

"You can't set things straight if you're dead," Giselle said.

One thing could be said about Giselle—she'd survived in the world a long time. Maybe having her along for the ride wasn't the end of the world, even if it meant sleeping with one eye open. Melcher wasn't the only one aligning himself with past enemies.

"We could head east toward Canada," I said. "Cross the border on foot through the wilderness."

"No," Dante said.

"You've got a better idea?" I asked.

Dante studied the passing scenery, taking his time answering. Finally he said, "We go north toward Denali and we keep heading north. Why do you think Melcher always sent me to Fairbanks? Because I know that area better than anyone." Dante leaned into me. "Including everything in between."

I clenched my jaw.

Cozy.

Until I had a chance to meet up with Fane, hiding out with Dante and Giselle made the most sense. I couldn't risk going home to pack a bag or speak to Noel. It was only a matter of time before Jared found a phone and alerted Melcher.

"Do you have an extra phone in here?" I asked, eyes on the glove box.

"No more phones," Giselle said.

"Where can we pick up some burners?" I asked.

"No phones of any kind from now on," Giselle said.

My jaw tightened. "I need to call Noel and let her know Dante and I are okay. While I'm at it, I can give her Gavin's location. There's no reason to leave him locked up. He never hurt anyone."

"We can look for a pay phone once we're out of Anchorage," Giselle said. "Until then, I'm not stopping."

"She's right," Dante said. "We have to keep moving."

I looked between the two of them, mouth ajar. My gaze settled on Dante. I could stare all I wanted. His eyes were intent on the road.

Then it occurred to me. I couldn't call Noel—not even from a pay phone. Her phone was electronic road kill on the Seward Highway. There was no way to reach her. No way to reach Fane.

There had to be someone who could pass on a message to Noel. Daren, Reece, Whitney or Hope. Too bad I didn't know any of their last names.

❄ ❄ ❄

My gut twisted as we passed through Anchorage. Fane had to be worried about me—probably livid, too. I'd told him we'd be right back. Instead, I took off without him.

The weekend had been one unending emotional roller coaster—more of a dropping elevator really, hurtling straight down to ground zero.

Tommy rested his face on the truck's seat back. There wasn't much room for him. Dante scratched behind the dog's ears.

"What's the plan?" Giselle asked.

Funny she was asking us when we were on the run because of her actions to begin with.

Dante faced forward. "We need more weapons and supplies. Guns, ammo, flashlights, walkie talkies, sleeping bags, and freeze dried food."

Speaking of food, in the heat of the moment, I'd left my backpack with the blood bag inside the Subaru. Dang it! It wasn't as though I could run into a convenience store and pick up another one.

Giselle wrinkled her nose. Freeze dried food probably sounded even less appealing to a two-hundred-and-something-year-old vampire than it did to me.

"Did you really not know you were a vampire?" Giselle asked.

Dante stretched his legs in the space we were sharing. "Jury's still out on that one."

I turned to him. "There is no jury. We're undead. Forever young."

That got a smirk out of him. His eyebrows jumped. "If we truly are forever young, that means we can fight the undead forever."

He found out he was undead, and that was the first thing he had to say about it? Should I really be surprised?

I sighed heavily.

"What?" Dante asked. "We need all the advantages we can get."

Giselle cleared her throat. "The way I see it, neither of you has much of an advantage right now."

"We have all the advantage we need," Dante said. "The only way anyone's going to find us is if I want them to."

My chest tightened. "I'm worried about my mom and Gran."

Dante's hand touched my thigh before I ever saw it move. He gave me a gentle squeeze. I knew it was supposed to be reassuring, but it was anything but. Plus I wanted his hand off me, but he left it there.

"The first call we make will be to Mrs. Sky."

I squeezed my hands together and jerked my head in acknowledgement.

"What about Noel? My phone was taken, so I borrowed Noel's. Giselle made me throw it out the window."

Dante removed his hand from my leg. "I'll give my roommate your home address and have him pass on a message."

My body relaxed now that Dante had his hands to himself. "Does your roommate know anything about the agency?"

"Not a thing."

"What will you tell him?"

"That me and my girl decided to get out of town." Dante turned to me and winked.

"What about Gavin?"

"I'll have him pass the address along—say a friend is traveling with us and she needs her plants watered."

My jaw clenched. "Friend?"

"I am your friend," Giselle said. It was spoken as a statement—without emotion. "We all want Jared dead and for that agency of yours to leave us alone. That make us allies."

Allies, okay. I could accept that. Friends? Never!

I wasn't about to befriend someone who threatened me at gunpoint and kidnapped Dante. The fact that he wasn't getting more upset about that part made me want to shake him. Dante struck me as eager, showing the same excitement he got on mission.

We weren't on an operation. We were retreating. Hiding. Running for our everlasting lives.

Part of me wanted to tell Giselle to pull over and let me out of the car. I'd walk or hitch my way back to Anchorage—back to Fane. The other part of me wanted to survive.

What would happen to me if I went back? Melcher could easily grab me and toss me inside one of his cells. After everything I'd been through, I sure as hell wasn't going to make anything easy on the agency. I'd take the open road and backcountry over a cell on base any day of the week.

I'd come back for Fane. I'd come back for Joss. And by using everything the agency taught me, I'd take it down.

※ ※ ※

After driving up and down Wasilla's side streets, Dante at last spotted a pay phone. Phone booths were about as obsolete as drive-ins, but at least they still existed.

Giselle pulled over and put the truck into park, leaving it running. The clock on the dashboard read just after two o'clock. Dante exited first. I slid out after him. Good thing there were a couple quarters in my wallet. I didn't want to waste a second making change at a gas station.

Dante stopped at the booth's open entrance and gave me a slight nod. There were three sides to the booth, but no door. I stepped inside, a quarter pinched between my fingers.

The whole thing felt surreal. Even the clack of the phone as I lifted it from the receiver sounded archaic.

It was just after five p.m. in Florida. Poor Gran was probably getting ready to eat dinner. Both her and Mom were completely unaware that their lives were about to turn up-side-down.

Welcome to the club. We were all on this sinking ship together. Mom had put us there. If anyone should listen up and understand, it was her.

I punched in her phone number. After a short delay, I heard ringing and more ringing.

A sick sense of dread came over me. What if she wasn't home? What if Melcher had gotten to her first?

"Hello?" Mom answered.

I gasped in relief. "Mom."

"Hi, honey. I don't recognize this number."

"I'm calling from a pay phone."

"A pay phone? Are you on assignment?"

I turned and met Dante's eye. His chin dropped. He gazed into my eyes. In his face I saw the concern he shared for my family, and it gave me renewed purpose.

"No, Mom, I'm not on assignment, but I'm okay. I'm with Dante. We ran into a bit of trouble. Dante's life was in danger. Getting him back meant going against the agency. Now we have to disappear for a while. You and Gran do, too."

No use sugar-coating it.

"What do you mean disappear?" Mom asked, voice rising.

"The less you know the better. Right now you need to worry about yourself and Gran."

"Aurora," she said, her voice rising even more. "I want to know what's going on right now."

"Sorry, Mom. Telling you would put my own life at risk, as well as yours. Trust me, everything's going to be okay."

A brief silence passed. Then Mom spoke.

"I'm coming home." Her voice brokered no argument.

My heart lodged itself inside my throat, tight as a fist jammed inside a boxing glove.

"No! You can't come up here."

"This isn't up for discussion."

Tears swarmed my eyes. I'd only just gotten Dante back. Now I had to worry about losing my mom.

My knuckles ached under the bone crushing death grip I had over the phone.

"Aurora," Dante whispered behind me. "Let me try talking to her."

I took in a shaky breath. My fingers loosened slowly.

"Mom, Dante wants to speak to you."

Good thing because I was about to yell or cry—or both. None of us were safe. The worst thing my mom could do right now was fly up and walk right into Melcher's hands.

I held the phone out to Dante.

Our eyes locked briefly. He stepped forward, blocking me inside the booth with him. Dante took the phone. He smiled the moment he began speaking.

"Hi, Mrs. Sky. How are you?"

Normally my mom turned into cherry flavored Jell-O speaking to Dante, but standing that close, I could hear her agitated tone coming from the earpiece. Dante's body stilled as he listened. His expression turned neutral.

My jaw tightened. Although on the run, Dante and I had training. We had weapons. We had a centuries-old vampire at our disposal. What did my mom have? A tennis racket. A cake pan. My seventy-three-year-old grandmother.

Now that we weren't in imminent danger, the full weight of the situation pushed down on me with brutal force.

As my shoulders sagged, Dante's lifted.

When the chatter stopped he said, "Aurora's right. For now, you're better off not knowing the details, not to mention we're safer if you don't know where we are or where we're headed. Do you and Abigail have someplace you can hole up until we sort things out?" Dante listened for a bit. "That will work for now," he said. "I suggest you pack a few essentials and leave within the hour."

More chatter.

Dante's chin lifted as he listened. In that moment, his presence filled me with comfort. His tone with my mom was firm, but caring.

Dante wasn't the type to give up, and neither was I. Together we'd figure something out. Together we'd survive. I wanted a life free of the agency for my family, friends, and Fane.

"Are you friends with any of your neighbors?" Dante suddenly asked. "Okay, give me her phone number. We'll leave updates with her when we can. More importantly, we'll let her know when it's safe for you and Abigail to return home." Dante listened for a moment. "Will do, Mrs. Sky," he said somberly. "I'll make sure nothing happens to her. For now you need to get yourself and your mom to safety. Okay. I will. You, too. Bye."

Dante reached over me to place the phone on the hook.

I raised my eyebrows. "She didn't want to say bye to me?"

"I'm sure she did, but I thought it best to get her off the phone and on her way."

I nodded absently. "Good thinking."

"They're going to be fine." Dante leaned into me. "Your mom's a tough cookie—like you. She has friends with vacation homes in the area. She said some of them are unoccupied, and she can arrange for her and your grandma to crash at one of them. She also gave me the number of one of their neighbors. If we need to get a message to them, we can do so through the neighbor, but we agreed no locations—including your mom's. As soon as we've dealt with this agency issue, we can let her know it's safe to come out of hiding."

My jaw relaxed a fraction.

"Thank you, Dante."

He touched my cheek. "At least we're together. I've missed you."

Before I could respond, Dante leaned forward and kissed my lips.

My whole body froze, including my mouth.

Dante pulled back and frowned. "What's wrong?"

Air left my lungs. The space inside the booth was way too constricted.

My head gave a slight jerk. "We can't do this."

His eyebrows furrowed. "Why not?"

My stomach tied into knots. Why did we have to have this conversation now? Pressed together inside a phone booth? Running for our lives? The situation was tense enough already. But he'd kissed me, and being on the run meant shacking up. Dante needed to know there'd be no snuggling inside a double sleeping bag together.

I swallowed the lump in my throat.

"Because I have feelings for someone else."

Dante's eyes narrowed. Without taking a step, his body pulled away from mine. "That was quick. You managed to fall for someone else during my stint in Giselle's basement?"

I shook my head. Of course, not. I wasn't heartless. The trouble was my heart had never been free to give.

"This happened before you and I met."

"Francesco." Dante's nose wrinkled as though he'd said a dirty word. "You don't belong with riffraff like him."

I understood Dante was hurt, but this went beyond feelings. Like my mother, he was judging Fane on looks rather than merit.

"He offered to help both you and me leave the country."

Dante's chest expanded, filling the thin space between us.

"I'm not going anywhere. Alaska is my home. The residents here need me, and I won't allow any vampire or agency to scare me off. Jared and Melcher are going down."

With that, Dante took a big step backwards.

A moment ago, I had wanted out of the booth. Now I didn't want to step away until we were back on the same page. I also wanted to be beside Dante when he called his roommate to pass on a message to Noel.

His jaw clenched when he noticed me lingering.

"You can wait with Giselle and Tommy in the truck," he said.

I frowned. "What about the message to Noel?"

What about being in this together?

"I'll handle it."

I didn't move.

"I said I'd handle it."

His words knifed me in the gut. What happened to my happy-go-lucky friend? My partner?

I couldn't force myself to love him. Despite this, I'd put Dante's rescue in front of everything else. Joss had been captured as a result.

"Do you have any idea what I went through to get you back?" I asked.

Dante stared at me, his gaze as smooth as glacial ice.

How could he stand there saying nothing? I couldn't help who I loved. Yet, despite that, I had done everything to get Dante back, including put my own life at risk. If I could go back in time, I'd do it all over again in a heartbeat. That's how much I cared about my partner, my friend.

"I was worried sick the whole time you were gone."

Dante's nostrils flared. "I know the feeling."

I took a step closer, hoping we could move past this and figure out what the hell we were going to do next.

Dante turned away, as though the sight of me was too painful.

"Please, Sky, just wait in the truck. I'll be right behind you."

I opened my mouth to protest, but clamped it back shut as Dante's stiff back met my eye. Instead, I pivoted and walked away.

As I approached the truck, I considered walking past it— walking all the way back to Anchorage if I had to. I'd rather take my chances with Fane and Noel in the city. And yet, to do so would put their lives at further risk.

My feet slowed as I stormed up to the truck. Tommy stuck his nose against the glass of the backbench window.

A sense of calm purpose washed through me. This was no time to get emotional or act rash.

I glanced back at Dante, who stood inside the booth, back to the truck, phone cradled between his ear and neck.

For better or worse, we were in this together. Partners until the end.

Everything had changed since I last saw him.

Everything was about to change again.

We were no longer hunters. We'd become the hunted.

WHITEOUT

Want to know what happens next? Get the next Aurora Sky book: WHITEOUT.

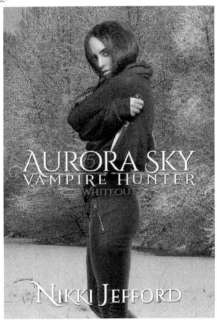

Say Hello!

Sign up for Nikki's spam-free newsletter. Receive cover reveals, excerpts, and new release news before the general public; enter to win prizes; and get the scoop on special offers, contests, and more.

Visit Nikki's website, nikkijefford.com, to put your name on the list, then confirm your email so you won't miss out.

See you on the other side!

MORE PLACES TO FIND
NIKKI JEFFORD

Website:
nikkijefford.com

Instagram:
www.instagram.com/nikkijefford

Facebook:
www.facebook.com/authornikkijefford

Twitter:
twitter.com/NikkiJefford

BookBub:
www.bookbub.com/profile/nikki-jefford

Slaying, Magic Making, Running Wild & Ruling Across Realms

Discover your next fantasy fix with these riveting paranormal romance titles by Nikki Jefford:

AURORA SKY: VAMPIRE HUNTER
    Nightstalker
    Aurora Sky: Vampire Hunter
    Northern Bites
    Stakeout
    Evil Red
    Bad Blood
    Hunting Season
    Night of the Living Dante
    Whiteout
    True North

SPELLBOUND TRILOGY
    Entangled
    Duplicity
    Enchantment
    Holiday Magic
WOLF HOLLOW SHIFTERS
    Wolf Hollow
    Mating Games
    Born Wild
    Moon Cursed

ROYAL CONQUEST SAGA
    Stolen Princess
    False Queen
    Three Kings

About the Author

Nikki Jefford is a third-generation Alaskan now living in the Pacific Northwest with her French husband and their Westie, Cosmo. When she's not reading or writing, she enjoys nature, hiking, and motorcycling. The dark side of human nature fascinates her, so long as it's balanced by humor and romance.